Spring
Break

ALSO BY KAYLA PERRIN

We'll Never Tell

The Delta Sisters

The Sisters of Theta Phi Kappa

Spring
KAYLA PERRIN
Break

St. Martin's Griffin
New York

SPRING BREAK. Copyright © 2010 by Kayla Perrin. All rights reserved. Printed in the United States of America. For information, address St. Martin's Press, 175 Fifth Avenue, New York, N.Y. 10010.

www.stmartins.com

Design by Kathryn Parise

Library of Congress Cataloging-in-Publication Data

Perrin, Kayla.
    Spring break / Kayla Perrin. — 1st ed.
        p. cm.
    ISBN 978-0-312-54728-8
    1. African American women—Fiction.   2. Female
friendship—Fiction.   3. Vacations—Fiction.   I. Title.
    PR9199.3.P434S67 2010
    813'.54—dc22

                                        2009040013

First Edition: March 2010

10 9 8 7 6 5 4 3 2 1

This book is dedicated to my "Auburn Crew"—the group of students from Auburn University who I met and hung out with in the Bahamas in 2007. They were on their spring break vacation; I was with my young daughter.

It was truly a blast to have hung out with y'all—for both me and my daughter! I told you then that I was going to write a book about spring break, and here it is. I hope you enjoy it—keeping in mind that none of you are the characters in this book!

And to those of you I asked questions of, thanks for taking the time to answer them!

War Eagle!

Spring
Break

Prologue

PRIVATE NAME. *Private number.*

My heartbeat began to accelerate, the response I'd had every time this week when I'd seen those words on my caller ID. I quickly placed the cell phone to my ear, cautiously hopeful and sick with anxiety at the same time.

Please, let this be the call.

"Hello?" I said, then held my breath as I waited for a response.

Scratchy static filled the line, evidence of a bad connection. I strained to hear the person on the other end of the phone.

And then, the faint sound of *something* on the other end of the line. A voice, a movement—I wasn't sure.

"Hello?" I repeated. "Is someone there?"

"Chantelle . . ."

My back went rigid. I was certain now. Someone had whispered my name.

"Help . . . please."

"Ashley?" Excitement washed over me in waves. The voice was faint, but it was female. It had to be her. "Ashley—is that you?"

"Help me . . ."

"Why are you whispering? Where are you? Who's there with you?"

"I was stupid," she went on, sobbing between her words. "This was . . . all a mistake. A stupid decision. And now . . ."

The rest of her words were drowned out by the static.

"Ashley? Ashley!"

When I heard more soft sobbing, I was relieved. For a moment, I thought the call had been disconnected.

"Ashley, we must have a bad connection. Can you speak up at all? Tell me where you are. I'll come get you. Or I'll send someone."

I again strained to listen, hearing static and the faint sound of a voice. So faint I couldn't make out the words.

"Ashley, please speak up." Now I was crying. I was relieved, but terrified. I had to get to my friend. Save her. "Please tell me where you are."

"I . . ." More crying. "I . . ."

My voice rose an octave as hysteria set in. "Where are you?" No answer. "Ashley? Ashley!"

The dial tone sounded in my ear.

The line was dead. And Ashley was gone.

Just like a ghost.

Chapter
One

IT STARTED the way any trip to paradise should. The sun was bright, the sky that shade of perfect blue you only find in the Caribbean. The thirty-three of us had filled the plane with lively chatter and spontaneous bursts of laughter ever since we'd left Philadelphia, probably annoying the heck out of everyone around us.

But I didn't care, the way I suspected none of us did. As we descended onto the island of Artula, we were all excited and happy and looking forward to a much deserved break from the daily grind of college life.

We being a group of spring breakers from Lancaster

University, which we often referred to as Lan-U, about an hour outside of Philadelphia, Pennsylvania. Off to the Caribbean island of Artula for seven days of fun in the sun.

I stared out the plane's window at the gorgeous ocean below, awestruck by its varying shades of blue—turquoise, azure, and royal. The only thing more enticing was the stretch of white sandy beach. Sand I couldn't wait to sink my toes into.

I heard giggling coming from the row in front of me—not for the first time during this flight—and tried to block it out as I enjoyed the view. But when the giggling turned to moaning, I couldn't help sneaking a peek through the opening between the seats, where I saw the two of them engaged in yet another open-mouthed kiss.

In front of me, my best friend, Ashley, and her boyfriend, Ryan, were the two in our group off in their own world. Ashley hadn't turned back once to make conversation with me or Erica since we'd gotten on the plane. Ashley and Ryan were arguably the happiest of all of us, if their inappropriate public displays of affection were any indication. They were currently sucking face as if they couldn't wait to get to their hotel room.

Ashley tended to bring that out in a guy—totally wanton behavior. She was stunningly beautiful. With long, blond hair, full breasts, and tempting curves, she had the kind of good looks that the boys couldn't resist.

Boys like Ryan—her newest boyfriend of only two weeks.

"I don't know how she does it," Erica said in a low voice beside me, indicating Ashley with a nod of her head. "How long do you think this one will last?"

I stole another glimpse of Ashley and Ryan. They were still necking. "She seems to like him," I whispered. "But more importantly, *he* seems totally into her."

That was the most important thing as far as I was concerned—
that Ryan was the one into her. As lucky as Ashley was in the
looks department, she was just as unlucky when it came to love.
She jumped headfirst into relationships and almost always
ended up hurt.

"Speaking of relationships lasting," Erica went on, "I still
can't *believe* Carl gave you an ultimatum."

I refrained from rolling my eyes, though I wanted to tell my
friend to put a sock in it already. At least twice every hour
since we'd left Lancaster, she had brought up the subject of
Carl. It had been her favorite topic for the day, which I could
understand given that we'd just broken up, but still. Hadn't
we discussed him enough over the four-hour flight? There was
no new ground to cover, and I was on vacation. I didn't want to
land on Artula thinking about Carl when all I wanted to do
was forget him.

Instead of answering Erica, I picked up the in-flight magazine and perused it, playing like I hadn't heard her.

"I know I said he'd come to his senses," Erica continued,
clearly not needing my input to continue the conversation.
"But what kind of fool is he? To dump you because you're going on a trip? That's like saying, 'You have my blessing to make
out with some hot island man on the beach.' What was he
thinking?"

"I don't know," I said, my voice deadpan.

"I bet he's regretting his words already."

My stomach tightened. I didn't want to think about whether
or not Carl had had a change of mind, or if he had made a voo-
doo doll in my image. I had vowed to forget him for the next
seven days.

"I'm sure he'll be begging you to forgive him by the time

you get back—but in the meantime, girl, you have a free pass." Erica chuckled. "Make the most of it."

"Hmm," I replied noncommittally, then gazed out the window again. We were over trees now, going lower. Any second we would be touching down on the island.

If you go on that trip with your friends, you're choosing them over me.

No, Carl. I'm not. I just—

Yeah, you are. And we'll be through, Chantelle. I mean it.

Carl's ultimatum sounded in my mind, and just like that, I was pissed off. After a two-year relationship, he was going to dump me because I went away with my girlfriends for a spring break trip? I had scrimped and saved for this vacation—my first to a Caribbean island since I'd been a kid—and I deserved it. How dare Carl break up with me in an effort to ruin my fun? It wasn't as if I hadn't asked him to come with me. He'd said no, so then I'd asked my friends.

The plane hit the runway, and people began to clap, grateful for a safe landing. And suddenly, I had a whole new perspective.

I was on Artula now. A free woman because Carl had been a big jerk. Erica was right. What had he been thinking?

I faced Erica as I stuffed the magazine back into the pouch on the seat in front of me. Then I grinned. "Free pass, baby."

Her eyes lit up. "What happens in Artula stays in Artula."

"Damn straight," I agreed.

I looked out the window again, but I wasn't really seeing the view. Instead, I was thinking about the adventures that awaited me. Adventures as a single college girl with six nights and a guilt-free conscience.

"Come on, Ash. Don't leave me hanging like that. What is it?"

"You'll see, baby. When we get to the hotel."

The sound of Ryan and Ashley suddenly speaking got my attention. Wow—they'd actually come up for air.

"I hate surprises, Ash," Ryan went on. "Tell me now."

"When we get to the hotel," Ashley repeated, and there was something in her insistent tone I found odd. An edge I didn't expect after she'd just been kissing Ryan as though he was the last man on earth.

But she stroked Ryan's face as she spoke, and I figured I'd misread her tone. I watched as Ryan captured her hand with his and planted a kiss on the inside of her wrist.

And then Ashley turned suddenly, her eyes catching mine.

I looked away quickly, feeling as though I'd just been caught spying. But as I did, I felt a chill.

I'm not sure why. All I know is that the chill felt sort of like a premonition.

A premonition of something bad.

Chapter
Two

WE'D ALL STARTED drinking on the plane—a cocktail or two each—but once we got to the resort, we kicked it up a good ten notches. The hotel had an all-inclusive plan—all the food and alcohol we could consume—and given the rate at which we were downing booze, we were going to bankrupt them before the week was out.

We'd gotten to the hotel minutes to four, and now it was just after seven. I'd decided to ignore the odd premonition I'd had on the plane and settle in to having fun. After all, it made no sense. Ashley and Ryan had gone back to being as lovey-dovey as ever. And the atmosphere at this beautiful resort couldn't be more festive. What could go wrong?

A live reggae band was playing in the lobby bar, and most of our group from Lancaster was milling about, downing margaritas and piña coladas and the local beer. I had a good buzz going, and Erica was definitely drunk. She was by my side, both of our backs pressed to the bar as we gently rocked to the music and took everything in.

We looked good. I knew it. Because while *we* took everything in, guys were definitely checking *us* out.

Erica was what I liked to call pretty with an edge. Not the sweet, girl-next-door look of Ashley's, but one who was pretty and didn't doubt it. Not cocky, but confident. She wasn't the type to lament over whether or not she looked good in an outfit. She knew she did.

And who could fault her? Erica looked great in everything. She had a narrow, caramel-colored face, prominent cheekbones, and silky black hair that fell past her shoulders. Tonight, she wore dark makeup around her eyes, giving them a smoky, sexy look. A body-hugging black dress clung to her trim physique, emphasizing her narrow waist, while the low-cut V-neck showed off breasts that looked larger because of a push-up bra.

I lacked the natural confidence Erica possessed, but when my clothes and makeup came together just right, I had as much self-assurance as anyone. Tonight was one of those nights. I was decked out in a loose black skirt that came to above my knees, and a red top with a low scoop neck. Red looked great against my dark complexion—and the good amount of cleavage I was exposing looked even better. Guys liked my hourglass figure: big breasts, big booty, small waist. I wished my face was slimmer, not so full, but I was still cute, if not the most attractive girl in the world.

"Still no sign of Ashley and Ryan," Erica said, her tone exaggerated because she was drunk.

"Not since they got their welcome drinks and made a beeline for their hotel room."

Erica laughed. "Beeline is right! I never saw anyone disappear so fast."

"Wanna bet me five bucks we won't see them until morning?"

Erica looked at me askew. "I'm drunk, Chantelle—not stupid."

We giggled at that, then Erica turned and placed her empty glass on the counter. I watched her flash a seductive smile at Joey, the bartender on our end of the bar, and he came right over. Erica had a way with her teasing looks.

"That rum punch was awesome, Joey," Erica told him, her tone and eyes flirtatious. "I'll have another. And one for my friend, too."

Moments later, Erica was passing me another drink. I was mixing my alcohol in a way I'd never do back home. But what the heck? I was on vacation.

"I don't want to be the only one not getting laid on this trip," Erica said after a moment. "And none of the guys in here are doing it for me. Let's head outside—see if there's anyone decent there."

"All right," I agreed.

I followed her, stumbling a little in my tipsy state. I was on my way to feeling no pain.

We walked past the people dancing and went to the large patio doors, which were open to let in the breeze. Among all the warm bodies, the breeze had been nice, but as I stepped outside, I shivered. Though the day had been sunny and pleasant, the evening air was cool. I supposed that was March in the Caribbean—or at least on the island of Artula.

"Ah, now *that's* better."

I followed Erica's line of sight to a group of buff guys who were sitting at a table. They were dressed in jeans and tight T-shirts, the kind that showcased their bulging arm muscles.

"Big, black, and beautiful." Erica sighed dreamily. "Now *that's* what I'm talking about."

Two of them turned our way, making me wonder if they had heard Erica's comment. And for a moment, I was embarrassed. Until one of them met my gaze and smiled.

"Free pass," I found myself saying. I downed my rum punch.

"That's right, girl." Giggling, Erica looped her arm through mine, and together we made our approach.

All four of the guys' eyes lit up. No surprise there. A Caribbean island and endless booze—hookups were part of the equation.

"Hey," Erica practically sang as we reached the guys. Being close enough to check out their physiques, I was certain they had to be football players. They were all muscular—bulging arms and big pecs. Two had their wide backs to us around the circular table, so I couldn't see their faces well, but the two I could see were quite attractive. The one on the right was taller than the guy seated next to him by about two inches, with a medium brown complexion and hair closely cropped to his head. I'd put him at about six-foot-one, six-foot-two. He was cuter than the one on the left—but not by much. The slightly shorter one had light brown skin, was bald, and sported a sexy goatee. His arms were far more ripped than the taller guy's.

The taller one stared Erica up and down in an obviously lustful gaze—but who could blame him for checking out my friend's long legs and the cleavage that she was showing off? The shorter, more muscular one fixed his gaze on me, one full of heat. I preferred the taller man's looks, but this one would do. As the saying went, I wouldn't kick him out of bed in the morning.

They pulled out chairs, and we joined them, and soon we were all drinking and laughing. At one point I realized that Erica was on BJ's lap, the one who'd first been checking her out, and I wondered when that had happened. Perhaps when I'd been peeling the touchy-feely Kevaughn's fingers from my thigh.

In fact, I suddenly realized that I'd somehow missed the two other guys leaving the table, making me wonder when they'd disappeared. Perhaps I was drunker than I thought.

But I was still in control. Enough to keep taking Kevaughn's hands off my thighs whenever they ventured there.

I liked him, but I wasn't feeling him.

I was, however, enjoying the stories that he and BJ were regaling us with, tales of crazy players on their team and a quarterback who was addicted to every substance imaginable, but somehow still managed to lead them to victory more times than not.

"The guy's insane," BJ said of the quarterback, "but I'm gonna miss him when I graduate this year."

"Are you gonna play in the NFL?" Erica asked.

"I wish," BJ said. "The truth is, I'm not that good. Kevaughn, however, he's got some serious skills."

I looked at Kevaughn, who merely shrugged.

"Don't be modest, man," BJ said. He looked at Erica, then me. "The Arizona Cardinals are taking a serious look at him."

"We'll see what happens," was all Kevaughn said. He put

his hand on my thigh again, and this time, I didn't move it away.

What the heck? We were having a good time.

"Another round of shooters?" BJ asked. "I'm buying."

The line got the intended response. We all burst into laughter. Of course, there would be no shelling out of any cash since all the food and drinks were included in the price we'd paid to come here.

"Hey, BJ," Kevaughn said, his voice low. "Maybe it's time we offer these lovely ladies that extra-special something."

Giggling, Erica secured an arm around BJ's neck. I was pretty certain what that extra-special something was. I was also pretty certain that Erica was about to do something she'd likely regret in the morning—if I didn't intervene. For all her talk about getting laid, she wasn't good with casual hookups.

"One of the bartenders hooked us up," Kevaughn began, his voice a whisper. "We've got some weed back in our room. And even better, some X."

"What?" I asked, floored.

"X," Kevaughn repeated. "You know—Ecstasy."

I knew what he'd meant. But I'd been shocked that barely an hour into getting to know me and my friend, they would even *think* of offering us drugs.

I abruptly pushed my chair back and stood. "All right. Time to go."

"But the party's just getting started," BJ protested, an easy smile gracing his lips.

"Yeah," Erica concurred, pressing her face against his.

I went over to her and took her by the arm. "It's time to say good night."

"Why?" Erica protested.

I tightened my grip on her. "Because you're way too drunk."

"Jesus, loosen up," BJ said. Then he laughed, as if that would soften the blow of his insult.

"Look, y'all are nice," I said, "but we don't do drugs. And I'm not about to let my friend do something she'll regret."

I yanked Erica up, and she stumbled to her feet, still giggling as though everything was funny.

I started to walk away, dragging Erica with me.

"Aw, come on," BJ said. "Don't leave."

I looked over my shoulder at him and Kevaughn as I led Erica away. "Good night, guys."

"The night's young, ladies." This from Kevaughn. "We'll be here if you change your mind."

As if.

I pulled Erica along, leading her toward the opening of the shrub-lined stone path that would lead to our room. Initially, she let me lead her. But when we were passing the disco, she pulled her arm from my grip.

"Damn it, Chantelle. Let me go!"

"Hey," I said.

"What—are you planning to take me to the room and tuck me into bed?"

"You're too drunk to stay out here with two guys you don't know."

"I want to stay with them. I'm on vacation!"

"You say that now." I took her arm again and urged her forward. "Until tomorrow morning, when you're puking in the toilet and crying your eyes out because you don't know what happened to you."

She stiffened momentarily. "You don't have to worry about me."

"Right." I rolled my eyes. "Like the last time?"

Erica stopped again, facing me. "So, you think you're saving me?"

I looked at her in disbelief. Had she forgotten what had happened at the Halloween party five months earlier? That she'd been drunk and stoned, and had ended up in a room with three guys she had only a passing acquaintance with? She'd woken up to find one of them on top of her, and the other two watching the X-rated show. Her horror had been not knowing if only one of them had had sex with her, or if all of them had.

"I was the one who was there for you as you cried your eyes out the next morning," I reminded her. "I was the one who went with you to the doctor."

"Stop!" she snapped, holding up a hand. "I know what happened. And it's not like I was forever scarred or anything. It happened, I got over it, so don't bring it up again."

I frowned, taken aback by my friend's attitude. "Hey, I'm just looking out for you."

"Jeez, Chantelle, that's always been your problem. You act like you're a mother. Not a college kid in paradise who should be letting her guard down and getting over an asshole boyfriend."

"Huh?"

"At every party you stand around watching and waiting for someone to get into trouble so you can call them on it. As if that'll prove how superior you are."

"What?"

"You know what I'm talking about." Erica scowled. "Mother Superior."

Why was she turning on me? Yes, I knew that she had changed after the rape, lost her softer side and become harder. I understood that, because she had to be going through her own private hell trying to emotionally come to terms with what had happened. But still, I didn't expect the attitude from her now. Not when I had her best interests at heart.

"I'm your friend," I said, trying to be calm. "Friends look out for each other."

"No—you want to act like you're better than all of your friends."

Erica stormed off, leaving me to comprehend her baffling outburst. At least she continued in the direction of our room, instead of turning back to the terrace.

But what the hell was she talking about? I didn't act like I was better than my friends. No, I wasn't the one to get out of my mind drunk at a party, and yes, I would try to steer my friends out of trouble's path if I saw them heading on it. But that didn't make me superior to them. I did that only because I cared.

Someone had to be the designated driver, or the clear-headed one.

In the two and a half years I'd known Erica, I could count on one hand the number of times she'd gone off on me. And I knew her well enough to know that there was usually a trigger for her outbursts.

In this case, that trigger was likely jealousy. With that whole better-than-everyone comment, it had to be.

Erica was no doubt pissed because I'd gotten interest from a publisher for a manuscript I'd submitted.

Erica, Ashley, and I had met and become friends during a creative writing class, and since that day in freshman year, we'd all joked that the competition was on to see who'd get published first. A few weeks ago, I'd finally gotten a nibble—a major publishing house in New York was interested in my novel. I'd contacted enough of my favorite writers over the past few years to know that an interest was far from a guaranteed sale, but still, I was excited. It was part of the reason I'd been so looking forward to this trip. It was time for me to celebrate.

Yeah, that has to be it, I told myself as I started to walk back to the room. And I decided I wouldn't ask Erica about her comment when I got there, because I didn't want the drama. I hoped that she, too, was ready to put the matter to rest.

But when I stepped into the room, Erica was already out cold on the bed. Her body was spread out at an angle over the covers, with her feet dangling over the sides. She was on her back, and snoring.

Good, I thought. Drama averted.

And still no Ashley.

At least I was certain that she was with Ryan, not off with some stranger who wanted to ply her with drugs and alcohol to take advantage of her.

Mother Superior. The comment still stung.

But given the chance, I would pull Erica away from BJ and Kevaughn again. How could I not?

She was my friend. And friends looked out for each other. Erica would do no less for me.

I made my way onto the small balcony and took a seat on the white plastic chair, remembering the circumstances under which Erica and I had met. Her intervention on my behalf was the reason we'd grown close in the first place. After receiving back a creative writing assignment with a big red C marked on it, I'd burst into tears in the hallway outside of the classroom. Other students had walked by me as though I was invisible, but Erica had stopped. Asked what was wrong. So I'd told her about the crushing mark I'd received on a project I'd poured myself into.

She had wanted to read it, so we went to the cafeteria where she did so, and once she was through reading my story, she was outraged. Not only did she believe that my fictional account of a young woman searching for her parents after being adopted was fantastic, she went to our professor the next day and told him so. At Erica's urging, Professor Young decided to reevaluate my story. He later admitted to me—when he decided to change my mark to a B—that his marking of my story had been based on his own bias. He'd been adopted and had never had the desire to find his birth parents, and simply didn't understand the motivation of my main character.

What Professor Young didn't know—and what I'd shared with Erica after she'd read my story—was that what I'd written had been deeply personal because of my own life. I'd never known my father. He had passed away when I was a baby, and while his absence in my life didn't affect me often, there were times I desperately missed him. Wished that I could turn back time and erase the day he'd been killed so I could have grown up with a daddy.

Ashley had also been in that creative writing class, and she'd overheard what Erica had said on my behalf to Professor Young, after which she'd approached me to ask me about it. That's when I learned that she and I had something in common—both of us had grown up without our natural fathers, though the circumstances were different. Her father had simply left the family, never to be heard from again.

Our bond, much like mine and Erica's, had been instant. Ashley, because she understood firsthand what I was going through, and Erica, because of the way she'd stood up for me. My story had brought us together, and a friendship had easily formed among the three of us. Our love of writing connected us, but our bond was deeper than that. Our different personalities complemented each other, balanced each other out. Ashley was sweet and spontaneous, and thought too often with her heart instead of her head. Erica had that biting sarcasm that always made us laugh, and she went to bat for those she cared about without blinking an eye. I was the studious one with the habit of overthinking things, but I could also be a total goofball when the mood struck. We had clicked, and it hadn't taken me long to realize that we would be friends for life.

And here we were, on our first spring break vacation together outside of the United States. Erica was drunk, passed out, and mad at me. Ashley was probably having sex with Ryan for the umpteenth time.

And I was sitting on the balcony, alone, staring at the darkening sky.

Not the way I had hoped this first night in paradise would go.

The bushes rustled, and the feeling returned then, that odd premonition.

My heart beating fast, I glanced around, searching the area before me. I saw beautiful palm trees and neatly trimmed bushes and a well-manicured lawn. Nothing out of sorts.

But still, I quickly rose and went back into the room. And then I locked the balcony door for good measure.

Chapter Three

THE NEXT MORNING, Erica was as sweet as pie, as though we hadn't argued the night before. Which was fine by me. I was happy to pretend our little tiff hadn't happened. The last thing I wanted was any drama in paradise.

"Should we call Ryan's room to make sure the two of them are still alive?" Erica asked me as she applied mascara to her lashes in the bathroom. "I've heard of older guys croaking during sex, but what if both Ryan and Ashley exerted so much energy that instead of simultaneous orgasm, they went into simultaneous cardiac arrest?"

"Right," I said, giggling as I secured my hair in a ponytail. I was glad that Erica's warped sense of humor was back. It was one of the things I loved about her. "We can tell you're a writer."

We waited five more minutes for Ashley to show up, and when she didn't, we headed to the main restaurant for lunch.

We'd spent a quiet morning at the beach after breakfast, both of us reading a novel as we listened to the waves lap at the shore. It was just what I'd needed—a relaxing start to my day. Still, I knew that after lunch, I'd be ready to be a little more festive, and I'd hoped Ashley would be around to join me and Erica in that quest.

But given we hadn't seen or heard from her yet, I wondered if she was planning to stay locked away with Ryan for the rest of the trip. Maybe she would end up leaving the island without even one tan line.

Sex was great, sure. But still. What about the shopping trips we had talked about, and just hanging out together, period?

Half an hour later, Erica and I were finishing our desserts when Erica suddenly said, "Well, well, well. Look who's finally made an appearance."

I jerked my head around, following her line of sight. And there was Ashley, breezing into the restaurant sans Ryan, wearing a white bikini covered with a white knit dress. She was rolling her carry-on luggage behind her, something that gave me pause. Trouble in paradise?

Stopping, Ashley glanced around. Her large black sunglasses made her look like a diva, but those who knew her best knew that she lacked the confidence to pull off the diva attitude. The truth was, Ashley didn't even know how beautiful she was.

And she was gorgeous—a fact that all the men around her

on the restaurant floor didn't miss. Their eyes followed her movements as she looked around, clearly trying to determine where to go.

I stood and raised a hand, and I saw her shoulders visibly relax when she saw me. She hurried toward our table.

When Ashley got to our table, I pulled out the chair beside me. She fell onto the seat, heavy and ungraceful.

It was her body language that told me something was wrong. I'd known her for two and a half years, the same amount of time I'd known Erica, and she was always graceful . . . except under pressure.

"I seriously need coffee," Ashley said, not bothering to even say hello.

"Good morning," I said, pointedly but good-naturedly.

"You mean *afternoon*," Erica corrected me.

"Whatever," Ashley quipped, her response making me eye her with surprise. She didn't catch my look, because she was whipping her head around the restaurant. "Where's the damn waitress? I need a coffee like now."

"It's a buffet," I said. "You get the coffee yourself from the back wall over there."

"Oh. Good."

Ashley pushed her chair back, about to stand, but I put a hand on her arm. It wasn't like her to snap at people. "Hey—what's going on?"

My gentle question cracked her tough facade. Her lips twitched, and then she began to cry. Heaving sobs that got the attention of the people around us.

Erica met my gaze across the table, her eyes registering surprise and concern. We were both stunned by this unexpected display of emotion.

"Erica, get her some coffee," I said, as though that was the answer to the problem. Erica scrambled to her feet. Then I began to rub Ashley's forearm in a consoling gesture. "Sweetie . . . my God. What is it? What happened?"

"I don't know what I'm doing wrong." Ashley pushed her sunglasses up into her hair, revealing eyes that were red and swollen. "Every single time this happens. Every time . . ."

You didn't have to be a trained psychologist to figure out what Ashley was saying, even though her words hadn't been explicit. Whatever had happened to devastate her had to do with Ryan.

The jerk. I *knew* he'd hurt her. Just knew it.

Ashley continued to cry, and I let her get it all out, consoling her by rubbing her back. This wasn't the proper place to get into whatever the drama was.

Erica returned to the table a minute later, placing a steaming cup of coffee in front of Ashley, who didn't even lift her head.

"Fresh coffee," Erica said, trying to keep her tone light. "Black, just the way you like it."

"I don't want it. I don't want anything anymore. I just want to die."

Erica and I exchanged a worried glance. Without a word, we both got up. I took Ashley by one arm, and Erica took her by the other. I also took hold of her luggage. It was time to get out of this public place and go to the room where we would have some privacy.

Ashley was inconsolable as we walked with her back to the room, making me wonder if something worse than a breakup had happened. I'd seen her upset over a guy dumping her before, but this . . . this was different.

"We're here," Erica announced when we got to the door. "It's gonna be okay, Ashley."

Erica opened the door, and Ashley broke free of us, hurrying inside. She went straight to the bed closest to the window and collapsed onto it, crying even harder now. She curled into a ball, her gut-wrenching sobs breaking my heart.

I looked at Erica, who shook her head in response to my silent question: *What do we do?*

For about two minutes, we watched her, helpless.

But two minutes were enough. I had to do *something*. Slowly, I went to the bed and eased down beside her. "Ashley, sweetie," I began gingerly. "We're here for you, okay? Whatever it is, it's not that bad."

"Yes, it is," she sobbed.

"I'm sure it feels that way right now, but—"

"It's not just how it feels," Ashley snapped, raising her head. "It *is* that bad. You . . . you don't know what he did."

"Then tell us," Erica urged, sitting on the opposite side of the bed.

"Yeah, tell us. So we can go kill him." I said the last words playfully, hoping to elicit at least the hint of a smile from Ashley.

She didn't smile, but she did sit up. Brushing her hair out of her face, she made a concerted effort to stop crying. "I'm sorry I yelled at you," she said. "I know you both want to help." She sighed. "Without you two, I don't know what I'd do."

"Did Ryan break up with you?" Erica asked.

It seemed pretty clear that that was what must have happened, but Ashley still needed to say it. To give us the exact details of what had gone down.

Ashley sniffled, and I quickly reached for the box of tissues and offered it to her. She took out about three and wiped her nose. Then she took more tissues and dabbed at her eyes.

"Gosh, I must be a mess," she said.

"Who cares about that?" I said. "If Ryan dumped you, you're entitled to a few tears."

"God, I wish that was it." Ashley sighed. "I so wish that was the problem."

I didn't understand. "What do you mean?"

Erica gasped. "Oh, no. Tell me that asshole didn't give you an STD."

I shot a glance at Erica, my mouth falling open, wondering if she was right.

"No, not that," Ashley said.

"Thank God," I said, relieved.

"Of course, I wouldn't be surprised," Ashley said bitterly. "That would be the icing on the cake."

"Sweetie, you've just got to tell us," I went on. "Do you think we're going to judge you or something?"

"No." She shook her head, and then began to softly cry again. "It's not *you* I'm worried about."

"Who are you worried about?" Erica asked.

"Everyone else." Ashley whimpered. "I can't show my face again. I just want to go home right now."

"Look, sweetie," I began, "we can't help you if you don't tell us what happened."

"Okay." Ashley inhaled deeply a few times, further pulling herself together. "It's just hard."

I nodded, encouragement for her to continue.

"Ryan is the biggest asshole on the planet. I thought he loved me, but . . . he's a pig, that's what he is." Ashley paused. "This morning, when I was out cold, he must have let Blake into the room. No big deal, right? Except that it was. Because it was all part of some sick plan. Blake hid in the bathroom, and when Ryan and I started to . . . to fool around—"

"Oh, shit," I cursed. "He let Blake watch the two of you in bed?"

Ashley's face contorted with pain. "He didn't just watch. He . . . he took a cell-phone video of what I was doing."

"Jesus—they taped you two having sex?" Erica all but shrieked.

"What a fucking jerk."

Ashley shook her head. "No. That might have been better, when I think about it. But Blake took a video of me . . . giving Ryan a blow job," she finished, in a horrified whisper. "Then he came out of the bathroom laughing, with his pants down, saying I'd done such a good job that he wanted one, too."

As she got the words out, Ashley began to cry again. But while she cried, I was enraged.

"The asshole had the nerve to say that to you?" I asked. "After demeaning you not just by spying on you, but taking a dirty video of a private moment?"

"Why would someone do that?" Erica asked, but her tone said the question was rhetorical.

"Because they're assholes," I answered.

"And he's going to show it to everyone!" Ashley went on, panic creeping into her voice. "I saw Samantha when I was going into the restaurant, and she looked at me and started to laugh, and said, 'Nice performance.' I'm *mortified.* I swear to God, I want to die."

I wanted to commit murder.

I'd never liked Blake. He was tall, blond, and gorgeous— and a self-proclaimed God's gift to women. He was a first-rate asshole, and the fact that Ryan was his friend was the main reason I'd never liked the idea of Ashley dating him.

Birds of a feather, and all that. Unfortunately, it turned out that I was right.

"To think Ryan's the son of a minister," Erica said. "I don't expect him to be perfect, but to do something so evil?"

"Children of ministers can be the worst," I said. "They're raised feeling they're deprived, so they act out the moment they get their freedom."

"And his father's not just any minister," Erica began, nodding her head. "He's the head of that popular Baptist church in South Carolina, so maybe he felt even more deprived with the constant spotlight on the family. Maybe that's why he chose Philadelphia to go to college—to get away from that spotlight."

I didn't care if Ryan had been flogged daily and given sedatives in order to sit quietly during his father's televised sermons. Wrong was wrong. And taking advantage of Ashley, one of my two best friends, was wrong.

He would have to answer for what he had done. But first, I needed to get Blake's phone.

I rose from the bed and started for the door.

"Where are you going?" Ashley asked, and I could hear the alarm in her voice.

I faced her and said calmly, "To take care of this. I'm gonna get that phone."

Chapter Four

"WHOA," Erica said, and flashed me a worried look. "I don't know about that, Chantelle."

"Why not?" I asked her.

She shrugged. "Because."

"Look, someone's got to deal with this," I told her frankly. "Before the situation gets out of control."

Samantha had seen the video, and God only knew who else, but not everyone could have yet. I wanted to put a stop to Blake before he got to show off his disgusting porn-film-making debut to everyone from Lancaster.

"I know," Erica said, sounding noncommittal.

There was a time when Erica would have been the first one charging through the door to confront Blake. When it came to defending her friends, she took no prisoners. But that side of her had changed after the rape. There was a wall around her no one could quite penetrate, and I wasn't sure why.

"You'd want me to do the same for you," I told her.

"Blake is . . . he's big."

"Meaning he'll hurt me?" I asked. I didn't think so. He might be a jerk, but I didn't think he'd hit a woman.

"Meaning it will be hard to get his phone from him. He's at least six-foot-one."

And I was only five-foot-seven. But that didn't concern me. "How much taller was Goliath than David?"

Erica made a face. "We're not talking biblical parables, Chantelle."

"So, what? He should just get away with this?" My gaze volleyed from Erica to Ashley, who looked totally devastated. "No way." I shook my head. "I need to get the phone now, before he shows it to too many people."

Ashley smiled faintly, letting me know that she approved.

It was all the encouragement I needed.

I left the room and marched toward the hotel's main play area, where the large pool, the outdoor bar, and the hot tub were. The hot tub had been Lancaster Central the evening before, and with another day in the low seventies, I was betting it would be again.

If Blake wasn't there, I would check the main restaurant, then the lobby bar, and then the beach.

Wherever the pig was, I would hunt him down.

My instinct had been right: Blake was at the hot tub. His tall, muscular form was splayed out on a lounge chair. Two other football players were sitting next to him, all of them laughing as Blake had his cell phone in his hand.

The fucking bastard.

Inhaling an angry breath, I marched up the steps to the hot-tub platform, heading straight for Blake. He didn't see me coming, not until I was right above him. I grabbed the cell phone from his hand before he realized what was happening.

"What the—"

"You have got to be the biggest pig on the planet," I told him, my anger barely contained.

He glared at me. "Give me my fucking phone."

"You want it?" I challenged him. "Go get it." Acting on instinct, I tossed the cell phone into the bubbling hot water a few feet away.

Blake jumped up instantly, and my heart pounded as the thought entered my mind that Erica's concern had been well founded. He *was* going to hit me.

But instead of trying to strike me, Blake jumped right into the hot tub, groaning loudly as the scalding water enveloped him.

"You stupid bitch," he yelled. "You stupid, fucking bitch!"

For a moment, I'd been afraid—that was only natural—but with the immediate danger out of the way, I was back to feeling in control. In fact, with my goal accomplished, I flashed a smug smile.

"You think you can mess with people and it's all a joke?" I asked him.

Blake didn't respond. He dove down into the water for his phone, while those surrounding the hot tub laughed like drunken idiots.

This brave, angry person wasn't me, not in the least, but I

was acting on adrenaline because this bastard had hurt my friend. I hadn't been able to help Erica that day at the Halloween party, after which I'd vowed never to let anyone hurt my friends if there was anything I could do about it.

And now, with the cell phone in the water and surely destroyed, I *had* done something. Blake wouldn't be able to show his dirty porn to anyone else.

Mission accomplished.

I grinned as I stormed away from the hot tub.

Back in the room, Ashley was sitting on the edge of the bed, and Erica was beside her, nodding her head as Ashley spoke.

At least she wasn't crying anymore.

"I feel like a fool for ever trusting him."

"You're not the fool," Erica told her. "Ryan's the fool. And so is Blake. Lord knows, every woman he dates ends up sorry."

I went to the small path between the two beds and sat on the edge of the other one, facing them. They both looked at me expectantly.

"Well?" Erica asked.

"I got it," I said, triumphant.

"You did?" Ashley asked cautiously.

"Not only did I get it, I took the phone from the smug bastard and tossed it in the hot tub. It's destroyed, Ash." I leaned forward and took her hands, giving them a reassuring squeeze. "Girl, you should have seen the look on his face!"

The caution slowly ebbed out of Ashley's face, and her eyes lit up. "Oh, Chantelle." She framed her face with both hands. "I can't believe it. Thank you! Thank you!"

Erica let out a whoop of joy.

"He was showing it to some people, laughing as he did, but I snatched the phone from him before he saw it coming and, oops, it fell in the hot tub." I laughed now, giddy from my success. "That'll teach him."

Ashley laughed, too, a warm, happy sound that lifted my spirits. But after a few seconds, the laughter abruptly stopped and her expression once again turned grim.

The situation sucked. There was no denying that.

"This'll pass, Ash," I told her. "It will."

"Maybe," she said softly, but the look on her face said she wasn't convinced. "But what happened with Ryan . . ." She exhaled sharply. "It was a huge red flag for me. I pick the wrong man every single time."

"That's pretty easy when there are so few decent guys out there," I commented wryly.

"Nice," Ashley said. "It doesn't make me feel better when the one girl in the room with a steady boyfriend starts complaining about the lack of decent guys."

Ashley and Ryan had been so completely lost in each other that I hadn't had a chance to tell her what had happened with Carl. And it might have seemed to people that Carl and I had a great relationship, but I wasn't so sure about that.

"If it's so great," I began, "why did he dump me because I was going on this trip?"

Ashley's eyes widened as she regarded me. "He dumped you?"

"Yep. Right before I left. Told me that if I got on the plane it was over." I shrugged, feigning a nonchalance I didn't truly feel. I was angry with Carl for doing what he did, but the truth was, I wasn't really upset. Not in the way that Ashley had been so utterly devastated about her breakup with Ryan, a guy she'd been dating for two weeks.

"I'm sorry, Chi-Chi," Ashley said. Chi-Chi was her nickname for me, pronounced *chee chee*. I didn't know where it came from, though she'd once said that it was loosely based on a combination of my name and where I was from: Chicago. To me, it was one of those silly nicknames friends came up with for you when they were drunk, and it stuck.

"It's okay," I told her. "I'm just trying to tell you that I understand."

"At least he just dumped you. He didn't make a video of you giving him a blow job."

I said nothing, because she was right—there *was* no comparison.

Ashley pushed herself up off the bed and trudged to the mirror on the wall. I watched her go, wishing I could do more to help her. But there was only one thing that would help her now, and that was time.

She checked out her reflection, and groaned. "Look at my eyes. I look like shit."

"Nothing a little rest won't cure," Erica said.

"Naw." Ashley turned back to us. "I'm gonna see if I can change my ticket. Get on the next flight home."

"Why?" I asked. "So Ryan and Blake can laugh at how much they hurt you? No—you don't run. You stay here and hold your head high."

"While everyone talks smack about me. Laughs behind my back."

"Everyone will know that Ryan and Blake are the fucking jerks," I told her. "At least if they dare to talk to me about it."

Again, Ashley smiled faintly. "I know it shouldn't bother me, but I can't deal with everyone talking about this."

"You mean all the people who are insanely jealous of you?" Erica asked. "Those are small-minded people who wish they could *be* you—remember that. They've got nothing on you. And Ashley, you did nothing wrong. You have no reason to feel any shame."

"Exactly," I agreed. "Erica's right. And hell, it's not like anyone we know is still a virgin. The video's embarrassing, but no one can act like you're some kind of freak because of what happened. You need to show your face and have a 'big deal' attitude."

Ashley shrugged.

"I'm serious, Ash. Think about it—that'll be the best revenge. Showing Ryan and Blake that what they did isn't bothering you in the least."

"I wish I could pull that off," Ashley said. "I just don't think I—"

"You *can*," I interjected, insistently. "But if you don't feel like being around here for a bit, I get that. So why not a change of scenery? We can head into town tonight, show this island what we've got." I smiled, nodded. "Get dressed up, meet some new people. Dance and have fun. After all, I'm single now, too. I need a pick-me-up." When Ashley didn't say anything, I continued. "Why let Ryan and Blake ruin your whole vacation? Don't give them that power."

Ashley glanced down, thinking, and I got the bad feeling that I hadn't gotten through to her. That she was going to say she'd made up her mind about returning home.

Which would put a serious damper on the rest of the trip.

Finally she said, "You're right."

"You're gonna stay?" Erica asked.

"The phone's destroyed," Ashley went on. "And anyone who saw the video here will spread the word back home anyway. Maybe they're already Twittering about it. So what's the point in running home? If I stay here, it'll show Ryan that he can't push me around."

"Yay!" I exclaimed, relieved.

But my relief wouldn't last more than twelve hours.

Because I would soon live to regret not letting Ashley get on a plane and head home.

And to safety.

Chapter
Five

ZACK'S SHACK was filled to capacity with a raucous crowd of partyers. Pretty much everyone here was in their twenties, and most appeared to be tourists, but there were definitely some native islanders in the mix.

The place was easily the most popular spot in Artula's downtown core, based on the number of people both inside the club and spilling out onto the terrace. The music was loud, and the bass extra deep—the kind of music you felt in your bones with every pulsing beat.

I'd expected an island flavor at the club, but the vibe was very much American. For the fifteen minutes we'd been inside, the music had been a mix of hip-hop and R&B.

All eyes were on me, Ashley, and Erica as we made our way through the crowd in the general direction of the bar. We'd moved from our spot near the edge of the dance floor because of some drunk guy who was trying to touch Ashley, but I knew that someone else would approach her.

It was only a matter of time.

To look at Ashley now, you wouldn't know that only hours earlier, she had been dismally unhappy. Dressed in a shimmery red halter top and a white denim skirt, men were staring at her as if she was some kind of sex goddess who'd come from heaven to fulfill their every fantasy.

It was a typical reaction.

And Erica and I didn't look too bad ourselves. Also in mini-skirts and halter tops—yes, we'd coordinated our wardrobes—we looked like women on a mission to get laid.

And just maybe I was.

Ashley's earlier experience with Ryan, plus my own experience with Carl, had me thinking that all men were assholes. Only an asshole would give his girlfriend an ultimatum. Why shouldn't I do what Erica had suggested—consider Carl's breaking up with me a free pass?

Lord only knew what he was doing while he was pissed off with me for leaving.

"If you are thinking about Carl right now . . ." Erica grinned to soften her unfinished threat.

"I'm not. I promise I'm not."

She gave me a knowing look.

"All right—maybe I was. But not anymore. Right now, I'm thinking 'free pass.'"

I was thinking more than free pass, actually. I was thinking that maybe there would be no working things out with Carl when I got home.

Erica's lips curled in a grin. "That's what I'm talking about."

Ashley, who was leading the way, turned to face us. "What?"

"I was just telling Erica that there are some real cute men in here," I said, speaking loudly to be heard over the music.

"Mmm-hmm." Ashley smiled her agreement. But her grin faded a moment later as her eyes settled on something beyond me. "Oh my God."

"What?" I asked.

"Blake. And Ryan. Over there."

I spun around, my eyes quickly scanning the area behind me, near the restaurant's front door. My stomach twisted when my gaze landed on the arrogant jocks, smiling easily as if they didn't have a care in the world.

As if they hadn't tried to crush Ashley's spirit.

They were chatting up two redheads who appeared to be twins. No doubt, they were next on the list of their conquests.

"I can't believe they're here!" Ashley exclaimed.

"Don't worry about them," Erica quickly said. "Look at you—practically every guy in the room started salivating the moment they saw you. You can have your pick of men in here."

My stomach continued to twist with anxiety. Why did they have to be *here,* of all places?

I knew why. It was an island hot spot. Of course they would find their way here sooner or later.

Our being here at the same time was coincidence, but still I was nervous. I didn't want a confrontation with Blake, who might get on my case about what I'd done to his phone.

I faced Ashley again, faking bravado. "Remember what I

said. This is your chance to show them that they haven't hurt you forever with their childish antics. The fact that you're out having a good time will prove to them that they haven't gotten the better of you."

"And flirting with other hot men won't hurt in proving that to them, either," Erica said.

The last thing I wanted was for Ashley to jump headfirst into another relationship to prove she was over Ryan. It was just the kind of thing she would do. So I said, "This doesn't have to be about you getting revenge. Just about having a good time."

"Mother Superior," Erica muttered.

Even with the music, I heard her perfectly. I whipped my head around to face her. She smiled sweetly.

I ignored the comment, saying instead, "Let's get a drink."

Before we even reached the bar, men vied for position around us, something I was used to on occasion—but definitely every time I was with Ashley. Despite her sweet nature, because of her looks, she didn't have many female friends. Most girls on campus couldn't handle being friends with a girl more attractive than they were. With a woman who was always going to get the most attention when you went out anywhere.

I saw past Ashley's looks to her core, which is why she was one of my best friends. She wasn't the type who boasted about her looks, nor did she even seem to realize how pretty she was. It was stupid that some girls hated her on sight.

But it was funny to watch men fall all over themselves around her. Before we could even get near the bar, men were already offering to buy us drinks. It was the typical men-in-lust routine.

Some brave enough only to look, their mouths hanging open as if they'd seen a celebrity. Others crowded in around us, just wanting to get close. And others still—the bravest ones—dared to ask what beverages we wanted.

The attention seemed like liquid adrenaline for Ashley, whose gait grew more confident and flirty with each passing second.

We all smiled our appreciation at the various men, and continued to the bar without breaking stride. I had my eye on an available spot. But before we could snag it, the spot was suddenly occupied by a man—one who was casually resting an elbow on the bar's surface and wearing a confident smirk as he stared at us.

Well, as he stared at Ashley.

He was cute, *very,* with wavy blond hair that reached his nape. The rimless glasses he wore gave him a sophisticated look. He wasn't from Lancaster—that was certain. He wasn't even in college. He looked around thirty, give or take a couple of years.

As though he realized I was checking him out, his gaze suddenly met mine. And for a few beats I held his gaze, stared into his deep blue eyes—and felt an unexpected jolt of heat.

But then the man's eyes jerked quickly to his right, and I looked to my left to see what had gotten his attention.

Ashley was starting toward him.

She walked slowly, moving her hips in a deliberately sexy gesture. She even flicked her long, blond hair over her shoulder—a none-too-subtle sign that she was interested. She was exuding more confidence than I'd known her to do in the past, but after what had happened with Ryan and Blake, who could blame her for wanting to boost her self-esteem by flaunting her sex appeal?

I watched her advance farther still, wondering where on earth she was going when this gorgeous stranger was occupying the last available space at the bar. But that didn't stop her. She squeezed in beside him, making a cozy space for herself.

And just like that, I knew we'd lost her for the night.

I shot a look at Erica and shrugged, feeling a little miffed, though I wasn't sure why.

Then I looked back at Ashley and the guy. He said something, and Ashley tilted her head to the side and giggled.

She was flirting.

Oh yeah—we'd lost her.

"Seems like Ashley's already found a catch," I said, stating the obvious.

"Yep," Erica agreed. "He's a little old, but very cute."

"Too cute to be here alone," I found myself saying. "I wonder if his girlfriend is in the bathroom." It wouldn't be the first time a guy who'd hit on Ashley suffered the consequences when his girlfriend returned to his side.

"The way he's looking at Ashley, he can't have a girlfriend," Erica said. "Otherwise, he's risking getting smacked upside the head. In public."

Men always looked at Ashley that way—with lust in their eyes. They reacted to her on a carnal level, and often didn't see past that. Which was too bad, because Ashley had more than that to offer in a relationship. It was a shame she hadn't yet found a man who truly adored her.

"Well," Erica went on, "this is a car that doesn't need two extra wheels. Let's find another spot at the bar."

We started to turn to the right. But out of the corner of my eye, I saw a hand frantically waving.

I pivoted back to the left. Ashley was beckoning us over, her eyes alight with excitement.

So damn clueless, I thought. Ryan had just broken her heart, yet she was already going ga-ga over someone new. When was she going to learn?

But I made my way over to her nonetheless.

"Chantelle and Erica," she said, "meet Jason."

"Hello," Erica and I said in unison. I met the man's eyes and once again, there was that pull of attraction. I quickly averted my gaze.

"My friends and I are all aspiring novelists," Ashley explained.

"Nice to meet you, ladies," Jason said, speaking loudly to be heard over the pulsing music. "What do you all want to drink?"

"A margarita," I said. Hey, he was buying. We'd get a drink and then leave. I looked at Erica. "You want a margarita, too?"

She nodded. "It's my new favorite drink."

"Two margaritas," I told Jason. "Over ice, not frozen."

He turned to the bar, and I took the opportunity to look at Ashley and mouth, *What are you doing?*

Either she couldn't read my lips, or she deliberately played dumb. She simply smiled and swayed her body to the music.

"Be careful," I told her, the words spilling from my mouth on their own.

"What?" she asked.

I leaned closer to her and repeated my warning. "Be careful, Ashley. Seriously. You don't want to get hurt again."

Chapter Six

ASHLEY'S EYES narrowed a little at my comment, but that was the only response I got from her. Because Jason turned around then, a margarita in each hand.

With a charming smile, he extended them to me and Erica. "Here you go, ladies."

Erica and I thanked Jason for the drinks. We stood in front of him and Ashley as we began to sip from the plastic cups, but it didn't take more than a couple of minutes for me to feel stupid. Ashley and Jason quickly settled in to chatting while staring only at each other.

Erica and I were so clearly third and fourth wheels that it was time for us to roll away.

Erica knew it, too. "Let's hit the dance floor."

I was about to tell Ashley that we were heading off, but she wasn't even looking in our direction, so I didn't bother.

I turned and followed Erica, who led the way through the crowd toward the dance floor. We were almost there when she stopped short of the goal. She put her drink to her lips and I understood. No point heading onto the dance floor with drinks in our hands.

So instead we stood near the dance floor's edge, moving our bodies to the music as we sipped our drinks.

When the next song came on, Erica's eyes lit up. "Ooh, ooh. I've gotta dance." She downed her drink, then took my hand. "Come on."

She grabbed me so hard, the green margarita mix sloshed around in my plastic cup, spilling over the edge and splashing onto my top.

"Shit," I mumbled, but Erica didn't notice. She already had her hands in the air and was shaking her hips wildly.

I glanced down at my cream-colored top, frowning at that huge wet spot marring my perfect outfit.

I needed to go to the bathroom. Or at least to the bar to get some napkins.

I glanced around. The signs for the restrooms were on the other side of the establishment. The bar was actually closer. But I opted for the restroom, which would have a mirror where I could see what I was doing.

I raised my head, ready to tell Erica that we needed to head to the restroom, and was surprised to find a guy dancing with her. A local, by the looks of it.

I decided to head off by myself. I was on a mission, and ignored the men who looked my way and the few who were brazen enough to reach for my hand.

But the attention was nice.

The lighting in the bathroom was poor, and the mirrors smoky, which wasn't ideal. But at least I could see the wet spot on my halter top.

I wadded up a paper towel, wet it, and set about getting the stain out.

Suddenly, the bathroom door opened, making me jump. I whipped my gaze to the left.

And there was Ashley.

She stopped short when she saw me. Then a smile burst onto her face.

"Hey, girl!" She sauntered over to me, teetering slightly on her low heels. Surely she couldn't be inebriated already. Of course, we'd all consumed alcohol before leaving the resort.

"I like him," Ashley said in a sing-song voice.

"You like him? Already?"

"You don't have to worry, Chi-Chi."

"But Ash, you just met him."

"Isn't that how every relationship starts?" she challenged. "With that first moment when you know you like someone?"

Yes, but . . . Those were the words that popped into my mind. And then I thought about Erica's references to me being Mother Superior, and I stopped myself.

Ashley was smiling, not sulking. She was still here, not on a plane back to the States. If a little harmless flirting was what she needed to feel better after the earlier disaster, who was I to object?

So I said, "You're right. Tell me about him."

"It's fate, I swear," Ashley all but squealed. "He's an *editor*. From New York."

I felt a stab of jealousy. "An editor?"

"Mmm-hmm." Ashley squeezed my arm. "Chantelle, this could be my big break!"

"What publishing house?" I asked.

"Horton House."

I hated myself for feeling even a bit of happiness over her answer. I'd never heard of Horton House, which meant it wasn't a major New York publisher.

An editor from a major publishing house was considering *my* work.

Then something popped into my mind. What if Ashley had mentioned that she was an aspiring writer, and Jason had come up with a fictional publishing company to impress her?

"Horton House?" I said. "I've never heard of it."

"He's legit." My tone must have clued Ashley in to my doubt. She produced a business card. "See?"

The words HORTON HOUSE in a cursive, gold script graced the top of the business card. Obviously the company *did* exist.

"So that's why you like him?" I asked, hearing a hint of snark-iness in my voice. God, what was wrong with me?

"No. Of course not. He's also gorgeous—in case you some-how failed to notice that."

I *had* noticed. And I suddenly realized what my problem was.

Perhaps for the first time since I'd been friends with Ashley, I wished that just this time, she wasn't the one who had her pick of men first. I'd felt an attraction to Jason on sight, same as she had.

But like all men, he'd gone for the pretty blonde—not me.

It wasn't just jealousy fueling my reaction; I was concerned about her making a mistake. The news that Jason was an editor only made the concern greater. I didn't want to see Ashley jump into something with Jason with an ulterior motive. That could only end in another disaster.

"And he's supersweet," Ashley went on. "And much more mature than Ryan."

"I'm sure."

Ashley stuffed the card back into her purse and rushed into a stall. I continued trying to clean my shirt while she did her business.

And I tried to fight my jealousy—on more than one level. Jason was supercute *and* he was an editor?

So what? An editor at a major publishing house had requested my full novel. I had my own good news to celebrate.

And if Jason was attracted to Ashley, there was nothing I could do about that. There were other guys in the bar for me to flirt with.

So I shouldn't feel any bit of jealousy.

But a connection to a live editor—one who was possibly physically attracted to you as well . . . I couldn't deny that was the kind of connection that got results.

Ashley exited the stall and washed her hands. "I'm heading back out to Jason. Want to come meet him? I mean, really meet him? Maybe you can pitch something to him, too."

"You pitched him a story?"

"Mmm-hmm. And I think he likes it."

Another stab of jealousy. "Which one?"

"I'm not gonna say which one yet. I don't want to jinx it." She grabbed my hand. "Come on."

"No, that's okay." When Ashley looked surprised, I went on. "Look at my blouse. I'm a mess."

She checked out the wet spot. "Ah. Well, that's no big deal. You can hardly see in the club, anyway."

"No," I repeated, and stepped toward the sink. "Maybe later."

"You're sure? It's not every day you get to make a great connection like this."

I rolled my eyes, then faced her. "Congrats on making a connection with someone so great. Enjoy it. I'm sure you'll get a book deal out of it."

"What?" Ashley's eyes narrowed in surprise as she stared at me. "Why are you acting like this?"

"Like what?" But I knew. And I wished I could stop my feelings of jealousy.

I should be happy for my friend.

"Like you're mad at me or something."

"I'm not mad. I'm just . . ." I took a moment. Inhaled deeply. "I'm thinking about Carl, and I guess I'm in a bit of a funk." I offered her a smile. "It's not you. Honest."

Ashley's lips curled in smile. "All right."

"I'll find you guys later," I told her. "Besides, Erica's waiting for me on the dance floor."

"No prob."

Ashley exited the bathroom, and I waited several beats before doing the same. I needed a moment to collect myself, to let my irrational jealousy pass.

I checked out my blouse in the mirror. The big, wet spot wasn't going to disappear. I could only hope there wouldn't be a stain.

I exited the bathroom, and instantly stopped dead in my tracks.

Because there was Ashley, about ten feet from the door, kissing Jason.

A kiss that was far too inappropriate for two people who had just met.

Chapter Seven

"THERE YOU ARE!" Erica exclaimed when I rejoined her on the dance floor, as though I'd been gone for forever. She held up two shot glasses with what looked like Irish cream. "Here you go!"

There were two men standing beside her. The one she'd been dancing with earlier, and someone else. Both men had glazed eyes. They were either drunk or stoned. Or both.

I accepted the shot glass, but eyed it warily. "Did you buy these?"

"Don't ask questions, Chi-Chi. Just drink it."

"I'm serious, Erica." I gave her a stern look. I wanted to make sure that no guy had had a chance to slip something into a drink that might knock a girl out.

"Oh, stop worrying. Yes, I bought them."

"Irish cream?" I asked, stealing a glance at the two men. Standing with their legs slightly askance, their vibe was easygoing, and my threat radar wasn't up. I decided they were harmless. And if they proved to be a distraction, even better. Clearly, I needed to get out of my funk.

"Rum cream," Erica said. "Which is kind of like Irish cream, but better. I've already had one—it's delicious." She smiled. "On three, okay?"

"Okay."

"One, two, three."

I downed the shot. So did Erica. And she was right—the creamy shot was delicious. It warmed a path to my stomach, already making me feel better.

"Good, huh?" Erica asked.

"I need another one." There was a cocktail waitress near us with a tray, and I made my way toward her. I bought two more rum cream shots, which Erica and I quickly downed.

"So, who are your friends?" I asked Erica.

"Ivan and Billy. They're brothers."

I glanced at them, and they smiled. I smiled back.

We all began to dance to the upbeat reggae tune, a comfortable distance between us. Ivan and Billy were being respectful, something I appreciated.

I danced closer to Erica and spoke into her ear. "Guess what? That guy Ashley met—he's an editor."

Erica eased her head back and looked at me with wide eyes. "Wow."

"Yeah. Looks like she might get published first after all." I tried to sound gracious, but I couldn't help thinking that Ashley had just gotten an unfair advantage in what had been a good-hearted competition between friends.

"You know what they say: it's not who you know, it's who you blow."

I laughed at Erica's crude comment, feeling good that it was a genuine laugh. I did need to loosen up and have a good time.

A waitress passed by with a tray of red Jell-O shots, and Erica flagged her down. This time, the guys bought a round for all of us. We made quick work of finishing them off.

"Hmm." Erica raised an eyebrow. "Maybe Ashley won't get published first after all."

"Why not?" I asked.

"Look," she said, indicating the area behind me with a jerk of her head.

I turned and looked. At first I didn't see Ashley. But when I did, my mouth fell open.

She was standing with Ryan and Blake.

And Ryan had his arm on her shoulder.

"What the—"

Before I could finish my statement, Ashley shrugged violently out of Ryan's touch, quickly making me realize that their interaction was not cordial. Then her hand flew up, and she jutted a finger into his face.

"Oh, shit." I was already moving through the crowd.

Blake moved to Ashley's other side, looking as if he was about to manhandle her. But Ashley spun toward him, wagging her finger in his face as well.

I made it to Ashley, throwing my arms around her and

acting like a buffer between her and Ryan and Blake. "Hey!" I
exclaimed. "What the hell are you doing?"

When neither Ryan nor Blake spoke, I supplied an answer
for them, muttering, "Being jerks, of course. Haven't you done
enough?"

Again, no response. But Ashley was my biggest concern.

I looked at my friend. "Are you okay?"

"Yeah, I'm fine." Her eyes were brimming with tears. She
brushed them away. "I'm fine."

I threw a hateful gaze over my shoulder at Blake and Ryan,
then guided Ashley away from them. There was no point in
arguing with those two jerks.

"What the hell is going on?" I asked Ashley when we were
safely away.

Ashley shook her head. "Nothing."

"Nothing? That didn't look like nothing."

Erica, who had been standing back a bit, now joined us.
"What happened?" she asked.

"Ashley was just about to tell me," I said.

Ashley sighed. "Ryan . . . He actually said that the wanted
me back. That he deserved my forgiveness. When I told him
no, he got angry. He grabbed me."

I was baffled. "How did you even end up talking to them?"

Ashley shrugged, but didn't meet my eyes. "I thought . . ."

She didn't finish her statement, but I could figure out what
she'd been about to say. With a few drinks in her, she'd probably gone over there to give Ryan and Blake a piece of her mind.

"Bad idea, Ash," I said.

"I know . . ."

"Stay away from Ryan," I continued. "From both of them. If

you see them coming, go the other way. Hell, threaten to call the police if you have to."

"I will. I will. I just . . ."

"You don't have to prove anything to them."

"I know."

"She knows," Erica concurred.

I shot her an annoyed look. As far as I was concerned, I'd just helped to avert potential disaster. I didn't need Erica giving me the 'you're acting like Mother Superior' attitude right now.

Ashley's eyelids fluttered. Then she looked toward the bar. "I need another drink."

Her speech was slightly slurred, and she'd wobbled as I walked with her away from Ryan and Blake. "I think you've probably had enough," I told her.

She chuckled softly. "Please tell me you're not going to lecture me."

Lecture?

"No. Of course not. I . . . I just—"

"Stop worrying. Damn, girl. You're the one who convinced me to stay. The one who got me excited about going out tonight. And you were right. We're on vacation." Ashley patted my cheek, then gazed around. "Oh—there's Jason."

She walked off, clumsily, and I stood there with Erica at my side. I didn't dare look at Erica, for fear she'd give me a knowing look.

Even still, a part of me wanted to go after Ashley, make sure she was okay.

But I didn't. Because the bigger part of me didn't want to look like the nagging mother hen.

Chapter
Eight

I STARTED toward the bar with a purpose. That purpose being to shed what Ashley and Erica clearly saw as my uptight side.

To do that, I needed another drink.

Erica fell into step beside me. "Slow down, Chantelle," she said. "Ash is—"

"I'm going to the bar," I interjected before she could finish voicing her dissent. "Another margarita?"

"Oh," Erica said sheepishly. "Sure."

"I'll bring them back to the dance floor. Don't keep Ivan and Billy waiting."

I continued on to the bar, going straight to an open space.

No sooner than I was there, I felt a strong body settle in beside me.

I looked to my right and started, stunned to see Kevaughn standing there.

He smiled down at me with an easy, confident grin. His eyes roamed lazily over my face, then landed on my chest. Was he simply noticing the wet spot—or ogling me?

"Wow," he said, lifting his eyes to mine. "You are smokin' hot. Pardon me for asking this, but are your breasts real?"

I gaped at him, appalled.

"Of course they're real," he said, chortling as though his question hadn't been offensive. "It's just . . . *Damn*. You've got me mesmerized, your body's so amazing."

The bartender, a man with hazel eyes and long dreadlocks, approached me at that moment, for which I was grateful. I wasn't interested in getting cozy with Kevaughn.

"Two margaritas," I told him.

He nodded, then began to prepare the drinks. I was surprised when Kevaughn opened his wallet and placed a twenty on the bar.

"No, Kevaughn. It's okay. I've got it."

"Come on." That confident smile again. "Let me buy you a drink."

"Look," I said, my tone frank, "Erica and I are hanging out with a couple of other guys. So thank you, but I've got it." I pushed his twenty-dollar bill back toward him, then took one from my own purse.

The bartender set the drinks down on the bar, and I handed him my twenty before Kevaughn could pay him.

"So you're hanging with a couple of other guys," Kevaughn said, pocketing his cash.

"Yes."

"And yet you're buying your own drinks."

The comment caught me off guard. I didn't have a response.

"What kind of man lets a lovely lady buy her own drink?"

I flashed Kevaughn a smile. I had to give him an A for effort. The bartender brought me my change. I placed a dollar bill on the bar and stuffed the remaining money in my purse. Then I lifted the two plastic cups of margaritas.

All the while, Kevaughn watched me.

"See you around," I told him.

He just smiled, the kind of smile that said I'd be seeing him sooner, rather than later.

At least he didn't follow me.

I jiggled my body to the music, dancing my way onto the dance floor. When Erica saw me with two more drinks, her face erupted in a grin.

It was the kind of grin that was infectious—helping all of my reservations to fade away. I once again resolved to let loose and have a good time.

I passed a plastic cup to Erica, then raised my cup and touched it to hers. "What happens in Artula, stays in Artula."

"Ooooh," Erica squealed. "Now you're talking."

We both downed the drinks. By the time I was finished, I felt like a new person.

An older song came on, a Ja Rule tune, and I threw my hands in the air and whistled my approval. The next thing I knew, either Ivan or Billy—I couldn't see who—went behind me and started to gyrate against me. The truth was, I didn't care who it was. I was going with the flow, having a good time.

As I sang along to the lyrics, fingers curled around my hips. I glanced over my shoulder and saw Billy. He smiled and drew me closer—and I could feel the evidence of his attraction to me pressing against my ass.

I continued to move against him, the alcohol having loosened me up.

It had loosened Erica, too. Because when I spun around so that I'd be face-to-face with Billy, I saw her in a serious lip-lock.

My eyes widened as surprise shot through me. Not because of the kiss, but because something was off.

In the next second, I figured it out. It wasn't Ivan she was kissing, but Kevaughn's friend.

BJ.

What the heck?

And then I saw Kevaughn. He seemed to step out of nowhere, moving with confidence toward me, forcing Billy to step back. He curled a proprietary hand around my waist.

I should have moved backward, away from him. But I couldn't deny that I felt a little thrill at his persistence. And there was no doubt the brother was fine.

"This is for you," he said, handing me a plastic cup with his free hand.

"What is it?"

"A margarita."

I guess my eyes relayed my surprise, because he added, "I pay attention."

I was about to argue that I couldn't accept it, that I needed to go back to Billy. But that would be a lame excuse at best. After all, Billy had stepped away, effectively telling Kevaughn he could have me. And who was I kidding? Kevaughn was making me feel beautiful and desirable—enough to have me forgetting the offer of Ecstasy the night before. The old, mother hen Chantelle had been offended by it, but the new, easy-going me was determined not to be so uptight.

I accepted the drink, thinking that maybe I'd accept a whole lot more than that.

"What about a drink for my friend?" I asked.

"My boy already gave one to Erica," he told me.

I glanced at Erica. She and BJ were no longer kissing. But his hands were all over her body as Erica now danced with her back facing his front. He was groping her hips, her stomach. Her breasts.

The expression on Erica's face said she was enjoying his touch immensely. I wondered—not for the first time since the Halloween party—how my friend had changed so much. Before the party, she'd had a steady boyfriend, one she hadn't slept with until they'd been dating for a good three months. She was the type who took her time getting to know someone before jumping into anything. Since that party, she had lost her boyfriend and, in my opinion, had lost a part of herself. I'd expected her to become withdrawn where men were concerned, less trusting, more cautious. But strangely, the exact opposite had happened.

I felt a finger on my chin. Kevaughn turned me to face him.

"Drink," he said.

So I did. If Erica could throw caution to the wind after what she'd been through, certainly I could let down my guard a little. If things got hot and heavy between me and Kevaughn, I had condoms in my purse.

The margarita hit me immediately, slamming into my already inebriated brain with force. I swayed. Gripped Kevaughn's chest for support.

Circling both of his hands around my waist, he smiled

down at me. We danced for a while like that, our bodies close and intimate, even though the song was fast with a pulsating beat.

"Damn, girl." Kevaughn's gaze was full of dark lust as he stared down at me. "You are hot."

I'm not sure if he moved his head, or if I tipped up on my toes, but in the next instant, we were kissing. It was a deep, hot kiss, all tongue.

Kevaughn's hands went lower, covering my ass in a public display of affection that would make a sober person blush. But I wasn't sober.

And whether it was the alcohol, the thrill of a stranger touching me, or a combination of both things, I was turned on. His erection was large and hard against the base of my belly, and a part of me desperately wanted to have sex with him and forget all about Carl.

And Ashley and Jason.

The sound of someone wretching violently jerked me from the illicit thought. I broke away from Kevaughn and looked to my right, where Erica was doubled over, puking another stream of vomit onto the floor.

People screamed, groaned, and vaulted out of the way. Within seconds, there was a clear path around Erica. One girl was standing about ten feet to the left of her, intermittently looking down at her sandals in horror and staring at Erica in disgust.

I rushed to Erica's side and wrapped an arm around her. I didn't say anything as I guided her to the bathroom. She groaned and moved with difficulty, as if she was in pain.

She barely made it into a stall before she threw up again. As much vomit landed in the toilet as it did on the seat and the floor.

I rubbed her back, being there for her as a friend should.

And then she was crying. "Oh my God, Chantelle—I feel awful."

"I know you do." I didn't feel much better. My head was spinning, and I wondered if I would end up hugging a toilet like Erica was. "Come to the sink. Get some water."

Erica moaned as she lifted her head and exited the bathroom stall. I went ahead of her to the sink, turning on the cold water faucet.

"Here, sweetie," I said. I cupped my hands together to create a bowl of water. "Drink."

Erica braced her hands around the sink's edge and dipped her head to drink. She downed several gulps of water before easing back, sobbing like a baby.

"Why do I feel like this?" she wailed. "I feel like shit."

"Because you had too much to dr—" I stopped short of completing my statement. And like a lightbulb turning on in my brain, I wondered.

Had there been something else in her drink? Something to knock her out a little quicker? Or something to make her lose all her inhibitions and do something she might not normally do?

Kevaughn and BJ had offered us Ecstasy the night before. Was it a stretch that they might have put some in our drinks before giving them to us?

Erica wobbled, nearly collapsing. I secured an arm around her waist. "Come on. Let's find Ashley and get out of here."

She could hardly walk. Most of her body weight was supported by me as I pretty much dragged her to the restroom door.

Erica spoke just as we reached the door. "Ishouldn'thave . . . shouldn'thavetaken . . ."

"What?" I asked. She was slurring her words, making it difficult to understand her. "Shouldn't have what?"

"Taken . . . that . . . pill . . ."

As she finally got her words out, anger rolled through me like a locomotive, sobering me instantly. "Pill? He gave you a *pill*?"

"I'msorry."

Again, Erica began to cry gut-wrenching sobs. The only time I'd ever seen her like this was the morning after the Halloween party.

"It's okay," I told her. And it was. Because unlike at the Halloween party, no one had taken advantage of her sexually this time. I opened the door and helped her walk out. "You're gonna be fine."

I was all set to give Kevaughn and BJ a piece of my mind if I saw them when I exited the bathroom. But they weren't around. Instead, Ivan and Billy were there, genuine looks of concern on their faces.

Ivan stepped toward us. "Is everything all right?"

"Not really," I said. I glanced around for Kevaughn and BJ. "I need to get Erica back to the hotel."

As if to emphasize my point, Erica doubled over and moaned. I braced myself for her to vomit again, but she didn't.

Ivan hooked his arm through hers, offering her more physical support to stay upright. I was grateful for the help.

Someone appeared with a mop and a pail, and I cringed, embarrassed. But such was life. Erica couldn't have been the first person to puke on the floor here.

"What hotel are you staying at?" Billy asked. "We can drive you."

I hesitated. Already, one man had tried to take advantage of Erica. Everything in my brain screamed that getting into a car with someone we didn't know was a truly stupid idea.

Billy clearly sensed my hesitation. "You don't have to worry. We won't hurt you."

Maybe I shouldn't have, but I believed him. And I didn't have much choice. I wanted to get Erica out of here sooner rather than later. I didn't know if she'd be able to stand if we got outside to wait for a cab. Going right into a car was definitely the easier option.

"All right," I said. "But we've got another friend here. I have to find her."

"I'll take care of Erica," Ivan said. "You go find your friend."

I watched Ivan lead Erica past the dance floor to where the tables were. He pulled out a chair and helped her onto it.

"I can help you find your friend," Billy said. "What does she look like?"

"Blonde. Very pretty. Her hair is long and reaches her mid-back. She's wearing a shimmery red top and a white skirt. Her name is Ashley."

Together we walked around the club, which was no longer as packed as it had been before. People had spilled onto the exterior patio, most likely because of Erica's accident. The smell was far from appealing in a club that didn't have enough air to begin with.

I searched the crowd. I didn't see Ashley anywhere. I looked for Jason, but didn't see him either. A search of the patio also produced no results.

We went back into the club. This time, I searched for Ryan and Blake as well, planning to ask them if they had seen Ashley.

But I didn't see either of them.

After a good ten minutes of searching, Billy and I went back to Erica and Ivan. They were exactly where we'd left them, both of them on chairs. Erica's eyes were closed. I didn't know if she had simply fallen asleep or if she had passed out.

"I can't find Ashley," I announced.

Erica's eyes fluttered open at my words. "No?"

"No." I shook my head. "She's probably hooked up with Jason for the night, so I say we go. She's a big girl. She'll find her way back to the hotel."

Chapter Nine

BILLY AND IVAN proved to be gentlemen, taking me and Erica back to the hotel with no strings attached. They even offered to drive us to the hospital to have Erica checked out, if we thought that was necessary.

I had no clue what it might cost to go to a hospital out of the States, and unless it seemed like Erica was about to die, I didn't think it was necessary. The resort had a doctor on call, and if Erica got worse during the night, I wouldn't hesitate to contact him or her.

I figured what Erica needed was more water, some carbs in her stomach, and a good night's rest.

She had time only for the water before crashing on her bed. Within seconds, she was out cold and snoring.

Thank God for the annoying sound. If at any moment the snoring stopped, I would check on her, see if she was still breathing. If she wasn't, I would call for emergency help.

The plight with Erica preoccupied my thoughts the entire night, so much so that I didn't think much of Ashley's absence. I didn't put it past her to be partying all night, or to even have hooked up with Jason. Would she go that extra mile to make sure she snagged a publishing contract?

I didn't doubt it. With me being the first one in our group to get serious attention from a major publisher, I expected her to try to milk the connection to Jason for all it was worth. I had to admit, even I would do the same.

There was another possibility regarding where Ashley might be, one that disturbed me. Ashley had said that in the bar Ryan had tried to reconcile. Despite how he'd hurt her, I wouldn't be surprised if she and Ryan had patched things up.

When they'd started dating only a couple weeks earlier, Ashley had been over the moon. She'd had a crush on him for a very long time, and I feared that if he apologized to her for his behavior, as angry as she had been with him, she might decide to forgive him.

Whatever she was up to, she'd fill me in in the morning.

Sighing softly, I glanced across the room at Erica passed out on the bed. Right now, she was my main concern. And she was still snoring, thank God.

I prayed she still would be come the morning.

·   ·   ·

I woke up to silence. I thought nothing of it at first. Until I remembered Erica.

And then I bolted upright, panic washing over me as I quickly looked at my friend. My heart pounded as I stared at her, searching for any signs of life.

She was still on her back, though in a different position on the bed. That was a good sign. But it wasn't until I saw the steady rise and fall of her chest that my shoulders sagged in relief.

She was breathing.

She was alive.

But was she okay? I got out of my bed and went over to hers, where I gently shook her shoulder.

"Erica?" No response. "Erica," I repeated, shaking her harder.

Now she groaned. "Leave me alone."

I smiled. She was conscious, and irritated. Music to my ears.

"I'm going to get breakfast. You want to come?"

In response, she dragged the second pillow on the bed over her head.

No problem. I'd let her sleep. She was still on top of the bedspread, but I maneuvered the free edges so that at least part of it was covering her.

And though I'd slept fitfully and knew that Ashley couldn't have entered the room without me hearing her, I glanced toward her cot near the door.

It was just as it had been the night before—bedspread neat, with her suitcase open on top of it. That's where she'd left it after rifling through it to find the perfect outfit to wear to Zack's Shack.

The first inkling of alarm manifested itself in a cold chill across the nape of my neck. There was no real reason for it— except a gut feeling.

But I pushed the feeling aside and got dressed. Before I even showered, I needed coffee and some carbs. The alcohol I'd consumed the night before was a vile mix in my stomach, and I felt nauseous. I knew that if I didn't get something in my stomach—and soon—I would throw up everything I'd consumed the night before.

I went to the dining room, where I saw other Lancaster students. I waved as I passed them en route to the row of coffee machines at the back.

"Hey, girl," Rebecca greeted me at the coffeemaker. She and I had taken a philosophy course together. "If you're here alone, why don't you come join us?"

She wasn't a close friend, not even in my circle, but she was from Lancaster, as strong a connection as any here in a foreign country.

"I'm just getting coffee and a bagel, and heading back to the room. But thanks anyway."

"Oh, okay."

"Hey," I said before she turned to walk away. "Have you seen Ashley?"

Rebecca shook her head. "No. Not this morning."

"What about Ryan or Blake?"

"Um, I'm pretty sure I saw Blake walking near the lobby when I was heading to breakfast."

Good, I thought. That was good news indeed. If both Ryan and Ashley were missing, maybe they were holed up in his room. Not that I approved—but I would be relieved to know that she was here on the hotel property. I felt bad about leaving the club without her.

But what were you supposed to do? You looked for her but couldn't find her.

"Hey," Rebecca said, lowering her voice in a conspiratorial tone. "What was up with you throwing Blake's phone into the hot tub?"

I don't know why I was surprised at the question. I knew word would get around. But still I asked, "You heard about that?"

"Everyone heard about it," she said, her eyes alight. I got the distinct sense that she approved. "What did he do?"

"Well." I hedged. "Uh, he took a picture he shouldn't have. I didn't want him showing it to everyone."

"Figures. He's a total asshole. I don't know how he gets so many girls."

"Tell me about it."

My bagel popped out of the toaster, and as I set about buttering it, Rebecca wandered off. I was glad she hadn't pressed me for details about exactly what Blake had done. In fact, her question was a relief. Clearly, she hadn't heard about the video. Maybe I truly had helped avert disaster.

I put the bagel on a plate, then covered two coffee cups with plastic lids and balanced one cup on top of the other. The second one was for Erica—just in case.

I was almost at the exit when I stopped dead in my tracks, my eyes widening, my breath halting.

Ryan was entering the dining room.

With Blake.

Another chill kissed the back of my neck. And just like that,

I had this terrible sense of foreboding. A sixth sense that something was wrong.

My heart pounding wildly, I hurried over to them. Was Ashley back in the room? Or was she somewhere else, perhaps with Jason?

"Ryan," I said when I reached him. He looked down at me, an expression of mild surprise on his face. "Where's Ashley?"

He didn't answer right away. Something unreadable flickered in his eyes.

Then he asked, "How should I know?"

"She wasn't with you last night?" I pressed.

"Hell, no," he replied, scowling.

"Lost your whore friend?" Blake asked, the crudeness shocking me. "Don't worry—you know she's probably still in bed with some guy she just met."

He and Ryan laughed, as if Blake had said the funniest thing in the world.

I didn't really care if they wanted to slander Ashley. I simply wanted answers. "When was the last time you saw her?"

"Not long enough."

I glared at Ryan. "Can you stop being a jerk? For one second? Did you see her this morning?"

"No," Ryan replied. "Last time I saw her was last night at that club. Before you dragged her away as if Blake and I were gonna hurt her."

My stomach plummeted. Ashley obviously hadn't spent the night with Ryan.

So where was she?

It was nearly eleven. If Ashley had spent the night with Jason, wouldn't she have made an appearance by now? Wasn't that how vacation hook-ups went? A few hours of passion, followed by an early morning walk of shame?

Maybe Ashley had returned in the time I'd gone to the dining room.

I hurried out of the restaurant and back to my room.

When I got to the room and didn't see Ashley there, my heart began to pound harder.

You know she's probably still in bed with some guy she just met.

The words got to me. Not because of any moral judgment, but because it hit me then—really hit me—that leaving Ashley alone with a guy she didn't know was an incredibly stupid thing to do. I had failed my friend—something I had vowed not to do after what had happened to Erica.

I had no clue where this guy was staying, or if he even was who he said he was.

What if he'd raped Ashley?

Or worse?

Regret washed over me in waves. I shouldn't have let Erica's comments about me being Mother Superior affect me. It was a friend's duty to watch out for a friend—especially with a girl like Ashley, who was entirely too trusting and looking to numb her pain. A girl whom men looked at and instantly thought of having sex with her.

And we were in a foreign country, no less.

My eyes wandered to Ashley's cot and the open suitcase. Suddenly it seemed eerie.

I bit down on my bottom lip. I was worried. I couldn't deny it.

I put the plate with the bagel down on the table, as well as the coffees, then scurried over to Erica's bed. I plopped down beside her and pulled the pillow off of her face.

She groaned. "Damn it, Chi-Chi."

"Erica, you have to wake up. Ashley didn't come home last night."

Another groan.

I shook her. "No one has seen her. I thought maybe she made up with Ryan—but he hasn't seen her, either. And now I think . . ." I shook Erica again. "Erica!"

"Jesus, Chantelle—what's the big deal?" Erica didn't open her eyes. "She probably spent the night with that guy to get over Ryan. She does that shit all the time."

"He was way older than us, and we don't know who the hell he is, and he could have done anything to her. We shouldn't have left her with him last night."

"Why don't you just text her?" And with that, Erica dragged the pillow back over her head.

Text her. Of course. I'd had my phone in my purse last night, though it hadn't been turned on. I figured it was smart to keep it on my person in Artula in case of emergencies, but decided to turn it off. I knew the roaming charges from friends calling me from back home would be astronomical.

But maybe Ashley had her phone turned on, especially if she'd awoken in Jason's bed and was once again suffering a broken heart.

Because if he'd taken advantage of a drunk college girl, he was definitely the sort to kick her out of bed the morning after.

I found my phone and powered it on. I immediately sent a text to Ashley.

Where are you?

And then I waited.

I didn't expect her to text me back right away, but when ten minutes passed, my worry increased a notch.

So I called her, the cost of the roaming a small price to pay for peace of mind.

The phone went straight to voice mail. I wasn't surprised.

I waited an hour and tried her again. I called. I texted. But again, there was no response.

"It's still kind of early," Erica told me as we walked together to the dining room a short while later. She was awake and famished. "It's only one in the afternoon. I just got up ten minutes ago. If she was up all night, drinking a lot and maybe partying somewhere else as well, she could be sleeping until at least three. Easily."

"I guess so." Erica made a good point, but to my own ears, I didn't sound convinced.

"Remember in our sophomore year, when she met that guy after the football game? She spent two whole days with him without contacting anyone."

"I know . . ." Another good point. "I just wish she'd call. She's got to know we're worried."

"Right," Erica said, and chuckled sardonically. "Even on the best of days, Ashley's a hard one to reach on her phone—if she doesn't want to be reached."

That was true. Sometimes on the weekends, if we wanted to meet up with her, she wouldn't even respond to our texts until hours later. She wasn't like most of the other college kids I knew, whose phones had become like another body part. They'd text you while in the middle of a movie theater, or during a date, and sometimes just before they were about to make out with someone.

Not Ashley. I got the sense from her that when she was on her own time—like visiting family on the weekends—she wanted to escape Lan-U life.

"You're right," I agreed, and now I did feel better. Even if I was concerned about the fact that Ashley might be in over her head with this guy Jason. But it was totally like her to throw herself headfirst into a new relationship.

"Hey," I said, slowing as we neared the restaurant doors. "I think we should talk about what happened with you last night. Why would you ever accept a pill from BJ?"

"I don't want a lecture," Erica said.

Again, I was struck by how much she had changed. She was far more defensive, didn't want to listen to reason anymore.

"You might not want one, but I think you need one. After what happened to you, I would think—"

"What do you think?" Erica all but snapped, placing her hands on her hips. "Tell me, what do you know about being *raped*?" When I didn't answer, she went on. "Exactly. Nothing. You don't know what it feels like to just want to forget, to want to numb the pain any way you can. And the worst part is that I lost Mike, someone I thought I would marry."

"Erica, I'm sorry . . . I know this hasn't been easy for you. But I've always been here for you to talk to, same as before that night. The way I've always been able to talk to you about my father or anything else."

"Did it ever occur to you that I don't want to talk about it? That talking isn't going to change a damn thing?"

"I . . . I thought it would help to get your feelings out."

"I need to deal with what happened in my own way, on my own terms. I know you think I've changed, and I guess I have. How could I not?" She stopped. Sighed. "Maybe I can't allow myself to worry about someone else, when right now I have to be worried about myself."

"Of course," I said, nodding. I'd never considered that before, but I could see her point. Emotionally, Erica was dealing with a lot. She didn't need any added drama on top of that.

Again, she sighed. "I love you for caring. Please know that. If I've ever made you think otherwise, know right now that that's not the case. It's just . . ."

"It's okay," I said, and offered her a small smile. "On your terms, in your own time."

"And it's not like I'm not worried about Ashley," Erica went on. "But you know how she is. It isn't the first time she's disappeared after meeting a guy. She'll turn up when she's good and ready. Maybe just before we have to head to the airport!" She laughed, breaking the tension between us.

"Hopefully before that," I said. "She's gonna need clean clothes."

"You don't need clothes when you're spending most of your time naked!" Erica laughed again, and I forced one, too, mostly to let Erica know that she and I were cool again.

But in my heart, I didn't feel it.

Because I still had that uneasy sense, that feeling of foreboding.

I would only feel completely at ease when Ashley got in touch with us, letting us know she was okay.

Chapter Ten

THE REST OF the day came and went with no Ashley, and when the next morning rolled around and she still wasn't back, I literally started to feel sick.

Yes, as Erica had pointed out, Ashley had disappeared with someone new for two whole days once. But that had been back at home, not in a strange country. Surely she would exercise more caution here.

But maybe not. She could just as easily have exercised bad judgment in the hopes it would lead to a publishing contract. Was she off with that editor, mending her broken heart with countless orgasms, hoping that the icing on the cake would be a publishing deal? Or had something else happened—and had I been negligent by not already alerting the police?

Was I worrying for no reason? Overthinking things, as I had a tendency to do?

Erica and I had stayed close to the resort for the duration of the day and evening—partly to be around in case Ashley showed up, and partly because neither of us cared for some big night on the town. Neither of us wanted a repeat of what had happened with Erica at Zack's Shack. The concern wasn't far-fetched. Clearly, there were guys out there willing to drug women to take advantage of them.

Guys like Kevaughn and BJ. I wondered where they were. I hadn't seen them around the resort at all. Maybe their absence had been intentional. Because I think they knew that if they dared to show their faces in the lobby bar, I would have knocked them out.

I was worried about Ashley—Lord knew I was—but seeing Erica sick and loopy, I'd been terrified. If I hadn't been with her, disaster would have ensued. I was certain of that fact. But she was fine now, not in a hospital begging for a morning-after pill like she had the day after the Halloween party. Whatever BJ had given her appeared to be completely gone from her system.

But what about Ashley? My gaze fell on her unused cot. Three nights had passed in Artula, and not once had Ashley slept in that bed. What if someone had given her some kind of drug, like what Erica had been given? Something to weaken her inhibitions.

The thought made goose bumps pop out on the nape of my neck. Anything was possible. Ashley could very well be some-where against her will right now, hurt and terrified.

It was all I could think of the entire previous night, as I

practically slept with one eye open, waiting for the moment the door would turn and Ashley would appear.

And it was the first thought that popped into my mind when I woke up this morning, the fourth day of our trip, and saw that Ashley still wasn't in our room.

I stared at her cot. The open suitcase.

It was like a bad omen.

Something's wrong.

I knew it. Was certain of it in my heart.

"She's still not here," I said to Erica as she came awake a short while later.

"What time is it?"

"A little after eight."

"Well, it's early."

"This makes two nights since we went to Zack's Shack. Another morning she's not here. What if something's wrong?"

"It's not like she's gonna come waltzing in at eight in the morning if she was partying all night."

"We don't know that she was."

"We don't know that she wasn't."

That was Erica's response? I frowned at her, wondering what was up with the indifferent attitude. Yes, she'd explained that she was dealing with her own issues yesterday, but certainly now she had to be concerned.

"Why don't you give a shit?" I asked. "Last I checked, Ashley was your friend, too. Anything could have happened to her. Why am I the only one worried?"

"Because she's on fucking vacation," Erica snapped.

"What is wrong with you?" I asked.

"Wrong with *me*? What's wrong with *you*?" Erica sat up. "You can't keep dibs on Ashley, so you freak out?"

"This isn't about me keeping dibs on her."

"Hmm," Erica muttered. "You sure about that?"

The way she said the words made my eyebrows shoot up. "What does that mean?"

"Oh, come on. I saw how you looked at Jason." Her lips twisted wryly as she stared at me. "You liked him, but Ashley snagged him."

"Are you serious? You seriously think that I'm—"

"Jealous?" Erica supplied the word, and gave me a challenging look. "You tell me."

I couldn't believe her! So what if she'd seen me check Jason out? I'm sure she'd done the same. That's what women do when they see a cute guy.

"That's ridiculous," I told her.

"Is it? Neither of us has ever been friends with an editor. Especially not romantically involved."

"That's *not* what this is about."

Erica shrugged, and I wasn't sure if she believed me. "I'm not worried because I'd bet my last dollar she's with Jason. I think you know she's with Jason, and it's eating you up."

"This isn't about jealousy!"

"Maybe you're not jealous of her and Jason, or the fact that she's made a connection with an editor. But I'm betting you wish you could be more like her, even if you can't admit it."

I gaped at Erica, incredulous.

"You wish you could be more easy-going, less rigid."

"So, because I'm *concerned*, that makes me rigid?" I was starting to get pissed off.

"The way I see it, you need to take a page out of Ashley's book. Find some guy you lose all track of time with. Lord only knows why you stayed with Carl for so long—he's as exciting as a seventy-year-old."

I shot up from the bed and stomped to the door, stopping only to grab the plastic key card on the dresser and slip into my flip-flops. I didn't know why Erica was trying to make this about me when it clearly wasn't. It was about Ashley potentially being in a bad situation, and not knowing how the heck to help her.

"Oh, so now you're gonna leave? Funny, you're always ready to talk to me about *my* problems. What about acknowledging yours?"

I jerked the door open and stormed out, dressed in my nightwear—an oversized T-shirt and shorts. I walked to the right, away from the center of the resort. I needed time with my thoughts.

The grounds were stunning, with lush green shrubs lining the stone path on one side, and bushes with bright yellow flowers on the other. Beyond the shrubs, majestic palm trees stood in the center of the row of buildings, and beyond that, I could glimpse the deep blue of the ocean.

The first day I'd walked the grounds, the view had given me a sense of excitement and awe. I was in the middle of paradise, after all. What could be better?

But today, I didn't feel excitement and awe. I felt ill. Because I believed something was horribly wrong. And it wasn't just the worrywart in me.

And I sure as hell wasn't jealous.

Maybe I had been initially, but my concern for Ashley was real.

I walked slowly, past the tennis courts. Beyond this part of the resort grounds, there was really nothing. And certainly no crowds. So it was a good spot to walk and think.

After a few minutes, it came to me. I had to find Jason. If Ashley wouldn't answer her phone, I would have to find him as a way of tracking down my friend.

But what was his full name?

Ashley hadn't mentioned it. Or had she?

But it had to have been on the card. I closed my eyes and tried to recall the image of the card in my mind.

Jason . . . Jason . . . Shit, I couldn't envision it.

And I couldn't very well call all the hotels on the island asking if they had someone named Jason registered.

Frowning, I continued walking, doing my best to make my brain remember.

Jason Horton.

No, that wasn't right.

Horton. Horton.

Horton House.

Jason was an editor at Horton House. That's what Ashley had said.

Excited, I pivoted on my heel and jogged back to the room. While calling every hotel on the island searching for a Jason was bound to be fruitless, contacting Horton House in New York, and asking for an editor named Jason would certainly yield some results.

Back in the room, Erica was either sleeping or pretending, but she had the covers pulled up over her face. Fine with me. I had no time to talk.

I didn't have one of those phones with Internet access, but the resort had computers in the lobby.

I got my wallet and made my way quickly to the lobby. Thank God, one of the three computers wasn't being used. I inserted my credit card into the appropriate slot and chose the least amount of time—ten minutes. Ten minutes should be enough to find the contact information for Horton House.

It took me about a minute to pull up the company's Web site, and another thirty seconds to find a direct number where I could reach them.

Victorious, I smiled—then scribbled down the number.

I admit, a part of me had been worried that Horton House didn't even exist. That this guy Ashley had met had been a predator of such skill that he'd been watching her from back home and knew that her greatest desire was to get published. Lo and behold, he showed up in Artula, sweet-talked Ashley with stories of working for a publishing house . . .

Far-fetched? Maybe. But you only had to watch the news to learn that nothing was impossible.

I went out the front door of the resort's main building to make my phone call. I wanted privacy, which meant going to the pool area was a no-no. With the Lancaster crew dominating the area, there would be questions about why I was on the phone instead of basking in the sun.

The bellman standing outside asked me if I needed a taxi. I told him no, then walked about thirty feet to the right where I was certain no one would overhear me.

My heart pounded as I dialed the number to Horton House. I was nervous, though I didn't know why.

Yes, I did. Clearly there *was* a Horton House. But what if Jason wasn't really an editor there?

A female receptionist answered almost immediately. "Horton House."

"Hi," I said, my voice faint. I spoke up. "I'm looking for some-one. Um, an editor. I only know his first name. Jason."

"That'll be Jason Shear. One moment."

"Uh—" I began to protest, but it was too late. The recep-tionist had already transferred me to Jason's extension, which rang until his voice mail picked up.

I hung up. Yes, I had his name, but I needed a bit more help. Talking to someone at the company about his trip to Ar-tula might help to narrow down which hotel he was at.

So I dialed the number to Horton House again. "Hi," I said when the receptionist picked up. "I called a moment ago about Jason Shear. His line went to voice mail, and I'm just wonder-ing if there's someone else I can talk to? I have some questions about the project he was working on in Artula . . ."

"I'll put you through to Phil Major."

Before I could ask who Phil Major was, the man's line was ringing. Again, my heart sped up.

"Phil Major."

"Hi." I paused a couple of beats, trying in that time to best decide what to say. "My name is Chantelle Higgins, and I'm not calling to pitch you a story or anything." Deep breath. "One of your editors, Jason Shear, is on the island of Artula. Right?"

"Yes," Phil said. "He's researching a story. What's this about?"

I exhaled, relieved. The confirmation that Jason Shear from Horton House was indeed on the island of Artula made me feel a whole lot better. He hadn't fed Ashley a line of bull. "He and one of my friends hit it off," I continued. "And I haven't seen her since a couple of nights ago, when she was with him. I'm hoping you'll give me a way to reach Jason. Or, I can give you my number to pass along to him." Yes, that was the better idea. "I can give you my cell number, and also the name of the hotel where I'm staying."

Silence. I wondered if Phil had just hung up. But then he said, "What was your name again?"

"Chantelle. Chantelle Higgins."

"And the gist of what you're saying is that you can't find your friend."

"Right. I think she's been staying with Jason, but she won't answer her phone. And . . . and her mother is trying to track her down. From back home in Philadelphia." The addition to the story felt right; this man might be more willing to help me if he thought that a student's family member was looking for her.

"I will pass along the message," Phil said, and my shoulders sagged with relief. "Where can you be contacted?"

Turning to stroll toward the bell stand, I began reciting my cell-phone number. Once at the bell stand, I looked for a business card or a notepad—something that would have the hotel's phone number.

Seeing a notepad, I snatched it up, smiling in thanks to the bellman. Then I gave the necessary information to Phil.

"I really appreciate this," I said when I was finished. "As I said, my friend's mother needs to speak with her, so it's kind of an emergency."

"I'll pass along the information."

Phil ended the call, and I palmed my phone in my hand.

All I could do now was wait.

Chapter Eleven

THE CALL came two hours later—two hours that seemed like twenty-four. I'd opted to spend some time under the shade of an umbrella on the beach, a book propped in my hands. To the world, it would look like I was reading and that I didn't want to be bothered. The truth was, I was too anxious to read—and until I heard from Ashley, I wasn't interested in small talk with anyone.

Before heading to the beach, I'd gone back to the room, where Erica was still under the covers from head to toe. She was a girl who liked to sleep in, even on vacation. It was just as well. Until her attitude changed, I wasn't interested in saying anything to her. And she probably needed a break from me.

I understood that she didn't want to think the worst—but this wasn't back home in Lancaster where Ashley had gone off on her own in familiar territory. We were on a strange island, and the last time I'd seen her, she'd been drinking like it was her last day on earth. Worse things had happened to unsuspecting women on vacation.

Then my cell phone sang. Literally. It was programmed to "sing" a Jennifer Hudson song. I snatched it up from the top of my beach bag before it could ring a second time.

A quick glimpse at the screen told me only that it was a private number. I flipped open the phone and put it to my ear. "Hello?"

"Chantelle?"

It was a man's voice. It had to be Jason.

"Yes, it's Chantelle. Is this Jason?"

"Yes, hi. I got a message that you were trying to reach me."

"Thank you so much for calling me back," I said, my relief palpable. "I've been so worried."

"From what my boss said, you seem to be under the impression that your friend Ashley is with me. I hate to be the bearer of bad news, but I haven't seen Ashley since two nights ago."

My stomach bottomed out. And despite the heat of the day, goose bumps popped out on my skin.

"Hello? Are you there?"

Jason must have said something, but the sound of the blood rushing in my ears had prevented me from hearing anything he'd said after *I haven't seen Ashley since two nights ago.*

"What . . . what did you say?" A numb sensation was spreading through my body.

"I asked why you thought she'd be with me."

Oh my God. Reality was hitting me, and it wasn't good.

"Chantelle?" Jason prompted.

"You and Ashley—that night—it seemed like you two hit it off. She didn't return to the hotel. And you're an editor . . . and . . . Oh, God."

"You think she's missing?" A note of concern crept into Jason's voice.

"If she's not with you, I have no clue where she might be."

"Is it like her to take off for days at a time?"

"No. Never." Except for that one time back home, but I wasn't going to tell Jason that. I honestly believed that Ashley wasn't missing because she was off having hot sex with some guy she'd just met. "And it's the last thing I would expect when she's on vacation with her friends. It doesn't make sense."

There was a pause, then Jason asked, "Have you called the club? Asked if anyone remembers seeing her leave with anyone?"

"No. I thought for sure she was with you." But the truth was, I'd been hoping that. In my heart, I'd felt that something was wrong. "Did you head outside the bar with her at all? Maybe to sit on the patio?"

"No."

"When did you both part?"

"I had to go to the bathroom. When I was finished, Ashley was nowhere in sight. She was pretty drunk. I assumed she found someone to hang with."

"And you didn't look for her?" I asked.

"No."

"Why not?" I pressed. "I mean, it looked like you two had hit it off."

"Look, I was flattered by her attention. But I didn't think Ashley was into me."

"Really?" I asked, doubtful. "That's what you thought, even after that serious kiss?"

There was a pause. "You saw that?"

"Who didn't?" My tone was a bit snippy, and I thought of what Erica had said—that I was jealous.

I guess I couldn't deny that I had been. I only hoped that Jason didn't pick up on that in my tone.

"That kiss came out of left field. Ashley came out of the bathroom, and the next thing I knew, she was planting one on me. I was shocked. But flattered. Who wouldn't be? She's gorgeous."

"Hmm." I inhaled deeply, trying to get over the inappropriate stab of envy.

"I wasn't flattered for long, though, because when she broke the kiss she said, 'Good—he saw that.' Obviously, she was trying to make someone jealous."

So that explained the kiss. I felt relief. Which was totally improper under the circumstances. I wished I could turn off my damned emotions.

"You're sure Ashley wouldn't be anywhere else?" Jason asked. "Maybe she made up with that guy she was trying to make jealous."

"I've already talked to him, and no. Ashley's not with him." I sighed, the gravity of the situation gripping me anew. "I know something horrible has happened. I have to call the police."

There was a long pause, then Jason broke the silence. "I can't believe this." I got the feeling he was speaking more to himself than to me. "I mean, what are the chances?"

"What do you mean?"

"If she's really missing . . . Whoa. What a shitty coincidence."

Now I knew he was talking to himself. And whatever he was referring to, it was important.

"What do you mean by 'coincidence'?" I asked.

"Aww, Jesus." Jason exhaled audibly. "Fuck."

"What?" I asked, desperate to know now, almost hysterical with fear.

"Look, I'm not saying this is the case. Seriously, I pray I'm wrong." He paused briefly. "Did Ashley get to tell you what I'm working on? Why I'm here in Artula?"

"All she told me was that you're an editor."

"I'm an editor, but I'm also a writer. And I'm here on the island doing some investigation for a book. A book about white slavery."

For a moment, I was too stunned to speak. I wasn't even certain I'd heard him correctly.

"White slavery?" I asked, for clarification.

"Yeah."

"You mean like the urban legends about women being taken for the purpose of becoming sex slaves?"

"Trust me, it's not an urban legend. It's a practice that's very much alive and well. And Ashley—she's exactly the type."

My head started to spin. A big part of me didn't compute what Jason was saying as even plausible—it seemed too outrageous. But another part of me wondered . . . With the stories of women who'd gone missing in the Caribbean, their bodies never found, it was possible . . .

My throat was dry, and I had to swallow before speaking. "What do you mean Ashley's 'exactly the type'?"

"Blonde. Beautiful. Oozes sex appeal. All a guy would have to do is put something in her drink, lure her away . . ."

I gasped. "Oh my God."

"I'm not trying to scare you, Chantelle, but it's possible."

I closed my eyes tightly. I didn't want to hear another word. "I . . . I . . . I have to call the police."

Jason snorted, an odd reaction.

"What?" I asked.

"Again, I don't want to be the bearer of bad news—"

"What does that mean?"

"I just pray for your friend's sake that she hasn't been abducted. Because if she has, I can pretty much guarantee you the police won't do anything."

I scowled at Jason's words. "What are you talking about? Why wouldn't they do anything?"

"Because from my experience, the police here are corrupt. Either that or they just don't give a damn."

Corrupt. White slavery. Jason was saying things that didn't make sense to me. I heard him, but I couldn't really comprehend.

Maybe he was a nut case.

"I have to go," I said abruptly. No matter what Jason thought about the police, they would have to be called.

Unless there was a reason he didn't want me to call them.

After all, he was one of the last people to be seen with Ashley.

If not the last one.

"Wait!" Jason said before I could hang up. "Let me give you my number. Will you call me if you find anything out about Ashley?"

I didn't answer.

"Or if you want me to go with you to the police," he continued, "I can do that."

"Why would you? You just told me you think the police are corrupt."

"I do—but I also know you'll call them. You have to. I just wanted you to be prepared for their reaction."

I wasn't prepared for any of this.

"I'd really like you to keep me—"

"What's your number?" I interjected. Again, I sounded abrupt, and Jason noticed.

"I get that you might not believe me," he said. "Hell, you don't know me. You're probably wondering if you can trust me. But I promise you, Ashley wasn't with me Sunday night. I swear to you on my mother's grave. In fact, I was looking forward to hearing from her again."

"Because she's exactly the type," I found myself saying, wondering if a jealous tinge had crept into my voice.

And then I realized that I'd caught him in a potential lie. Why would he be looking forward to hearing from Ashley again if he knew she hadn't been into him?

But before I got to say that, Jason spoke. "No, that's not why. There was no connection between me and Ashley."

"Really?" I asked doubtfully.

"Really. But as an editor, I was intrigued by something she said."

"What?" I asked, not sure I believed him.

"She told me that she had a juicy real-life story that I'd be dying to publish."

Real-life story? Ashley had never mentioned any such story to me. She was a fiction writer, like I was.

"What kind of story?" I pressed.

"I don't know. That's the last thing she said to me before I went to the restroom. And when I came out, she was gone."

Chapter Twelve

JUICY REAL-LIFE STORY.

I ended my call with Jason and ruminated on his comment. *Juicy real-life story.* What on earth could that have been?

Ashley had never once mentioned to me anything about a nonfiction story that she was thinking of, much less writing. She'd been working on a novel, a historical saga set in the antebellum South, as well as a bunch of short stories.

So what kind of real-life story could she have been talking about? Or did Horton House only publish nonfiction, and Ashley therefore gave Jason the teaser to a story she would have to create?

I would only know when I found her, and to do that, I had to contact the police.

I gathered my belongings on the beach and made my way to the front desk, passing fellow Lan-U students who were laughing as they frolicked in the pool and lounged by the bar. They had no clue that something major might have happened.

"Chantelle!"

At the sound of my name, I turned. Rebecca was jogging toward me. She was in a black bikini with a multicolored wrap around her waist, her hair pulled back into a ponytail.

"Hey, girl," she said as she stopped in front of me. "What are you up to?"

"Uh . . . nothing."

"Why don't you join me and Stef? We're getting a drink, then heading to the hot tub."

This was the second time Rebecca had seen me alone. She probably figured I could use the company.

"Actually, Erica is waiting for me in the room. Maybe we can both meet you in the hot tub in a little bit."

"Cool. See you soon."

Rebecca turned and jogged back toward the interior bar, and something about the simple sight of her reuniting with Stefanie made my throat swell with emotion.

That's what this vacation was supposed to be for me, Erica, and Ashley. Happy smiles, drinking margaritas, and lounging by the pool.

It's not too late, I told myself. *If Ashley shows up today, we'll still have three more days. Then everything will be back to normal and we'll show everyone here how to really have fun.*

But my heart told me that wasn't the case.

Swallowing the lump in my throat, I continued to the front

desk, where I asked a clerk if she could give me the number to the police station.

"Is there a problem, ma'am?" the woman asked, her island accent soft, delicate.

I paused. I didn't want to get into the issue of Ashley's being missing with the front-desk clerk. Who knew what she might say to someone else, and how quickly word might spread around the resort.

"Well," I began. "I just . . . I have a personal matter I'd like to discuss with the police, that's all. Nothing to do with the resort." I smiled pleasantly, hoping the woman wouldn't press the matter.

"Here is the number." The woman scribbled the number on a notepad and passed it to me.

"Thank you."

I headed out the front door, and back to the spot where I'd called Horton House, hours before. Anxiety swirled in my stomach like rolling waves crashing against the island's shore. Somehow, I'd held myself together when talking to Jason. But his words kept playing in my mind, and now I was terrified.

"Artula police department," a man's voice sounded in my ear.

"Hi." My stomach rolled again, and my head spun, and I had to lean against the stucco wall before my knees gave way. The emotions in me were vying for an outlet to be released.

"I need to talk to someone." My voice was faint, and I was on the verge of tears. Wherever Ashley was, I knew it wasn't a good place. "About my friend. She's . . . she's disappeared."

"I can hardly hear you, Ma'am. Will you speak up?"

I cleared my throat, and forged ahead. "I need to talk to someone about my friend. We're here on vacation from the

States and she hasn't returned to the hotel. I'm afraid something bad has happened to her."

"Hold please."

No hint of concern, just a detached "Hold please." It made
me think of what Jason had warned me about—that the police
wouldn't be much help.

Bob Marley's "One Love" serenaded me as I waited on the
line, the pleasant words like a mockery of my mood. A good
two minutes passed before someone answered—at least it felt
that long.

"Hello, Miss," came another male voice, this one deeper. "I'm
Sergeant Bingham. What's your name?"

"Chantelle Higgins."

"Miss Higgins, I understand you're concerned about your
friend."

"Yes, that's right."

"Why don't you tell me what happened?"

So I did. I explained that two nights before, Ashley and I
had been at Zack's Shack, how I couldn't find her when I was
leaving but figured she'd make her way back to the hotel. How
she hadn't been back by the next morning, nor the rest of the
day. That I grew gravely concerned by this morning when she
still hadn't returned, not even for a change of clothes.

I also explained that Ashley was an aspiring writer, how
she'd met and become chummy with an editor at the bar, and
that I had, at first, assumed Ashley could have been with him.

"But I was able to get in touch with him," I said, "and she
wasn't with him. Which is why I'm calling you now. I'm worried. And I need help finding her."

"So how long has she been missing?" the sergeant asked.
"Since the night before last?"

"Yes."

"Which is about thirty-six hours. Maybe forty."

Mentally, I did the calculation. "Yes. Around forty."

"A person has to be missing for seventy-two hours before you can file a missing person's report."

"But what if someone has her against her will?" I asked. "Waiting another thirty-two hours can be a crucial mistake."

"Please, Miss. Calm down."

"My friend is missing. I'm anything but calm."

"Didn't you say that you believed your friend was off with a man? The editor you mentioned."

"Well, yes," I said sheepishly. "But that was a conclusion I jumped to—one that was desperate, and erroneous."

"Nonetheless, you assumed she had disappeared with a man that she had just met. If that was your assumption, it says something about the character of your friend."

My lips parted, but I was too stunned to speak. Was this officer actually making a character judgment about someone I'd just told him was *missing*?

"My friend is a tourist. An American citizen," I stressed, hoping he would get my implication that this could turn into a big deal if he did nothing and Ashley actually was hurt somewhere—or worse. "She's missing on your island and you're not even slightly concerned?"

"If she's still missing after seventy-two hours have passed, we will be happy to help you."

"Seventy-two hours may be too late!"

"Miss, I know that you're concerned, but I've worked on the police force for twenty-four years. Twenty-four spring break seasons. Trust me when I say this is not abnormal behavior. I've known friends to disappear for five days and turn up married. Or show up just in time to head to the airport."

"Ashley wouldn't do that," I insisted. "Not without calling, at least. She wouldn't want us to worry."

"Again, in my twenty-four years on the force—"

"What about checking hospitals?" I asked before he could try to dismiss me. "She could have been sick and ended up there. Or what if someone raped her? Shot her? Stabbed her and left her in an alley?"

"Yes, of course—coming from America, I can understand why you would think this. Your country is rife with senseless violence. But do you know how many murders occur on my island, Miss Higgins?" He didn't wait for me to take a guess. "We have a small population. Only seventy-five thousand. Artula is probably the safest country in the world. Last year, there were two murders here. The year before that, one. All arising from domestic situations."

"I'm not saying someone from Artula hurt her," I told him, in case he felt I was making some sort of judgment about Artulans. "All I know is that she's missing, and in *my* country the police would help out in a situation like this."

"Unless there's a reason you can provide that would lead me to believe there's been any foul play—"

"What about white slavery?" I quickly said, throwing out what Jason had told me. I wasn't sure I believed it, but what if Jason was right? He certainly was right about the fact that the police wouldn't be eager to help. "I've heard that many young girls have gone missing from this island, abducted into white slavery. Tourists from abroad whose families have never heard from them again. How often have girls outright disappeared in your twenty-four years on the—"

"Miss Higgins," Sergeant Bingham interjected, an edge to his tone. "You would do well not to listen to the likes of Jason Shear. He cannot prove any of his allegations. Good day."

And then the phone went dead.

Slowly, I lowered the phone from my ear, my heart pounding so hard, I thought it would implode.

I felt light-headed. Nauseous. I staggered to the right, bracing my shoulder against the wall for support before my legs gave out.

It wasn't that the sergeant wasn't ready to help me find Ashley that bothered me the most.

It was that he knew, without me naming him, that Jason Shear was the editor I was talking about.

Which made the crazy story Jason had told me about white slavery suddenly seem far less crazy.

And frighteningly real.

Chapter Thirteen

As much as I had hoped to not have to alert anyone to Ashley's disappearance, praying that I would have found her or heard from her without that ever being necessary, I knew I couldn't keep it secret anymore. I had to talk to everyone from Lan-U, see if any one of them had by chance seen Ashley since I last had, two nights ago in the bar.

I went to the pool. Asked everyone. No one seemed at all concerned as to why I was asking, either too drunk or self-centered to give my question much thought.

After circling the pool, I headed to the hot tub, and abruptly stopped short when I reached its perimeter. Ryan and Blake were there.

I always knew Ryan was a snake, but the fact that he had his tongue down some random blonde's throat solidified the opinion. She was on his lap in the hot tub, his hands beneath the bubbling water, probably groping places on her body no one should do in public. His friends from the football team cheered and jeered, celebrating Ryan's prowess as a stud.

Slowly, I climbed the stairs and stood on the hot tub's landing. I watched, disgusted, waiting for Ryan to come up for air.

As the jocks began to turn toward me one by one, obviously wondering what I wanted, their raucous cheering faded. That's what alerted Ryan and the bimbo to the fact that something was going on. They broke the kiss and both looked up. But Ryan's hands stayed beneath the water—his fingers likely lodged in the girl's loose vagina.

"You want a piece of this, all you've got to do is say so," Ryan said, and everyone broke into hysterical fits of laughter.

I steeled my jaw. I hated this pig. But I wasn't about to let him know that he had gotten under my skin with his crude comment. I drew in a breath and asked, as calmly as I could, "Have you seen Ashley recently?"

"Since the last time she was sucking my dick?" Ryan shot back, and again everyone laughed.

I wanted to spit on him. But again, I played like his vile comment hadn't gotten to me. "After that," I said coolly. "Since that night at the club."

"Still can't find her?" This from Blake. A look of mock empathy played on his face. "You know where she is." He made the kind of hip motion that signified screwing. "Doing what she does best."

"Fuck you, you asshole," I snapped, no longer able to keep my emotions under control. Spinning around, I headed down the steps, back toward the pool. I moved so fast, I had to stop abruptly before slamming into another person.

It was Erica.

"Chantelle!" she exclaimed.

"Sorry, Erica. I wasn't paying attention."

She waved off my apology. "I don't care about that." She looked happy to see me. "Where have you been?"

I remembered Erica's earlier response when I'd brought up my concern about Ashley, and I didn't want to hear her say I was being Mother Superior again. Or worse, that I was disguising jealousy with concern.

But this morning, we'd both thought it likely that Ashley could have been with Jason. Now, I knew that wasn't the case.

I took Erica's elbow and led her several steps away from the hot tub, to the edge of the pool that was close to the path that led to the beach. "I know you didn't believe there was anything weird about Ashley being gone," I said. "You figured that I was jealous about her hooking up with Jason. But she *is* missing. I'm sure of it now."

I braced myself for her dissenting opinion, but instead, regret streaked across her face. "I'm sorry about earlier. I was tired, and felt like crap, and snapped when I shouldn't have. The truth is, I've been a bit messed up ever since what happened with BJ," she admitted softly. "It's made me remember some stuff I wanted to forget. I didn't mean what I said about you being jealous."

I didn't believe her. She hadn't made one offhanded comment that I could easily dismiss. She'd said far too much on the subject of my jealousy for her not to have meant it.

But none of that mattered right now.

"I tracked down Jason." When Erica looked at me in surprise, I explained how I'd called the publisher, and how that had led to a conversation with Jason. "I was hoping and praying that she was with him. But he hasn't seen her, and—"

"And you believe him?" Erica asked. It wasn't a sarcastic question, but a genuine one.

I nodded. "Yes, I believe him. It gets worse, Erica. He told me a crazy story about white slavery, that that's why he's on the island, investigating stories of girls who have come here on vacation and disappeared."

Erica held up a hand. "Whoa."

"I know. Insane, right? But guess what—he also said that if I called the police, they wouldn't help me."

"He could be lying," Erica interjected.

"That's what I thought," I pressed on. "Until I called them and the sergeant I spoke to acted like he couldn't care less."

Erica made a face, her expression saying that was hard to accept.

"I know—unbelievable, right? He said that I needed to wait seventy-two hours before I could report her missing, and I get that. But when I told him that this was completely unlike her, he basically implied that I probably didn't know her well. That she was likely off with someone and I was worried for no reason."

Erica said nothing, just continued to look at me with a puzzled expression.

I began strolling toward the path that led to the beach, and Erica fell into step beside me. "You want to know what really creeped me out?" I asked, my voice barely above a whisper. "When I mentioned to the officer that I'd heard some stories about white slavery, he told me that I'd be wise not to listen to Jason Shear. I'd never mentioned Jason's name."

Erica held my gaze for a beat before shrugging. "Well, you said he's here on the island investigating those stories. I'm sure he must have spoken to the police."

"I know . . . I thought that, too. It's just . . . it was the feeling I got when the sergeant said that."

We stepped onto the sand, and I kicked off my flip-flops. The sand was soft and warm, and a shade just a touch darker than white. Paradise indeed—but beyond the pristine beach and turquoise blue waters, did the island hold a dark secret?

"So what should we do?" Erica asked, pulling me from the bleak thought. "Because you're right—something's wrong. I'm sorry I didn't believe you sooner. I feel stupid for writing you off as jealous."

I shrugged. "I was asking everyone from Lancaster if they've seen her recently. I doubt it, but I figure I have to cover all bases here, just in case. After that . . ." I stopped, faced her. "I'm kind of thinking we have to get in touch with Ashley's family. If this *is* something serious . . ."

Erica nodded. "Yeah. I think you're right. I think we have to."

We both stared out at the Atlantic Ocean. Such an idyllic view.

We sighed at the same time, and I knew we were both thinking the same grim thought.

"All right," I said, turning on my heel. "Let's find a way to track down Ashley's parents."

While walking back to the room, I thought of the fact that I'd seen Ashley's parents only a few times over the years. They lived near Philadelphia, only about an hour from Lancaster University, but rather than visit their daughter on weekends, Ashley liked to return home. She had a fifteen-year-old sister she was very close to, that closeness having been forged ten years ago when their father had abandoned the family, never to be heard from again. Five years after that, her mother had remarried, and Ashley had gained a stepfather.

I didn't know much more about the family, other than the fact that Ashley seemed to adore her mother and her sister, and had reacted to her stepfather with the expected wariness of a teen who didn't have much reason to trust men. Five years later, her mother and stepfather were still happily married, as far as I knew. I hoped the new marital foundation would help Ashley's sister when it came to issues of trust, but I feared it was too late for Ashley. I couldn't imagine the psychological trauma a ten-year-old endured when her father up and left. But I was pretty much certain that she continued to replay that trauma by getting involved with the wrong man over and over again—one who would ultimately hurt her the way her father had hurt her.

Her mother was an OB-GYN, her stepfather a child psychologist. They lived in an affluent suburb of Philadelphia. I didn't expect their home number to be listed, but I knew I'd find the Hamilton family through a listing of medical professionals.

This time, Erica went with me to the hotel lobby, where we used the Internet to do our search. We found the listings for both of Ashley's parents with ease.

"Who do we call first?" I asked.

But even as I asked the question, I was pretty certain what Erica would say.

"Her mother. We should call her mother."

. . .

Mrs. Hamilton took the news well, all things considered. Perhaps because we weren't totally sure that something bad had befallen Ashley, there was no true reason to freak out. There was reason, obviously, to be concerned—but with the return home scheduled for three days from now, it was entirely possible Ashley would return before then.

Mrs. Hamilton advised me that she would be in Artula the next day to help search for Ashley. We would see her then.

"That went well," I said to Erica once I ended the call. "She was cool and calm, not freaking out at all. She said she'll be here tomorrow."

Erica nodded. "That's good. She should be here. In case . . ." Her voice trailed off, and she didn't finish her statement.

She didn't have to.

"I've been thinking," I began. "We need to retrace Ashley's steps. Go back to the club where we last saw her and see if we can find anything out. Someone there might know something—a bartender, a waitress. Someone. Because surely Ashley couldn't have vanished into thin air."

"I've got those pictures we took on my phone," Erica said. "That'll help."

For a moment, I didn't get what Erica was talking about. Then my eyes lit up as it came to me. Before we'd left for the club, Erica had taken a picture of me and Ashley in our outfits, then I had taken a picture of Ashley and Erica.

"Excellent!" I said. "We can show it around, see if anyone recognizes her."

My cell phone sang, startling me. I held it up and looked at the caller ID.

Private name. Private number.

Let it be Ashley, I thought, then flipped my cell open and put it to my ear. "Hello?"

"Chantelle, it's Jason."

My shoulders sagged in disappointment. I hadn't expected it to be her, but the confirmation of that fact left me cold. "Hi, Jason."

"Has Ashley returned?"

"No."

"Have you called the police?"

"I did. And you were right. They weren't the least bit interested in what I had to say. The cop I spoke to feels Ashley's probably somewhere on the island, with some random guy she just met. Said it happens all the time."

"I'm not surprised."

"I called Ashley's mother. Maybe I'm jumping the gun, but I figured I had to. My friend Erica and I are planning to head back to Zack's Shack tonight and ask the staff if they remember anything, show Ashley's picture around."

"That's what I was going to suggest," Jason said. "But wait until about six. The night staff will be working, but it'll be much quieter than later on. In fact, I'd like to come with you."

"Why?"

"If Ashley was abducted into white slavery, that's something I know a bit about. I can help you."

Having him around certainly couldn't hurt. Three heads would be better than two.

"We'll meet you there at six?" I asked.

"See you then."

Chapter
Fourteen

JASON WAS STANDING on the sidewalk in front of Zack's Shack when we arrived, at the edge of the club's enclosed patio. My heart picked up its pace when I saw him, a similar reaction to the first time I'd set eyes on him, surprising me.

At least under the circumstances.

His hair was wet, indicating he'd recently showered. His hands were shoved into the front pockets of a pair of faded jeans. He wore a white T-shirt with a cartoon picture of three men with dreadlocked hair on the front, banging away at a set of drums. The caption beneath the men read:

YOU'RE IN ARTULA, MON. BE HAPPY.

And the people on the patio were certainly happy. Almost all of the patio tables were filled, but it was a more subdued crowd than when the sun went down. These people were eating and enjoying the sunshine, which was slowly making its descent on the western side of the island.

I paid the driver, then Erica and I got out of the taxi. Jason smiled when we approached him, but it was a reserved smile. Wary, given the circumstances under which we were meeting.

"Hello," I greeted him. And when I met his eyes, I felt it. An undeniable zap of attraction. His gaze lingered, giving me the distinct impression that the attraction was mutual.

But mutual or not, it was ridiculous. How could I feel the slightest bit drawn to him when my friend was missing?

I broke our eye contact, glancing toward Erica. "This is my friend, Erica," I announced. "You remember her from the other night?"

"Yes, I remember." He extended his hand to her. "Nice to see you again."

Erica shook it.

I found myself watching to see if Jason looked at Erica the way he'd looked at me. To see if I had been reading anything into his gaze.

There was no intensity when he met Erica's eyes. Nothing but a polite expression, completed with a warm smile.

There is something, I told myself. But my next thought was, *Stop it. What the heck is your problem?*

"I guess we should go inside," I said.

We began to walk, but Erica stopped as we reached the door. She looked at me anxiously, before facing Jason.

"What's the matter?" he asked.

"That thing you said about white slavery," Erica began in a whisper. "You really think that happened to Ashley?"

"I can't say for sure. I only know that many women have disappeared while vacationing on this island, and that the prevailing theory is that they've been abducted for the purpose of human trafficking. I know it sounds crazy, but all you have to do is search the Web for stories about this, even talk to friends and family of the missing about the circumstances under which their loved one disappeared, about strange phone calls . . . and it starts to sound a lot less crazy. There are wealthy men all over the world willing to pay for beautiful women. Men in the Middle East, for example, who pay incredible amounts for a pretty blonde." Jason stopped abruptly, concern streaking across his face. I glanced at Erica, who looked as sick as she had before throwing up when we'd been at Zack's Shack Sunday night.

"I didn't mean to scare you," Jason said.

"Don't sugarcoat anything for our sakes," I told him. "If it's not pretty, it's not pretty. We need to know what we're dealing with."

Jason nodded. "For Ashley's sake, I hope she *is* somewhere with some guy she met. Because if this *is* about white slavery . . ."

Jason didn't finish his statement, but the grim set of his jaw made my body turn frigid. "Because what?" I prompted. "What were you going to say?"

Jason looked at me and Erica in turn before speaking. "Because as much as people know the crime of sex trafficking exists, it's almost like the stories about the Bermuda Triangle."

"I don't understand," I said.

"You know how there were always stories about ships and such disappearing in the Bermuda Triangle."

"Uh-huh," I agreed. Beside me, Erica nodded.

"But there's never any proof," Jason went on. "So in many ways, it's like a myth. Except that people *do* disappear."

"Right," I said, trying to follow his argument.

"The people who abduct young women, who control the sale of them, are so skilled, there's basically no evidence," Jason explained. "At least not enough evidence to lead to anything concrete. So if Ashley was abducted for the purpose of being a sex slave . . ." Jason made a face as he shook his head. "I hate to say this, but the chances of you ever seeing her again are slim to none."

That somber reality hung over us like a dark cloud as we opened the second set of doors that led into the club proper. But I wouldn't believe it. Wouldn't accept it. Not until I knew the truth.

I recognized the bartender with the long dreads and hazel eyes as the one who had served me drinks on Sunday night. He was wiping down the dark marble counter as we approached, the bar area scarcely populated. I knew that would change as the night went on.

The bartender looked up, giving us a nod and a smile in greeting.

"Sebastian." Jason extended his hand across the bar. "Good to see you again, my man."

Sebastian accepted his hand, and the two shook hands first before knocking their closed fists together.

"What's up?" Sebastian asked.

Jason remained standing, resting his forearms on the bar, while Erica and I took seats on the barstools. I was happy to let him take the lead.

"My friends and I were here on Sunday night," Jason said.

"I remember."

"They were also with another young woman," Jason continued. "Long blond hair, very attractive."

"Here's her picture." Erica lifted her cell phone and showed it to Sebastian. "I took this just before we came here Sunday night. So this is what she was wearing."

Sebastian narrowed his eyes as he examined the picture on the phone's small screen. I held my breath as I waited for some response from him. It took him several seconds before he nodded, saying, "Yes, I remember seeing her."

"Did you see her leave with anyone?" I asked. "Anyone she seemed particularly chummy with?"

"There were hundreds of people in the bar," Sebastian pointed out. "I don't keep track of who comes and goes."

"I know," I said. "But anything you can think of may help. She's been missing since that night, and we're worried about her."

"I remember seeing her with you." Sebastian looked pointedly at Jason.

I jerked my head to the left, also looking at Jason. Erica did the same. And I wondered about Erica's question, about whether or not Jason could have been lying. That maybe he had something to hide.

"Yeah, but I didn't leave with her," Jason said. Cool. Calm. Perhaps too cool, too calm?

And then he did something I'd only seen people do in the movies. He took his wallet from the back pocket of his pants and put a twenty-dollar bill on the bar. "Anything you can think of, my man. Anything at all."

Sebastian lifted the bill, his hazel gaze passing over the

three of us before he spoke. "Now that I think of it, I do remember something. This girl, she was talking to two white
guys. Tall. Muscular. One had blond hair, like hers. The other
had dark hair."

Ryan and Blake. My heart slammed against my rib cage.

"And they weren't just talking," Sebastian continued. "They
were arguing. I could tell it was something serious."

I'd seen them, too. That's when I'd gone and intervened. "I
know when you're talking about. They were near the bar and I
rushed over to them because I saw trouble was brewing."

Sebastian shook his head. "No, they weren't at the bar.
They were outside, on the patio. I know because I went to de-
liver some drinks, and I saw them in a corner. Whatever they
were saying, it didn't look like it was pleasant."

Jason nodded slowly. "I remember at one point Ashley told
me she needed to get some air, that she was going to head to
the patio. I asked if she wanted company, and she told me no.
She wanted a moment alone."

"Wait a minute," I said to Jason. "I thought you parted ways
with Ashley when you went to the restroom?"

"I did. That was the last I saw her, when I left her to go to the
restroom. But before that, she'd needed a breath of fresh air,
and made a point of saying she wanted to be alone. At first I
thought she might have been giving me the brush-off, but about
five minutes later she came back in, found me, and I bought a
couple of shooters from a cocktail waitress. It was after that that
I went to the bathroom and never saw her again."

I nodded. Jason's explanation was credible. I turned back to
Sebastian. "When you went outside to the patio, was that the
last time *you* saw Ashley? Or did you see her at the bar later?"

"I don't remember seeing her again, not after I served those drinks outside."

But she had obviously come back inside if she'd met up with Jason again. Jason had mentioned a cocktail waitress. I wondered if she could be of help.

But I doubted it. Based on what Sebastian had said, Ashley had obviously met up with Blake and Ryan again. And they'd been arguing again. It was obvious to me they had something to do with what had happened to Ashley.

"Ryan and Blake," I muttered, shaking my head. "Those fucking bastards. I bet they're behind this. I'm *sure* they are."

"So what do we do?" Erica asked. "Head back to the resort and talk to them?"

I looked beyond her, through the window to the outside, anger brewing inside me like a tornado spinning out of control.

And then I saw something I didn't expect to see.

"Well," I began, almost disbelievingly. "Looks like there's no need to go find Ryan and Blake. Because they've just come to us."

Chapter Fifteen

ERICA'S HEAD whipped in the direction of the front door. So did Jason's.

A sick energy made my hands shake as the door opened and the two slimeballs entered Zack's Shack. They were accompanied by two blondes who wore too much makeup and too little clothing.

I watched them, waiting to see their reaction when they looked my way. When they did, the smug smiles immediately faltered.

You bastards, I thought, and then I was rising, unable to stop myself from charging toward them.

"What did you do to Ashley?" I demanded as I reached them. I didn't give them time to answer before I pounded on Ryan's chest. The woman on his arm gasped and stepped back, as though she feared I would hit her, too. "You were fighting with her on Sunday night," I continued. "What happened next? Did you take her to the beach and drown her?" My voice grew louder, hysteria taking over. "What the fuck did you do?"

I tried to punch Ryan again, but he grabbed my wrist, holding it in his strong grip. Squeezing it. He looked around, as though taking stock of the various witnesses in the joint before deciding what to say.

"You need to calm down."

I fought to free my wrist from his grasp, but I was unsuccessful. He was too strong.

My eyes flitted to both of the women. The one who'd stepped back looked terrified. The one with Blake appeared indifferent. Maybe she was stoned.

I wanted to warn them to run before they ended up like Ashley, but I didn't. Instead I steeled my jaw and said to Ryan, "Let me go."

"Calm down and stop making allegations that will get you into trouble." His voice was low, but angry.

"Why will I get into trouble?" I challenged him. "Because you'll kill me, too? Is that it?" My eyes didn't waver from his menacing gaze, and he finally let me go. Maybe because he knew this public display couldn't look good in front of his date.

"You're insane," Ryan said. "I didn't do anything to Ashley."

"Why were you fighting with her on Sunday night?"

"We weren't fighting."

"That's a lie!"

I felt a hand on my arm, and looked to my left, startled.

Jason was beside me. "Chantelle, this isn't the way to go about this," he said. "If you really believe he's behind what happened, there's another way to deal with this. Like contacting the police."

The woman on Blake's arm widened her eyes slightly, the only sign she was more than a gorgeous mannequin.

"Who the hell are you?" Blake demanded, his gaze suspicious as he sized up Jason.

"Someone who wants to make sure that Ashley is found alive and well." Jason was a good four inches shorter than both Ryan and Blake, but he stood his ground, giving back a glare as strong as theirs.

"You're saying you think something happened to her?" Ryan asked. And for the first time, I saw a look of something other than arrogance on his face. A look that showed a hint of humanity—concern for another human being.

"That's exactly what we think." At the sound of Erica's voice, I glanced to my right and saw her standing there. I hadn't even realized that she'd come to stand beside me.

"We haven't seen her since Sunday night," I said. "When the three of you were clearly arguing over something."

"What were you arguing about?" Jason asked.

"We weren't arguing," Ryan said. "We were having a discussion."

"So heated that the bartender remembers it," I said, my tone doubtful.

Ryan and Blake exchanged glances. Concern for Ashley—or something else?

"This isn't the time," Ryan said. He glanced furtively at the bimbo who had once again come to stand by his side.

"When?" I demanded.

"Back at the resort. Later tonight."

"And you'll tell me what you were *discussing*?" I asked.

"Yes," Ryan agreed. "We'll tell you everything."

"Good." I nodded, satisfied. "Because if you don't, I'm going to the cops."

Smug, I turned. But I heard Ryan say behind my back, "You just might not like what you hear."

You just might not like what you hear.

The words bothered me—until I realized that they were vague. They could mean anything. They could mean, *Ashley left with some unknown guy.* Or they could mean, *We tried to hash things out, but couldn't.* Truly, it could be anything.

On the one hand, I was empowered by the way I'd stood up to Ryan and Blake, but on the other hand, I was terrified. Something had gone on between Ryan, Blake, and Ashley that night. That was clear. But did it have anything to do with why she was missing?

If it did, there could be only one logical conclusion. Something bad had happened. The kind of bad that could mean we would never see Ashley again.

The thought was so daunting, it put me in an introspective mood. I wasn't interested in hanging out and chatting. So I was glad when Jason offered to drop me and Erica off at the hotel, rather than suggest discussing our next move. For his part, he said he would try to see if any of his contacts on the island had any information that was useful.

I went back to the resort with Erica, where we tried to have a normal evening, which included dinner and a few drinks, but there was nothing normal about how either of us was feeling.

Erica tried to poke fun at the various people in ridiculous outfits in an effort to keep the mood light, but I could tell her
heart wasn't in it. We were simply passing the time.

I was anxious to talk to Ryan and Blake, hear what they had
to say about their argument with Ashley. All evening, I kept my
ears open for the sound of their laughter.

When, close to midnight, neither Blake nor Ryan had made
an appearance—at least not that we could tell—Erica and I
decided to head back to the room. I figured the two were likely
going to spend the night screwing the women they'd been with
at Zack's Shack.

The red light on the room's phone was flashing when we
entered, indicating that someone had left a message. At the
sight, my heart filled with hope.

Ashley.

I scurried between the beds, sat on mine, and immediately
picked up the receiver. A quick glance at the instructions on
the phone showed how to retrieve the messages. Moments
later, an automated female voice was telling me that I had one
message. I held my breath and waited for the message to play.

"I'm looking for Chantelle Higgins," a male voice began. "You
need to call me. This is important. It's about your friend."

Alarm shooting through me, I quickly sought a pen and
wrote down the number that the man had left.

"What?" Erica asked the moment I hung up.

"That was a message from some guy. He said to call him,
that he's got information about Ashley."

"Sebastian?" Erica asked.

"I . . . I'm not sure. The person didn't leave a name, but he's
definitely from the island. I guess it could have been Sebastian, but if it was, wouldn't he say so?"

"If it wasn't Sebastian, how did he get this number?"

Erica and I stared at each other, the magnitude of the question clear.

"Should I call?" I asked.

"We have to."

She was right. We had to.

This time, I used the hotel's phone to dial the local number. It rang one time before someone picked up.

"Hello?" came the gruff male voice.

"Sebastian?" I asked.

"Is this Chantelle?"

"Yes, it is. Seb—"

"I need to see you. It's about your friend. Can you meet me tonight?"

"Tonight?" I asked, and Erica's eyes widened in alarm.

"Do you want to find her alive or not?" the man snapped.

"Of course I—"

"Then meet me tonight. Three in the morning. In the alley behind Zack's Shack."

"But—"

The line went dead.

My heart was thundering in my chest as I met Erica's gaze. "Well?" she asked. "Was that Sebastian?"

"I don't think so. But whoever it was, he said that he wants to meet me tonight in the alley behind Zack's Shack. At three in the morning."

"What?"

"He said he has information about Ashley."

"Are you gonna go?" Erica asked, slowly shaking her head, as if trying to influence my answer.

"Do we have a choice?"

"Call the police," Erica said. "They can't ignore you now—
not after that call."

I stood, began to pace.

"Chantelle . . . we have to call the police. This is too much.
It's over our heads."

"We have to go," I said, not knowing where I was getting
the courage. It was from the same place that had allowed me to
grab Blake's cell phone from his fingers and toss it into the hot
tub.

"Chantelle . . ."

"Someone was able to track me down in this room. Maybe
it's someone who knows Sebastian. Maybe it's not. But the
bottom line is, if someone knows something about what happened to Ashley, we—we can't not go."

"Then let's call the police."

I laughed mirthlessly. "Right. Like they'll help."

"Jason, at least."

Erica sounded nervous, and I couldn't blame her. I was nervous, too. "I think calling Jason is a good idea. If he'll come
with us, I'll feel a lot better."

Erica expelled a shuddery breath and sat on the bed beside
me. "I'm scared."

"I know. Me, too."

I used my cell phone to call Jason's number. It rang until it
went to voice mail.

"Jason, it's Chantelle. Call me when you can, okay?" To Erica
I said, "Damn, he didn't answer."

"It's late," Erica pointed out. "Maybe he's already in bed."

I bit down on my bottom lip. "What do we do now?"

Before Erica could answer the question, my cell phone rang.
I quickly answered it. "Hello?"

"Chantelle, it's Jason. What's up?"

"I got a call from someone. A guy. He said he's got information about Ashley and wants to meet at three in the morning—in the alley behind Zack's Shack."

Silence ensued. I wondered if Jason was still there.

"Are you going?" he suddenly asked.

"I—I think I have to," I replied. "Erica said I should call the police, but—"

"No. Don't call the police."

"You think I shouldn't?"

"What was the cop's reaction when you spoke to him earlier?" Jason asked, his tone rhetorical. "I can guarantee you they won't help. They'll see you as a troublemaker."

"Is that how they see you?"

"I'm asking questions about the island's ugly secret. So yeah, they see me as a troublemaker."

"I understand." My stomach fluttered. "Erica and I are scared, but we have to do what we can to find Ashley. Will you . . . will you come with us?"

"You're damn right I will. Want me to pick you up at your hotel?"

"Yeah." I sighed softly, still scared but knowing we had to do this. "Definitely, yeah."

Chapter Sixteen

AT TWO-THIRTY in the morning, Erica and I were waiting outside the hotel for Jason. During the ten minutes we'd stood in the cool night air, I'd kept an eye out for Ryan and Blake.

We'd seen other Lancaster students returning to the hotel, climbing out of taxis rowdy and drunk from whatever parties they'd been at. But not the two people I wanted most desperately to talk to.

But was there really a reason to speak to them now? I'd figured for sure that they had something to do with what had happened to Ashley. But considering the reality that some strange man had called and set up a time to meet him in an alley, it was highly unlikely that Ryan and Blake had anything to do with had happened to Ashley, other than disrespecting her.

Jason arrived in his rented Ford Focus, and Erica and I got into the car. I sat in the front next to him, while Erica sat in the middle of the backseat.

As we neared the downtown area, I subconsciously held my breath for several seconds, releasing it only when my chest began to hurt. Some people bite their nails. Some people sweat. I hold my breath.

Quiet filled the car. It was eerie.

Jason made a right from the main road onto the street where Zack's Shack was. It was the third establishment on the left. Unlike before, there were no crowds on the patio. A few people walked the streets, but the bars had stopped serving drinks at two, and most people were either heading back to their hotels, or heading to one of the island's casinos, which were open all night, or looking for another place to hang out.

As Jason began to slow down, another car neared us, its headlights bright. As it got closer, I could see that it was a police cruiser. And suddenly, I was holding my breath again, afraid, but I didn't know why. I stared past Jason into the car as it passed us. The two male officers stared right back.

"Don't turn into the alley," I suddenly said, not wanting to arouse any suspicions with the officers. "Drive down the block. Don't stop until the cops turn the corner."

"Good idea," Jason said. "It's probably not the smartest thing for them to see us going into the alley."

"Exactly." Not that we were about to commit any crime, but why draw any attention to ourselves?

I craned my neck around, watching the taillights of the

cruiser. When it turned right onto Main Street, I released my breath.

Before righting myself, I caught the expression on Erica's face. She seemed small all alone in the backseat. Small and terrified. Not the same Erica I'd met two and a half years ago, full of attitude and fearlessness.

"It'll be okay, Erica," I told her.

"Will it?"

"Jason's with us, and that's a good thing. We'll get some answers—answers that hopefully will lead to us finding Ashley alive."

Jason did a U-turn at the end of the street, then headed back up to Zack's Shack. I thought he would turn into the alley, but instead he passed it, opting instead to pull up to the curb in front of the club. I'd spotted someone in the alley, someone heaving a bag of garbage into a bin. Could that be the person who'd called me?

I drew in slow, measured breaths as Jason killed the engine. Glancing at me, he asked, "How do you want to do this?"

"I . . . I guess just head out and start walking down the alley."

"All of us?" Jason asked. "Or do you think that will spook this guy?"

"I don't know. I didn't think about that. He didn't say to come alone or anything like that. But . . ."

"But if he sees someone he didn't expect to see, he might not be happy." Jason pursed his lips in thought. "Why don't you and Erica go? I'll get out of the car and stay hidden at the end of the alley. If you yell or scream, I'll come running."

I looked at Erica. She nodded.

"Okay. We'll do that."

I took another deep breath, summoning all of my courage. Then I reached for the door handle. "All right. Let's do this."

I opened the door first and quietly exited the car. Jason and Erica did as well, coming to meet me where I stood on the sidewalk.

Jason nodded, silently telling us to move forward. I took the first step, then Erica did the same. Together, we began a cautious walk down the alley.

My heart was beating so fast, I thought it might explode. I was terrified, and suddenly wondering if calling the cops would have been the better idea.

But that's why Jason was with us. In case of any problems.

If you can trust him. The voice sounded quietly in my brain. Instinct—or irrational fear?

My sandals clicked softly against the pavement. The sound wasn't loud, but loud enough to alert someone in the shadows of the alley that a person was coming.

A shadow came to life suddenly, moving in front of us without warning. I couldn't help it—I screamed.

As quickly as I opened my mouth, a hand clamped down on my lips to quiet me.

The man who held me looked like a nightmare come to life. He had wild eyes, a head of short, unruly hair, and a nasty scar on his cheek that I could see in the dim light of the moon.

It's over, I thought. *We're dead.*

"Quiet!" the man ordered in an anxious whisper. "Do you want to find your friend or not?"

I was scared and breathing hard, but I nodded. Slowly, the man lowered his hand from my face. I shot a quick glance at Erica, who looked horrified. Maybe she'd been too terrified to utter a sound.

"You shouldn't have screamed," the man hissed.

"I—I'm sorry," I stammered. "You came out of nowhere and you scared me."

The man looked anxiously around. His wild eyes widened as his gaze went over my shoulder.

I whipped my head around. Jason was running toward us.

"Who the hell is this?" the man said.

Of course. My scream had caused Jason to believe that something was wrong.

"He's a friend," I quickly said, turning back to the stranger. "He drove us here. I guess he heard me scream and got worried."

Jason's run slowed to a jog as he got about five feet away. He stared at all of us, seeming to figure out that there was no imminent danger.

"I don't like this," the man said. "Why did you bring someone?"

"Because we wanted to be smart," I said. "You know where Ashley is?"

The man looked toward Jason, his eyes wary.

"I'm not a cop, if that's what you're thinking," Jason said. "You can trust me."

The man didn't immediately speak, as if trying to determine if he could truly trust Jason. I suddenly feared he was too spooked and wouldn't tell me what I'd come to learn.

"Please," I begged. "Tell me where my friend is!"

"I'm not sure."

"What?" I asked, incredulous. "What do you mean you're not sure? You had me come here to meet you in the middle of the night—"

"I heard rumors," the man went on. "Rumors that a beautiful blond American was taken."

"Where?"

"It may be too late. They may have already taken her by boat."

"What do you mean?" I asked. "Who took her? What boat?"

"I thought we would be in time to stop them—"

"To stop who?" This from Jason.

"If they took her on the boat, it is too late. You will never find her."

The man was speaking in riddles I couldn't understand.

"White slavery," Jason said, no hint of a question in his voice.

"You know." The man's eyes registered surprise.

"I don't know enough," Jason said. "I've talked to the police, to members of your government—but no one takes me seriously."

The man laughed, a hollow sound. "That is no surprise. There is corruption on every level, more widesp—" He stopped abruptly, terror flashing in his eyes. "Shit!"

I heard the sound of a siren then. Spinning around, I saw the blue and red lights flashing atop a police cruiser that was speeding toward us.

I was too stunned to move, but Jason threw his arm around my waist and dragged me to the alley's side, where I landed against the brick wall with a thud. Both front doors to the cruiser flew open, and an officer sprinted down the alley after the mystery man who had taken off. The other officer approached us, gun drawn.

"Hands up!" he commanded. "Hands in the air!"

"Oh, God!" Erica started to cry, but she raised her hands. I did, too.

"We weren't doing anything wrong," Jason explained.

The cop leveled the gun in his direction. "Hands in the air!" he yelled.

Jason raised his hands.

"Against the wall. All of you."

I was already against the wall, but Erica took shaky steps backward until she was touching the wall beside me. Jason, knowing the cop meant business, did the same.

"We're simply taking a walk, officer," Jason explained. "Cutting through the alley to get to my car."

"Put your hands behind your head and turn around."

"Sir, is this necessary? We're tourists."

I wanted to tell Jason to shut the hell up, that lipping off with this cop would do us no good.

"Turn around," the officer said, his tone saying he was dead serious.

I got the feeling that if we didn't comply, we would get shot.

We all turned around. Erica was still crying. Through my peripheral vision, I could see the officer patting Jason down. He pulled the wallet from the pocket of Jason's jeans.

The officer moved to me. He patted my back near my waist, checking, I supposed, for concealed weapons. But then he smoothed his hands over my ass in a way that made a nervous tingle shoot down my spine.

When he slipped his hand over my crotch, I flinched. The pig wasn't checking for weapons anymore—he was violating me.

"Do you have drugs, Miss?"

"Drugs? No!"

"Women find very interesting places on their body to put them." He slipped his hands around the front of my body and fondled my breasts.

I wanted to scream—but I couldn't.

"Perhaps I need to take you to the station for a strip search."

"We were looking for a friend," I quickly said, hoping that explanation would satisfy the cop. Maybe he did believe that we were in the middle of a dark alley to do a drug deal.

He moved on to Erica, who cried quietly as the cop no doubt did the same thing to her that he'd just done to me.

"Our friend, Ashley Hamilton, has been missing for a couple of days. Someone called me—he said to meet him here in this alley because he knew where she was."

"The man who ran off?" the cop asked.

"Yes."

"What did he tell you?"

"Nothing," Jason said.

"Nothing?" the cop asked, sounding skeptical.

"There was some mention of white slavery," I supplied. "He said something about a boat and that we were too late. Can you help us?" I asked hopefully. "Can you help us find our friend?"

The sound of heavy footfalls had me looking to the left. The other officer who had taken off reappeared.

"I couldn't catch him."

"Are we under arrest?" Jason asked. "You've found no drugs on us."

A beat. I heard the jingle of handcuffs, and my heart pounded violently. Surely these cops weren't going to arrest us. They had no cause.

"What are you doing?" Jason protested as one officer secured handcuffs on his wrists.

The officer then placed his hand on my arm, and my brain frantically tried to make sense of the situation. But instead of securing my wrists behind my back, he gently turned me around. The other cop turned Erica around.

"You two may go," he said, looking at me first, then Erica.

My eyes shot to Jason. "What about him?"

"Jason Shear is coming with us."

"Why?" Jason protested.

"I believe we stopped a sexual assault," the cop explained, a hint of a smile in his evil eyes. His hypocritical words made me want to slap his arrogant face. "Did this man assault you?"

"No!" I exclaimed.

Erica didn't say a word. She was still crying.

"What about you, Miss?" the other officer asked her. "Did this man assault you?"

Erica was far too distressed to speak.

"Your friend is exhibiting the classic signs of a victim," the officer said.

"No—no," Erica finally managed. "He didn't hurt me."

"And Jason Shear matches the description of a man who has raped at least three tourists in the last week," the first cop went on.

Though I didn't think the words could be true, I threw an anxious gaze toward Jason nonetheless.

"You lying son of a bitch," Jason said. "That's not true—"

Fast as lightning, the second officer struck Jason in the stomach with his billy club. Crying out, Jason doubled over in pain.

"You cops know all about the women abducted on your island," Jason said defiantly, his voice strained and his breathing ragged from the pain. "Women abducted to be sold as sex slaves. You know and you do nothing to stop it!"

This time, the billy club hit him on the back. The cracking sound reverberated through the narrow alley, and I gasped as I saw Jason fall to the ground, barely holding my tears back.

"Go on, you two," the first officer said. "You're safe now."

Erica and I stood, immobile, both of us watching in terror as Jason writhed in pain on the ground.

"Go!" the officer yelled.

Erica took my hand in hers, tugging on it. She wanted to get the hell out of the alley.

I hesitated, not wanting to leave Jason. But Erica tugged on my hand again, her sobs growing louder, and this time I moved. Together, we ran.

Ran for our lives.

Chapter
Seventeen

I DON'T THINK either one of us slept. Curled up in the fetal position on her bed, Erica cried for a good hour after we got back to the room. I didn't allow myself to cry. My emotional pain had rendered me numb.

All night, I wondered what was going to happen to Jason. I didn't believe for a second that he was a suspected rapist. That was a trumped-up allegation made in order to take him into custody. And if they wanted him in custody, the bigger question was why.

A stab of pain pierced my heart as I thought of the answer

to that question, which was one I couldn't deny no matter how much I wanted to.

The police wanted to silence him.

Would Jason make it out of the Artula police station in one piece?

And was Ashley on a boat in the middle of the Atlantic Ocean, on her way to God-knows-where to become some wealthy bastard's sex slave?

Her mother would be arriving on the island, probably bright and early. Yesterday, she hadn't freaked out when I'd called to tell her the news of Ashley being missing. Without any concrete story of something bad that had befallen her daughter, Mrs. Hamilton had been able to maintain her composure.

But how would she react today? With the stories of white slavery and ships setting sail, and police corruption . . .

They were the kinds of stories that painted a very grim picture, which was why Erica had cried herself to sleep. Somehow, I had kept myself from becoming a weeping mess, but as the ugly reality hit me anew that I might never see Ashley—or Jason—again, my eyes grew moist with tears.

With the sun's early morning light beginning to filter into the room, I began to cry.

I couldn't stop. It was going to be an awful day.

The room phone rang just before ten, the loud sound like a death knell going off. I jumped up, terrified out of my slumber, reaching for the phone before it rang a second time.

Erica hadn't moved. In her bed beside me, she was finally sleeping after a mostly sleepless night. She'd always been the type who could sleep soundly, even if a fire alarm was going off. The ringing phone hadn't caused her to stir even a little.

"Hello?" I said, placing the receiver to my ear. My voice was groggy. I sounded like death.

"It's Jason."

I sat upright. "Jason! Oh my God! Where are you?"

"Home. Finally."

"How are you? What did they do to you?"

A pause. "I've been better. They beat the crap out of me, Chantelle. That shit about me being a rapist—it was an excuse to take me in. What they wanted to do was give me a warning—a warning not to ask any more questions."

Most of the night, as I'd lain awake unable to sleep, I had thought long and hard about what had happened in the alley. That experience, along with the fact that the first cop I'd spoken with had done nothing to help, led me to believe that there was a bigger story here.

There is corruption on every level.

That's what the stranger had said before the sudden arrival of the cops in the alley.

Corruption. Conspiracy theories. It all seemed too incredible to be true, especially on a small island like this one, where a tourist's biggest concern was what sights to see. And yet, it *was* true. I knew that. Because it was one thing not to take an allegation of a missing person seriously, but the way the cops had attacked Jason . . . There was something they wanted to cover up.

"But I got off lucky," Jason said. "Probably because they can't kill an American without explaining that to the world."

"Have you been to a hospital?" I asked. "How badly are you hurt?"

"I'll be okay."

"Don't say that, Jason. You need to get checked out."

"I said I'll be okay."

"But you could be bleeding internally, or—"

"Chantelle, listen to me," Jason said, cutting me off impatiently. "Because this is important. And you're gonna be scared, but you need to know what happened." Jason paused. "They killed him, Chantelle. The guy who met us in the alley—he's dead."

"What?" I shrieked. Finally, Erica moved, turning her head on the pillow—but she didn't open her eyes.

"His name was Paul Dunlop, and his body was found this morning. In a park downtown." I heard a heavy sigh on the other end of the line. "Chantelle—they cut his tongue out."

Waves of nausea instantly rolled through me. The image, the horrid reality, left me wanting to retch. "Oh God in heaven."

"It's what they do to people who talk," Jason went on. "Cut out their tongues as an example for others to stay quiet."

"Who?" I asked hoarsely, my throat clogged with emotion. "Who would do this?"

"The cops. Some government official. Or whatever thug they hired to do their dirty work. They knew he planned to tell you about the island's dirty secret, and he paid for that with his life."

I couldn't speak. I could hardly keep from throwing up.

"I've heard stories that sometimes people who talk simply vanish, the only thing left of them is their severed tongues."

"No bodies?" I asked.

"The north side of the island isn't like the south. The water there is treacherous. There are rocks, not soft white sand. It's the perfect place to dispose of a body because the current is so strong, the body will probably never be seen again."

I closed my eyes, a shiver washing over me while my head swam.

"I know you figured Ryan and Blake had something to do with Ashley's disappearance, but I think it's fair to say they didn't. To me, it's pretty clear what happened to your friend."

I swallowed. White slavery.

If only I could turn back time, I would have stayed with Ashley the entire time. Gotten on her case about drinking too much, and not cared if she and Erica called me Mother Superior. I would have made sure she was never out of my sight.

If only I'd done that, she would be safe right now.

If only.

But I couldn't turn back the hands of time.

"Chantelle?"

"I'm here," I said softly, holding in tears. "What did you say?"

"I said it's also pretty clear we're not going to find Ashley without help. Real help."

"Gosh, Jason. Do you think we can? Find her? I mean, if you're right . . ." My voice trailed off. I wanted to remain positive, to never give up hope. But was that realistic? Ashley could be on her way to the Middle East, with no way for anyone to save her.

"We can't stop trying, Chantelle. Never. You hear me? There's still hope."

I would cling to that hope, however fleeting. "Who should we call?"

"Authorities from the United States. But we have to get the media all over this, create a compelling reason for the U.S. authorities to get involved."

"Ashley's mother is arriving today. Probably any minute."

"That's good," Jason said. "It'll take a family member to raise some hell before people are gonna start hearing."

"Maybe you can meet with her. Tell her everything you know about the conspiracy here."

"I can't. I'm going back to the States."

"What?" Panic gripped me. And something else.

"They've given me twenty-four hours to get off the island, or they're putting me in jail. I was looking into flights when I heard the news about the murder and called you."

"Jason . . ." My voice trailed off. I didn't know what to say. I couldn't ask him to stay, not when I knew what was at stake.

"No, this is good," Jason said. "I'm going to get the story out. To CNN. Fox News. *The New York Times*. And with you on the island, you can take this story to the world."

"Me?"

"I'm serious about getting the media involved. Can I tell them to contact you?"

No. That's what I wanted to say. If the police had beaten Jason and killed someone else, hell no, I didn't want to be involved.

Jason must have sensed my hesitation, because he elaborated. "Once CNN, the BBC, and all the other news media get involved, there's nothing the cops can do to you. They won't be able to touch you. And maybe, just maybe, this kind of attention will be the exact pressure the island needs to bring Ashley and the other women home safely."

The other women . . . Though I knew there had to be others— after all, one missing woman did not a conspiracy make— hearing Jason say that struck me so profoundly, it was like being hit in the gut with a baseball bat.

The other families and friends. People whose loved ones had disappeared, and they had no clue what had ever happened.

Did the assholes who abducted women to sell them into sexual slavery care about the devastation they caused? About how hard it must be for a mother to go on each day, never knowing if her daughter was dead or alive?

Obviously not, or they couldn't do what they did.

Thinking about the gravity of the problem, the scope of people affected, made it clear what I must do. Jason was right about getting the story out to the media. I was here. I'd witnessed some of what had happened. If my speaking out to the media helped in any way, I would *have* to do it.

No island—especially not one that relied on tourist dollars—wanted negative publicity. If making this story public could lead to Ashley being found alive and well, then I would do whatever I could to help.

"Okay," I said softly. "I'll do whatever is necessary."

I looked over at Erica's bed and was surprised to see that her eyes were open, and she was staring at me.

"Great, Chantelle. I know you're scared, and you have every right to be. I can only hope that this is the story that makes a difference."

"What time is your flight?" I asked.

"Not sure yet. There's one around four, and one a bit earlier. I was gonna pack my things and head to the airport, see how it looks when I get there."

"Ashley's mother might already be here. I really think you should meet her, explain your suspicions. You know much more about this than I do. And she might believe it more coming from someone like you."

"If she gets here fairly soon, no problem. I can at least talk to her on the phone."

"I'll call you when I hear from her. We'll take it from there."

"Okay. I'll continue packing until you get back to me."

I hung up the phone, and once again looked at Erica, ready to tell her about the murder.

But her eyes were closed again, her lips slightly parted, her chest rising and falling in a steady manner that indicated she was asleep.

Chapter
Eighteen

UNLIKE ERICA, I could no longer sleep. With Ashley's mother arriving soon, I felt it was necessary to get the word out to everyone that Ashley was missing.

So I dressed quickly and headed toward the main area of the resort, figuring I would find at least some of the Lancaster students in the dining room, given the hour.

When I walked into the resort's main restaurant, everything felt surreal. All around, people were smiling, laughing, engaging in casual chatter. Life for them was going on as usual, while for me—for Ashley—nothing was normal anymore.

I thought of Ashley's warm laugh and infectious smile—

and my knees buckled as a wave of nausea hit me. Would I ever hear my friend laugh again?

Along the wall to the right, bordering the windows, I saw the first faces I recognized. A group of five girls from Lancaster was seated there, all of them with coffee and toast in front of them. Nursing hangovers, no doubt. There was a sixth seat at the table that was empty, and without asking, I pulled it out and sat down.

They didn't expect that, and they looked at me in mild surprise. But surprise quickly changed to alarm.

"Chantelle, are you all right?" Kelly asked me. "You look awful."

I shook my head. "No. I'm not all right."

And then I explained everything. That Ashley was definitely missing and likely abducted into white slavery. I told them about Jason, the editor from New York, and how a man who'd tried to tell us about Ashley had been killed.

"Spread the word," I said. "Ashley's mother is coming any minute, and I want everyone to know what's happening."

Numbly, I left that table and went to another, giving the same spiel to this group of students, which consisted of girls and guys.

"Chilling," one girl said. "Maybe that's why Ryan and Blake left this morning."

I'd been numb because of everything that had happened, but something inside me stirred at the girl's words. "What did you say?"

"You haven't heard?" another girl, Karen, asked. "Some people saw Ryan and Blake leaving with their luggage. They decided to cut their trip short."

I'd been unconsciously holding my breath, and had to

force myself to expel it before I could speak. "Did they say why?"

"Apparently they said something about the island not being for them. I was starting to get a creepy feeling here, too," Karen added. "And if Ashley's been abducted, maybe we should all leave."

I had to get out of the dining room. I hurried outside, breathing in gulps of the tropical morning air. It was warm, but I felt cold.

Ryan and Blake had left the island.

Why?

Suddenly, I was doubting them again. Why leave your vacation two days early?

Unless you had a reason to get off the island in a hurry.

Was that reason Ashley?

I scrambled down the stone path to my room, thoughts spinning in my head like a cyclone. I didn't know what to think anymore.

But by the time I was slipping the electronic key into the slot to open my room door, I told myself that their leaving had nothing to do with Ashley. Not after what had happened with the police and the stranger last night.

A stranger who had been killed to keep the island's dirty secrets quiet.

When I got to the room, Erica was awake. She told me that Ashley's mother had called from the airport to find out if there was any updated news, and was on her way.

"What did you tell her?" I asked.

"I told her that Ashley hadn't come back yet, but I didn't

tell her anything about last night. She said she and her family will be staying at this resort."

"Oh." Well, I supposed that was easier. Neither of us would have to travel to get together.

"Guess what?" I said as I sat on the edge of my bed. "Ryan and Blake left. They checked out this morning."

I watched Erica, wondering if she would have the same confused reaction I had. But after a moment, she shrugged. "With all the shit going on, I want to get out of here, too."

"You don't think it's strange?" I asked.

She shrugged again. "Think about it, Chantelle. You practically accused them of being behind Ashley's disappearance. Maybe they don't want to get hauled into the police station. And after what happened last night, I don't blame them."

"They said they were going to tell me why they'd argued with Ashley."

"Jesus, Chantelle—you think that matters? Ashley's probably on a ship to the Middle East, or Morocco, or wherever men take women to be sex slaves."

"I know . . ."

"Then drop it," she snapped. "It's like you want to see someone arrested for kicking a person, when the bigger problem is that the person was stabbed."

Erica was right, and I knew it. I just didn't like the timing of Ryan and Blake's disappearing act, even if on some level I could understand it.

"I'm sorry," Erica suddenly said. "I shouldn't be snapping at you. It's just . . . the way that cop groped me last night." Her voice cracked, and as she looked at me, her eyes filled with tears. "It brought it all back, Chi-Chi. The night of the Halloween party, how those guys all took advantage of me. Only this was worse, because I didn't know if we were going to live or die. Because I couldn't muster the courage to fight." Her head fell forward, and she softly cried.

I went and got the box of tissues, then sat beside Erica and extended the tissue box to her. She took out a wad and dabbed at her eyes. "It became so clear to me last night that something inside of me has changed. I've been trying to go on since . . . what happened . . . acting like I've been completely fine, when that's not true at all. There was a time when I wouldn't have gone down without a fight. I would have kicked, I would have screamed, I would have threatened. But last night . . ."

"Last night, we were dealing with cops who literally had our lives in their hands. Fighting would not have been smart."

"It's more than that," Erica said. "And I know that you know it. I snap at my friends more often, I'm not there in the way I used to be . . . it's like I've got a wall up so I can't feel, and it's all because of what happened to me. I don't like who I've become."

"Oh, Erica," I said. I gave her hand a comforting squeeze. Yes, she had changed. And while I could understand it, I'd been frustrated by the way she'd bottled up everything, by the way she had been less accessible. The carefree, sarcastic friend who had been such a rock had disappeared after the Halloween party.

"I hate even more that I'm thinking about *me* at a time when I should be thinking about Ashley. Here I am crying, wallowing in my own misery, when Ashley should be my number one focus."

"Hey," I said softly. "You're your number one focus. Especially when you've suffered trauma. It's called self-preservation. That doesn't mean you don't care about Ashley. I know you do."

Erica nodded, then said, "When I get back home, I'm gonna

get some therapy. But before that, I'm telling my parents what happened to me." Erica faced me, her eyes glistening with tears, looking more vulnerable than I'd ever seen her. "I think it's been eating me up inside that I've kept it from them."

"They won't blame you," I said, voicing a fear she'd mentioned more than once before.

"Maybe not, but they'll be disappointed. And my dad . . . I don't know how he'll take it."

"Your father will be nothing but supportive," I said, feeling a twinge of sadness as I thought of the gentle, older man, wishing that I had a father like him in my life. What I wouldn't give to have a father to call right now and share the burden of Ashley's disappearance with. Lord knew, my mother wouldn't be able to handle learning the news.

"Your parents will want to be there for you and help you through whatever you need to go through," I went on, my tone reassuring. "Just like your friends."

Erica's face crumpled. "Gosh, Chi-Chi, do you think it's possible we'll never see Ashley again?"

Erica's question hung between us for a few seconds, dark and heavy. I swallowed before speaking. "We *will* see her again," I said, trying to be strong. "We can't believe anything else . . . not until we know otherwise."

Erica nodded, but the pained expression on her face told me she couldn't let herself trust my words.

I couldn't handle looking at her, couldn't handle the truth of what I saw in her eyes. So I got to my feet, saying, "I'd better call Jason back. I'd like him to meet Ashley's parents, if he's got time."

"Yeah, of course."

I felt as though my emotions, at any moment, could spill

over the dam I'd erected to keep them in check. So I took a deep breath and held it, trying to keep the dam in place while I went to my purse and got my cell phone.

Moments later, I was calling Jason's number.

"Chantelle?" he said when he picked up.

Just hearing his voice lifted my spirits—if only slightly. "Yeah, it's me. Ashley's mother is on her way from the airport. Can you come to the hotel now?"

"Yeah, that'll work. My flight is at five. I was just about to call you and ask what's happening."

"How long will it take you to get here?"

"I can be there in ten minutes," Jason replied. "You'll need to wait for me at the hotel entrance though. I don't know if they'll let me come in, since the resort is all-inclusive."

"Hmm." I hadn't considered that. "I'll talk to the manager. Explain the situation. Hopefully there won't be a problem."

Because given what we were going to discuss, we needed a place to have a private conversation.

Once I explained the situation to the manager, he agreed to give Jason a pink band, which would indicate he wasn't allowed to drink or eat while at the resort. Which was fine. He wasn't here on a social call.

After about five minutes of waiting outside the hotel's front doors, I saw Jason's car approach. A bellman started for his car the moment it came to a stop, then opened the driver's-side door.

Jason stepped out of the car—and when I saw him, all the air left my lungs in a rush.

It was clear to anyone who looked at him that he had suffered a beating. He had a black eye, and there were visible bruises on his arms and legs.

Those were the marks I could see.

Yet his lips spread in a grin when he saw me, even as he limped toward me, as though he hadn't been through an excruciating ordeal the night before.

I wanted to cry again. I wanted to scream. I wanted to have the Artulan police who had done this to him charged with assault.

But my hands were tied, and I knew it.

I made my way over to Jason and opened my arms to him. He stepped into my embrace and I gently wrapped my arms around his body.

"Hey," I said softly. Then, "Oh, Jason—I'm so sorry. If I hadn't involved you—"

"No, don't apologize. If you hadn't called me, things could have been a lot worse."

As he said the words, my stomach twisted. It was something I hadn't considered. But he was right. What if the cops had done something worse to me and Erica without him around?

Maybe nothing would have happened.

But maybe something would have.

The way something had happened to Ashley.

Jason pulled away first, but his hands lingered on my arms for a moment, as though he was reluctant to let me go. And I felt something then. A spark pass between us.

I looked up into his eyes. Was I imagining the feeling? Or was it simply that this whole crazy ordeal had bonded us, making me believe something might be brewing between us when it wasn't?

"Is she here yet?" Jason asked me.

It took me a moment to get what he was asking, given where my thoughts just were. Then I shook my head. "No. Ashley's mother hasn't arrived yet. But I'm sure she'll be here soon."

He nodded. "Okay. Why don't we go back to your room? I've got some stuff on my laptop that I want to show you."

The expression on his face said that whatever he wanted to show me was serious, so I didn't ask him about it. I would learn soon enough, in the room. And I knew I wouldn't like it.

As soon as we were inside my room, Jason greeted Erica. Her face registered the same kind of surprise mine must have exhibited at seeing his appearance. He didn't hug her, however, just said a simple hello.

Then he got down to business, pushing aside some of our personal stuff on the table and making room for his laptop. "I've got some things to show Ashley's mother," he explained as he booted up the computer. "Files with my research about Artula and its history of white slavery."

Erica and I watched as Jason opened one file, complete with photos of a blond girl. I reeled backward—the girl on the screen looked a lot like Ashley.

"That's Deborah Matheson, who came to the island two years ago from England. She disappeared after a night of partying with her friends. Went to the bathroom and wasn't seen again."

Jason clicked more keys, bringing up another file. Another pretty blonde smiled at us from the screen. "Jennifer Probst, from Vancouver, Canada. She was on a cruise ship with her friends when she stopped here for the day. She was supposed to return to the ship at six in the evening. She never showed."

There were more files. More pictures of beautiful young women. Most were blondes, but there were some brunettes and a couple of redheads in the mix.

I'd lost count after twelve. "How many women are in your files?" I asked.

"Nineteen. More, really. But I decided to concentrate on the ones in the last seven years."

"Nineteen women in seven years, and no one has done anything?" Erica asked, sounding totally dumbfounded.

"Twenty," Jason corrected. "Including Ashley."

His words hung over us like a dark cloud, and for several moments we were silent. I didn't want to believe that we would never find Ashley, but with nineteen other women who had vanished in seven years, the odds were against there being a happy ending.

"It's almost unbelievable that something like this could happen without there being an international outcry," I said. "You only hear about the odd girl going missing, every so often. Like the Natalee Holloway story."

"I don't know how a problem of this magnitude can go unanswered," Jason said. "I guess the government supplies answers and people believe them. And when you cry conspiracy theory, people think you're nuts. No one wants to believe that people in positions of trust could be responsible for anything heinous."

The phone rang then, loud and shrill, and I nearly jumped out of my skin. When it rang a second time, I looked at Erica and Jason in turn. "Ashley's mother," I said, my voice barely a whisper.

Then I hurried to answer the phone.

Chapter Nineteen

ALTHOUGH I'D MET Anabelle Hamilton on a few occasions in the past, seeing her in the hotel lobby that morning, I couldn't help doing a double take. It was the resemblance to Ashley. I had a split-second hope that it was my friend, and not her mother, who had just arrived at the hotel.

Anabelle Hamilton had the same shade of blond hair as her daughter, and was also strikingly beautiful. She was an older, more sophisticated version of Ashley.

Her hair was pulled back, her face bare. Like her daughter, she didn't need makeup to look beautiful. She was naturally stunning without any makeup enhancements whatsoever.

The only thing marring the woman's pretty face was the stress, which I could see in her eyes.

But she held her head high, kept herself composed, in a way that told me she was emotionally very strong.

I thought of my own mother, how she might have reacted in a similar situation. She would have been hysterical, an emotional mess.

Bill Hamilton, Ashley's stepfather, was beside Anabelle, but I noticed that they weren't standing closely together. He didn't have his hand looped through her arm, nor was his arm protectively draped across her shoulder. Instead, his hands were shoved into the front pockets of his khaki shorts. Perhaps the stress of the situation had them at odds. Traumatic situations either brought couples closer or drove them apart.

I didn't see the young girl, another blonde, until she shifted behind her mother. She was Megan, Ashley's younger sister by five years, whom I'd met only twice. She stood behind her mother as though trying to shield herself from the brutality of the world.

Yes, the stress of their missing family member clearly had affected the family unit. They weren't huddled together like a close-knit family. They stood apart. Disconnected in the face of this awful situation.

They were near the doors in the lobby, Anabelle's eyes scanning the vast area. I began my approach, smiling softly when I reached them. "Mrs. Hamilton?"

She finally noticed me. "Chantelle," she said, sounding relieved, and her lips pulled tightly in what must have been an attempt at a smile. "Hello. It's good to see you again."

"Hello." I offered her my hand, though I wanted to offer her a hug. "I'm glad you could make it, but I'm sorry the circumstances aren't better." I looked at Bill. "Hello, Mr. Hamilton."

"Hello," he replied. His hands stayed in his pockets.

I turned to Ashley's sister. "Hi, Megan," I said gently. "I'm not sure if you remember me."

She shrugged, indifferent. Or perhaps, just too stressed to engage in small talk.

"Has Ashley returned?" Mrs. Hamilton asked me, matter-of-fact, getting down to business.

"No." I shook my head to emphasize the point. "She hasn't come back yet. But there's . . ." I glanced around and lowered my voice. "There's some news. We can talk about it back in my room."

Mrs. Hamilton's eyebrows rose, the question evident in her eyes. And for a moment, a flash of despair clouded her expression. But only for a moment.

"Not the worst kind of news," I quickly said, realizing how my words must have sounded. "In fact, it may be a lead. We don't know."

Anabelle Hamilton's eyebrows shot up. "We?"

I glanced around the populated lobby, conveying with my eyes that this wasn't the right place. "I'll explain everything when we get to my room."

Anabelle and Bill nodded their understanding, while Megan, looking miserable, stared at the floor, her arms folded over her chest.

"Maybe you should check in first," I suggested.

"We're not staying here," Mrs. Hamilton said.

"But you said you'd reserved a room here."

"I had. But then I changed my mind." Ashley's mother's eyes flitted around the lobby. "I wanted someplace quieter, where there'd be no distractions. I made some calls on the way here from the airport, and a travel agent is securing us a guest house."

"Ah." I understood. "Then let's talk to the manager so he can give you wrist bands that will allow you access to the resort."

They followed me to the front desk, where the manager gave the three of them the same pink bands he'd given to Jason. Then I led the way out of the lavish lobby and to my room.

Everything about this situation was surreal, like it was happening to someone else. I knew I was smack-dab in the middle of it, and yet, a part of my brain wouldn't accept that anything that had happened was truly real. I kept hoping that Ashley would show up, alive and well, with a doozy of a story to tell us all.

I guess it was my brain's way of coping. Because the moments when I let myself accept the awful truth, that Ashley might never come back or ever be found, those were the moments when I felt on the verge of losing it.

I knocked softly on the door when we got to the room. Erica opened it almost immediately. And I noticed then the change in her. In the short time I had left her, she seemed to have aged ten years. There were dark circles under her eyes, and a deep worry crease across her forehead, as though she had frowned for a week straight, which literally changed the makeup of her face.

In the time I'd gone to meet Ashley's parents in the lobby, she'd fallen off the tightrope of her emotions into the pit of despair. I suspected that the arrival of Ashley's parents had made it all far too real for her. That, in addition to the personal trauma she was dealing with, had clearly pushed her over the edge.

I was close to going over that edge, too. But I knew I couldn't let myself go emotionally or I might never pull myself together.

"Mr. and Mrs. Hamilton, this is Erica. We were both rooming with Ashley."

Anabelle's eyes took in Erica, but went past her almost instantly, to Jason. "And who is he?"

Jason spoke before I could. "My name is Jason Shear," he explained, walking toward her with his hand outstretched. "I'm an editor and writer from New York. I've been here on the island for the past two weeks, investigating stories of white slavery."

"White slavery?" Anabelle asked, doubt and shock emanating from her voice. She didn't take Jason's proffered hand.

"You think Ashley has been abducted into white slavery?" Bill asked, his tone echoing Anabelle's doubt. I was surprised he'd spoken at all. Oddly, he seemed to be letting his wife take the lead. Because Ashley wasn't his biological daughter?

"I know it sounds far-fetched." Jason lowered his hand to his side. "But I assure you, it's not only plausible—as far as I'm concerned, it's likely. I've been researching this very issue for quite some time, and I've discovered that it's the island's dirty secret."

Anabelle and Bill exchanged skeptical glances, but remained quiet, and Jason spent the next few minutes laying out his theory.

"So you're saying," Anabelle began when he was done, "that there is an organized group on the island that abducts girls like Ashley—for a price—basically selling them to rich men in the Middle East, or God-knows-where."

"That's exactly what I'm saying."

Anabelle looked to Bill, then began to pace the floor. I watched her, watched her face as she processed the news. Again, I was struck by the fact that Bill didn't touch her. Didn't try to comfort her.

Several seconds later, Anabelle stopped walking, closed her eyes, and pressed a fist to her forehead. When she opened her eyes, she looked at Jason.

"I've never been one to believe conspiracy theories, Mr. Shear. And what you're saying now . . ." She shook her head. "I need to call the police. I need to retrace my daughter's steps. I need to hit the streets and get flyers into as many people's hands as I can."

I, I, I. Anabelle was speaking like a woman here on her own, without her husband. Maybe she was hopeful while Bill wasn't. Maybe one was mad at the other for agreeing to let Ashley go on this spring break vacation. Because something was clearly keeping them from being a couple.

She faced me, and I noted that her hands trembled as she drew in a deep breath. "Where was she last seen?"

"We were with her at a club called Zack's Shack."

"And have you been back there? Have you asked if anyone's seen her?"

"Yes. We spoke to the bartender."

"And what did he say?"

"He remembered her. Remembered seeing her talking to Jason, and—"

That was all I got to say. Anabelle's hand shot up and she said, "Whoa. Jason? *This* Jason?"

"Oh, Jesus Christ," Bill uttered.

"*You* were one of the last people seen with my daughter?" Anabelle went on.

I hadn't even thought of my words, of the picture they would paint.

"Yes," Jason began. "I—"

"White slavery, Mr. Shear? Do you think I'm a fool?" Anger contorted Anabelle's face as she closed the distance between herself and Jason. She pounded both her fists on his chest. "Tell me where my daughter is, you sick son of a bitch! Tell me right now!"

Chapter
Twenty

ANABELLE HAMILTON kept pounding on Jason's chest, the wall guarding her emotions finally crumbling. "Tell me!" she screamed at the top of her lungs, and then began to sob. The gut-wrenching sobs of a mother who feared the worst had happened to her child.

Finally, Bill ran to her side, scooping her into his arms just before her legs gave way. She bawled like a baby as he held her, the once strong woman a quivering mass of despair.

"Tell me. Please . . ."

Hot tears spilled onto my cheeks. I could no longer keep my emotions contained, not in the face of this woman's grief. Megan was crying, too. Their devastation was immeasurable.

Jason looked stricken, and on the verge of crying himself. "Yes, I was with your daughter, Mrs. Hamilton. But I swear to you, I never hurt her. I care about what's happened to Ashley, and I want to help find her. I don't want another woman on this island to go missing."

"Because you care about a girl you met one night in a bar," Anabelle shot back, her tone sarcastic. Having regained her composure, she stepped out of Bill's arms.

"Yes," Jason answered, the word truthful. "I do care about Ashley."

Bill moved toward Megan, reaching for the sobbing girl, but she sidestepped him and ran to her mother, throwing her arms around Anabelle's waist.

Anabelle smoothed a hand over Megan's hair, ignoring Jason and everyone else for a few seconds as she comforted her daughter. And then she suddenly laughed with scorn. "Of course, Mr. Shear. Now I get it. This is all about a book deal for you. You care so much you want to profit from a family's pain."

My eyes flew to Jason's. I don't know why I hadn't considered that angle before. That for him, this ultimately boiled down to dollars and cents.

Slowly, Jason began to nod. "All right. I admit that I have an ulterior motive."

"You bastard," Bill spat out. "You sick fuck."

My heart sank. I'd let myself start caring about Jason, believing that he was as concerned about Ashley as I was. But how stupid that was. Why should he care about her? He didn't know her. He wanted to be embroiled in the story because it would further his career.

"But it's not what you think," Jason quickly said. "I didn't endure being beaten by cops and almost killed for a bloody story."

He paused, looking at everyone in turn before his eyes met mine. But my disappointment—in him, and in myself—wouldn't let me hold his gaze, and I glanced away.

"In 1987," Jason began, "there was a girl who came to this island on her first college spring break vacation. A beautiful blond girl, just like Ashley. After a night of partying, no one ever saw her again. She simply disappeared."

Jason paused, and for some reason, a chill ran down my spine.

"Her name was Hilary Shear," Jason continued. "And she was my older sister."

No one said a word.

It was as if we were in a bubble with no sound, no air. One where time was suspended.

Jason's bombshell had rendered us all speechless, and I had stopped breathing.

But after several seconds, I drew in a gulp of air, and once again looked at Jason. He was nodding, silently saying that yes, the story was true.

Oh my God. His sister.

His sister.

I saw movement in my peripheral vision, and I turned in time to see Erica collapsing. She fell onto the floor like a sack of potatoes.

I sprang into action, sprinting to her side. So did Anabelle and Bill. Megan sank onto my bed and buried her face in her hands.

"Erica!" I exclaimed. Her eyes were closed. She was out cold. I tapped her face. "Erica!"

"Get a damp cloth," Anabelle ordered, taking charge. Jason started for the bathroom. Dropping to her knees, Anabelle moved between me and Erica, and I eased backward, out of the way. She pressed two fingers to Erica's neck, then nodded, satisfied. "I've got a pulse."

I gasped in relief, sucking in air.

"Where's that cloth?" Anabelle asked.

Jason scrambled from the bathroom. "Right here."

It clicked in my brain that Ashley's mother was a doctor; of course she knew what to do in a medical crisis, how to stay in control.

Jason passed her the cloth, and Anabelle pressed it to Erica's forehead. Her eyes fluttered slightly.

"She's okay, just in shock," Anabelle explained. "Help me get her on the bed."

Jason and Bill crouched down and lifted Erica, and carried her to the nearby bed. Even as they laid her down on the mattress, she still didn't move.

I looked at Jason again, seeing him with new eyes. His words had hit me like a sledgehammer to the gut, giving me a clarity I hadn't had before. I understood now why he was so interested in this story.

It wasn't business—it was personal.

Twenty-plus years of not knowing what had happened to a beloved family member.

The very same nightmare scenario I had wondered about was something that Jason and his family had lived through. What did that do to a person? How could you move on?

Jason clearly hadn't.

"I'm sorry for your loss," Anabelle said suddenly. "And maybe you're right. Maybe there is a conspiracy going on here. But regardless, we have to go to the police. Get their cooperation."

Jason nodded his agreement. "You do. You're Ashley's parents. They'll likely take you more seriously than they did Chantelle. My only advice is that you need to get the media involved. Call CNN. Call every media outlet you can think of. Get them all over this story, and the sooner the better. Enough heat might break the people behind Ashley's disappearance—and get you results. Results my family . . . my family never got."

My eyes filled with tears, and I blinked them away. I wanted to go to Jason and put my arms around him. Hug him until his pain went away.

But I knew it wouldn't.

"Oh, Jason." I tried to swallow the lump that had formed in my throat.

Erica moaned, drawing our attention. Then her eyes popped open. She looked startled, her eyes traveling over all of us frenetically, as though she didn't know where she was.

I saw the moment when it clicked. When the brutal reality registered.

And then she began to softly cry.

"We have to go," Anabelle said. "The sooner we go, the sooner we find my—our—daughter."

The confidence, the hope . . . I supposed it was her way of coping, even in light of what Jason had said.

I walked toward her. "Before you go . . . you talked about retracing Ashley's steps. We did that. And there's something you should know, something that may or may not be significant."

"What's that?"

"There are two guys from home—one of whom Ashley was dating. She was having problems with them because of something they did, and if this whole white slavery angle is way off base where Ashley's concerned, they might have some answers. The bartender remembers seeing the three of them arguing that night at the bar. Their names are Ryan and Blake. Ashley and Ryan broke up the day after we got here."

"Ryan and Blake," Anabelle repeated. "Where are they now?"

"They left. This morning, apparently. It's not proof of guilt, but I find that suspicious."

"What did they do to my daughter?"

I hesitated, looking over my shoulder at Megan on the bed. "I . . . it's kind of . . . a grown-up matter."

"Tell me."

"Yes," Bill said. "Tell us. Whatever it is, we need to know."

So I lowered my voice and briefly told her the details of the cell-phone video that had been taken of Ashley, but also assured her that I'd destroyed the phone.

Anabelle's face grew red from barely suppressed anger. "What are their full names?"

"Blake Crawford and Ryan Sinclair."

"Blake Crawford and Ryan Sinclair," Bill repeated, his nostrils flaring. "It's a good thing they're back in the States. Because I'd rip their heads off if I saw either of them right now. And if they're behind Ashley's disappearance . . ." His voice trailed off, but his unspoken threat was clear.

Megan glanced up at her stepfather sheepishly, an expression on her face that I couldn't quite read. Sensing her gaze, Bill met her eyes. Megan quickly looked away.

That was an odd exchange. But perhaps Megan was surprised

at her father's sudden defense of Ashley, when all along he'd been content to let Anabelle lead the charge.

"I'll call the U.S. authorities on the way to the police station," Anabelle said. "Tell them about Blake and Ryan." She paused briefly. "Thank you, Chantelle—all of you—for helping."

I teared up again. "I want Ashley home as badly as you do."

Anabelle hugged me, briefly but warmly. I knew that she was once again trying to keep her emotions under control.

As was I.

She collected her purse and started for the door, and Bill followed closely behind her. Megan lagged behind.

I watched Anabelle and Bill disappear through the door. But Megan stopped at the threshold and stood there for several moments. I wondered if she was crying.

She turned around suddenly, her eyes dry. She glanced furtively in the direction of her parents, then back at us.

"What is it?" I asked, sensing she wanted to ask something.

"Are you . . . are you sure this is real?" she asked, not directly meeting my gaze.

"Real?" I repeated, confused by the question.

"You know." She shrugged. "That she's really missing?"

I didn't understand the question. "Of course. Why would you ask that?"

Finally, Megan made direct eye contact with me. "Because before Ashley left on this trip, she said that before the week was over, she would have a story to sell. One that would make her famous."

Chapter
Twenty-one

FOR SEVERAL MOMENTS after Megan had left, Jason and I stood in the doorway, neither of us saying a word.

Her words were ridiculous and baffling. Why would anyone doubt their sister was missing under circumstances such as these?

And yet, an uneasy tingle shot down my spine.

Megan's words echoed something Jason had said to me.

I turned to him, my chest heaving, fragments of questions spinning around in my mind like dots that needed to be connected.

"Why would she ask that?"

"I don't know," Jason said, shrugging.

"What kind of sister asks that kind of question?"

"It doesn't make sense."

I moved slowly, walking past Jason as my thoughts continued to spin around in my mind.

He was right. It didn't make sense. Unless what Megan had said was true.

A story that would make Ashley famous. Something else was going on here. Something that I needed to understand.

I turned back to Jason. "You said that Ashley told you she had a story for you. Something that you would be so excited about, you would have to make an offer to publish it."

"Yes." Jason eyed me warily.

"And you're sure that's all she said? She said nothing else?"

"We didn't get to talk about it. But I fully expected her to go into detail when we had a chance to talk outside of a crowded bar. When we were both sober."

One minute, I'd wanted to hug Jason and make his years of pain go away. Suddenly I was remembering that I didn't really know him. He could be spoon-feeding me bullshit for all I knew. The story about his sister, his involvement in Ashley's disappearance . . .

"You're not lying to me, are you?" I asked him, suddenly wary.

"About what? Ashley?"

"About everything!"

I hadn't meant to shout, but the whole situation was getting to me. And if it was some elaborate ruse on Ashley's part to become famous . . .

Anger made Jason's face flush. "You think I'm lying? You think these bruises on my face and my arms are fake?" He rubbed at them, proving that they wouldn't smudge.

"I don't know what to think!"

Jason's face fell at my words. If nothing else, his disappoint-ment was genuine.

"You think I'm in on some scheme with Ashley to get atten-tion? To get a story?" He dug into his back pocket and yanked out his wallet. "Then what the hell is this? Something I printed up on my computer before I came over here?"

He withdrew a folded piece of newspaper and extended it to me. I made no move to take it from his hand.

"Take it!" he demanded. "Read it. Then tell me you think I'm some asshole who would put a family through what mine suffered twenty-three years ago."

I took the folded newsprint, already feeling like shit for doubting him. It was fragile, and I opened it carefully.

The headline read CONNECTICUT GIRL GOES MISSING IN PARADISE.

There was a picture of a man, a woman, and a young boy huddled together in grief. A framed photo of a beautiful blond girl was in the woman's hands as they sat on a floral sofa, something that looked a lot like what my grandmother still had in her home from eons ago. Next to the photo of the fam-ily in grief was an insert of the same girl from the photo, wear-ing a graduation gown.

A Connecticut family is seeking answers in the disappear-ance of a beloved daughter and sister, Hilary Shear. Hilary, a freshman at NYU, went on vacation with classmates to the beautiful island of Artula. Her classmates returned home. She didn't.

My heart pounding, I stopped reading, carefully refolding the article. I got the point. And I didn't want to read about

Jason's family's grief, knowing it would only augment my own.

"I'm sorry," I said. "It's just . . ."

Just what? I'd seen the police viciously assault Jason. He'd told me what they'd done to the man with the scar.

"Hilary is the reason I do what I do," he said.

"You don't have to explain yourself."

"Yes, I do. I want you to understand."

"I do."

"No, you don't." He paused. Sighed. "Everything I've done—investigating white slavery, asking questions that could get me into trouble—it's the only way I know how to cope. I'm doing something, *anything*, and maybe I won't get answers, but at least I'm not sitting around being helpless. That keeps me going. That and the thought that if I can save another family from this nightmare, then Hilary's loss wasn't in vain. And that maybe . . . maybe I'll get the answers that will lead us to finally finding her."

"I'm sorry." It was all I could say. "I didn't mean to doubt you. Megan threw me for a loop, is all. And because Ashley said something about a story to you, too . . . I couldn't help wondering. . . . Stranger things have happened in this world."

"If this is some elaborate scheme on Ashley's part, I have nothing to do with it. I can promise you that."

"I know." I sighed wearily. "I know. I really am sorry."

Silence passed between us. Long moments of strained silence. I glanced over my shoulder at Erica, wishing she would interject on my behalf. But her eyes were closed, and she looked at peace in sleep. Thankfully.

"How old would your sister be right now?" I asked cautiously.

Jason didn't answer right away. I knew he was still pissed. And given all he'd gone through to help find Ashley, I couldn't blame him.

"Forty-two," he finally said.

"All this time . . . not knowing. How do you deal with that? It would kill me."

"It killed my mother," he said softly. "Literally. Broke her spirit. For years, every time the phone rang, her eyes would light up with hope. Only for the light to be snuffed out each time it wasn't Hilary. Ten years later, that light was gone for good. And then she was."

"Oh, Jason . . ."

"My father's still alive. Unlike my mother, he refused to give up all hope. But he's not stupid. He knows that if she hasn't been found in twenty-three years, it's unlikely she ever will be. I'm not gonna lie—I'd love to see my sister walk through the door one day, alive and well, even if mentally fucked up. But I think what we'd both like most is some closure. If we could find her body, finally put her to rest . . ."

"But if you truly believe she was abducted into white slavery, then you have to believe she's alive somewhere."

"When you're nineteen, you're young and beautiful and infinitely tempting to these sick bastards. But at forty-two, what man would keep you around for sexual favors? When they no longer have a use for you, will they really keep you alive? I've read that sex slaves are eventually killed. No one wants them going back to their families with stories of where they've been."

I shivered, yet I said, "But you don't know for sure. Someone could have fallen in love with your sister, made her his wife. Maybe she was so brainwashed, she no longer remembers her past life. Maybe she's happy with the life she's come to live. You can't think the worst. As long as you don't have a body, there's—"

"Hope." Jason finished the sentence, his expression sad. "That's what I used to think, too. In the beginning. And don't get me wrong—I think I still have to have a measure of hope to really deal with what happened. But that same hope, the never truly knowing, is like an albatross around a person's neck. Eventually, it can kill you. Like it did my mother."

I didn't plan to move toward Jason. Didn't plan to stretch out my hand and gently stroke his face.

I let my hand rest there, something else I didn't plan. What started out as comfort, and perhaps a physical gesture of apology, turned to something else.

Jason leaned his face into my palm. For a moment, he closed his eyes, as if drawing from my touch the strength he needed. Then his own hand reached up and covered mine, and he opened his eyes again. The sadness was gone, and now there was heat in his gaze. Heat that emanated from his body to mine.

I don't know who moved first. Maybe he did. Maybe we both did. But soon, our faces were only an inch apart, his warm breath fanning my skin.

He reached for my other hand, linking his fingers with mine. As he did, he urged me slightly forward, closing that inch-wide gap.

Our lips met, and for the first few moments we were both still, as if surprised to find our mouths connected. Our mouths were touching, but not intimately.

Then I drew in a much-needed breath, the audible sound serving as an icebreaker. Because that was all it took to break down the last bit of hesitation. Suddenly, Jason was kissing me, and I was kissing him back. Slowly, at first, our lips moving

over one another's with caution. With that new sense of wonder. Then his tongue thrust into my mouth, deep and urgent,
and we were all-out necking.

Jason was smoothing the palms of his hands down my back
when Erica sobbed, startling me out of the enchantment of
the kiss, and we both jumped apart. I quickly looked at her, my
brain scrambling for an explanation to give her.

But Erica's eyes were still closed, and it was soon clear that
she'd made a sound in her sleep.

I turned back to Jason, expecting to see regret on his face.
Instead, he smiled at me and circled his arms around my waist.

Heat and excitement spread through me. The excitement of
something fresh and new.

There *was* something between us. And it was mutual.

He gave me a soft kiss on the lips, one that was brief but
held the promise of something wonderful.

"What now?" I asked softly.

"Well . . ." Jason glanced in Erica's direction, as though he'd
misconstrued the meaning of my question.

"No—I mean what happens next. With this whole crazy
situation."

"I still have to leave the island. The authorities want me
gone today, and I don't want to piss them off."

The words were like a pinprick, bursting my bubble of hope.
How had I gotten so caught up in an unrealistic fantasy in the
span of five minutes?

I only knew that I didn't want Jason to leave. I wanted him
to stay around and help us through what was to come.

But I said, "I guess you have to go then."

What I'd wanted to say was, *Please don't go. I want to see
what can happen between us.*

A purely selfish and even crazy thought, given the circumstances.

"I'm going to be in touch with you every day," Jason said. "And keep your eyes on the TV. You might see me on CNN."

Stepping back, I nodded. The gravity of the situation had sobered me, sent me crashing down from my romantic fantasy. "I pray this helps. We have to find her. We have to."

I was surprised when Jason reached for my hand. He pulled me close and whispered, "Hang in there. You're gonna get through this."

I felt an electric charge. But it was immediately followed by a spate of sadness. I knew he wanted me to kiss him again, but it seemed pointless. Jason lived in New York. I lived in Pennsylvania. Not worlds apart, but far enough. Far enough when we had our own lives to keep us busy. Far enough that we wouldn't be able to sneak in time together in the evenings. What could come of this?

As if he sensed my question, he said, "I hate that I have to leave, but we're gonna stay in touch, right?"

"I want to," I admitted, but doubting that we would. Maybe for a few days, or a few weeks. But our lives would eventually pull us in different directions.

"Will you call me when you get back to the States? Not just about what's going on with Ashley, but . . ." His voice trailed off, but he seemed to finish the question with his eyes, eyes that were searching mine. "But about what's going on with us."

My heart rate instantly accelerated. There it was again, the hope. Irrational or not, it lifted my spirits, making me giddy.

I smiled up at Jason and stroked his cheek with the tip of my finger. "Yeah, I'll call you. Definitely."

Chapter
Twenty-two

"MY PARENTS want me to come home." Erica said the words the moment I stepped back into the room, startling me. When I'd left to see Jason off and to get a plate of fries, she'd still been sleeping. So I was surprised that not only had she woken up, but that she'd already called home about the situation in my brief absence.

"But you—you can't just leave. Now that Ashley's parents are here, the police are going to start investigating, and they're going to want to question us."

Erica laughed, the sound sardonic. "Like I want to talk to them! I don't trust the police. Not after what they did last night."

"You told your parents about that?" I asked, shocked.

"I had to."

I wanted to protest that fact, but how could I? Erica was clearly having a lot harder time dealing with all that had happened, and it was unreasonable to expect that during a crisis like this she wouldn't turn to her family.

"I know this whole situation sucks, but they're going to need to question us. We can't just take off."

"My parents don't want me involved," Erica said. Her tone said the decision had been made.

I didn't want her leaving me. But I couldn't fault her for wanting to get as far from Artula as possible.

"Did you already reschedule your flight?"

"There's a flight leaving at seven tonight. I was about to start packing."

I nodded. What could I say? Nothing about this situation was easy. Nothing about it was nice. We were all dealing with it as best we could.

"Is Jason gone?" Erica asked.

"He went back to the place he was renting, to pack as well." I said this with as much detachment as I could, not wanting to give away any hint of what had happened between the two of us. "Maybe you'll be on the same flight."

"Is he on American?" she asked.

"He's not sure yet. Whatever's cheaper when he gets to the airport."

"I wish you'd leave, too."

I didn't respond, just stuffed one of the lukewarm fries into my mouth. I couldn't leave—not yet. Not when there was a possibility I could do *something* to help find Ashley. But the knowledge that I would be alone in this room tonight left me feeling oddly uneasy.

"Have you called your mom yet?" Erica asked.

I shook my head as I swallowed.

"You should. I think this story's about to be huge. You don't want your family finding out about it on the news."

Erica was absolutely right. I'd already decided before heading for food that I would call my mother when I got back to the room. The news of Ashley's disappearance would break soon, and the last thing I wanted was for my mother to hear about it via CNN. My mother would hear the words, "Artula" and "girl's disappearance" and she would be a complete wreck until she knew I was safe. That's just the way she was.

I dreaded the call, because while I *was* safe, I had been rooming with the missing girl. The missing girl was one of my best friends. That connection alone would have my mother freaking out, and she would want me to return to the States as soon as possible.

But unlike Erica, I couldn't do that. The police—assuming they would finally begin their investigation of a missing college student—would want to question me. Especially if Erica wasn't going to be here.

Maybe I should have been scared, or at least worried. But I wanted to be on the island as long as necessary. I wanted to be here when Ashley was found.

My heart wouldn't let me believe anything other than that would happen. Not yet.

I extended the plate of fries to Erica, but she shook her head. I placed them on the table, then took my cell phone from the back pocket of my jeans.

I flipped it open. Then sighed. I couldn't do this. I couldn't call my mother . . .

I had to. It was just one more unpleasant thing in a line of unpleasant things since the night at Zack's Shack. If I could endure meeting a strange man in an alley in an effort to get a clue to Ashley's whereabouts, I could deal with telling my mother that, despite her protests, I couldn't leave the island, even if she believed that was for the best.

I wanted privacy, though, so I headed onto the balcony with my cell phone.

I punched in the digits to my mother's home number. Butterflies tickled my stomach as her line rang, and I waited for her to pick up.

"Hello?"

Deep breath. "Hi, Mom." I forced myself to sound as cheerful as I could. "It's Chantelle."

"Baby." I could hear the smile in my mother's voice. "How are you?"

"I'm good," I said. Technically, that was true.

"How is Artula? Are you having fun with your friends?"

I couldn't give the standard answer now. I closed my eyes and braced myself for my mother's response to what I would say next.

"Something's happened, Mom. That's why I'm calling."

"What do you mean something's happened?" Fear laced her tone. "Did someone hurt you, baby?"

I swallowed. The more I said it, the more real it was. But there was no avoiding the truth.

"Mom . . . Ashley—one of the girls I told you I was coming here with—she . . . she's missing."

"What do you mean she's missing?"

"We were out Sunday night. She never came back to the hotel. We think . . . we think she's been abducted."

"Oh my God." The fear in my mother's voice turned to dread. "Oh my God."

"I wanted to let you know what was going on before you heard about it on the news."

"On the news?" She asked the question as if to say that if the story made the news back home, it was that much more serious.

"Ashley's parents are here on the island, and I think they're going to try to get the story out. Anything to help find Ashley."

"Oh, Lord . . ." I could hear the rising stress in my mother's voice, bordering on hysteria. Exactly what I'd known would happen.

"I'm okay, Mom. I just wanted you to know what was going on."

"When are you coming home?"

The question I had dreaded. "I . . . I . . . Not yet. Mom, I can't."

"What do you mean you *can't*? Is it the money? The cost of changing your ticket? Because I'll give you my credit card number, so don't worry about that."

"It's not that. I was with Ashley that night. The police will need to question me, and that can help—"

"The police can do their job without you."

"Maybe. Maybe not."

"There's a madman on the island abducting students. I want you to come home right now."

"Mom—"

"I feel sorry for your friend, Lord knows I do, but you do not need to be involved in this."

"Yes, I do," I said firmly. "If I can be of help, I have to help. Ashley is my best friend. Wouldn't you want someone to help if it were me?"

My mother didn't respond, and as much as I knew she wanted to protest, that was a point she couldn't argue. If she were in Anabelle Hamilton's position right now, she would want a possible witness to stick around and help out with the investigation.

"Baby, I'm worried about you."

"I know you are. But I'm going to stay at the hotel, unless the police take me to the station to question me. And even though it's going to cost me a fortune, I'm going to keep my cell phone on. Call me whenever you want."

My mother was silent for a moment. Then she said, "I don't like this."

"I'm not going to do anything to put myself in harm's way. Like I said, I'll stay at the hotel. I'll only leave with the police, or with Ashley's family to help put up flyers and help search."

"Oh, baby." My mother sighed softly. "I'll be praying for you. And for Ashley, of course. Lord, you never know when you kiss your kids good-bye if you'll see them again."

"You'll see me again."

"Please be careful."

"I will."

"I love you, baby."

"I love you, too, Mom."

I ended the call and sat on the plastic chair on the balcony, staring off into the distance.

Where are you, Ashley?

I prayed that we found her sooner rather than later. First and foremost, for her sake. But also for my mother's. Because I knew that until I returned home, my mother was going to be an emotional wreck.

She'd already dealt with a lot in her life, losing my father when I was only eight months old, and being forced to raise me as a single parent. If she ever lost me, it would kill her.

There were days when I wished my mother had remarried. I didn't like seeing her alone. But having witnessed the divide between Anabelle and Bill, I couldn't help thinking that my mother had made a wise decision. That perhaps no man could love a child unconditionally who wasn't his own.

I didn't like what I'd seen of Ashley's stepfather. I didn't like how odd he and Anabelle had seemed together. How disconnected. Yes, a missing child had to put major stress on a relationship, but still . . . The picture of Jason's family in the newspaper, huddled together in their grief, was a stark contrast to the image I had of the Hamilton family.

I didn't like to judge people. I knew that everyone handled grief and stress differently, but there had been something about Bill Hamilton that rubbed me the wrong way. The way Anabelle had said *I* so often, coupled with the visible tension between them, made me wonder if he was just along for the trip but not offering any real support. He didn't seem anywhere near as invested in Ashley's disappearance as Anabelle and Megan did. He did get angry at the mention of Ryan and Blake, but to me the reaction had felt more like someone playing the part.

Perhaps there was more going on than the stress of Ashley being missing. Maybe Anabelle and Bill Hamilton were having marital problems. But in the face of Ashley's disappearance, they had to work together. That would explain a lot.

I nodded, thinking that yes, it made sense that they were having marital problems. And whatever those problems were, they'd affected Megan, too. Because I could see the tension between her and her stepfather as well. There was something about that look she'd given Bill that made me uneasy as I recalled it now. And her body language—the fact that she always stood closer to her mother, and even rejected Bill's arms when he'd tried to comfort her . . .

So what? I asked myself suddenly. Kids the world over preferred their mothers when hurt or sad. Was I making more of the Hamilton family problems than the obvious?

I stood and walked to the balcony's edge, gripping it as I stared toward the ocean. Maybe the writer in me was trying to find a story to explain behavior I didn't understand. Because I certainly couldn't understand anyone rejecting a loving embrace from her father. Not at a time like this.

There weren't many times in my life that I missed having my father in my life—since he'd died when I was a baby, I'd never known him. Mostly, I missed the idea of him. Of what it would be like to have a father around to talk to, to laugh with.

But I missed him now. Missed that I wasn't able to pick up the phone and call him, to tell him everything that was happening. In the past, on occasion, I would talk to the photo of him I kept in my wallet, but it wasn't the same. I needed my father right now—the living, breathing man—to be my rock in this crisis in the way I knew my mother couldn't be.

My thoughts ventured to Carl, the man I *should* want to call. But the very idea of talking to him made me feel on edge.

These days away from him had seemed like a lifetime. Would he hear about what had happened to Ashley and wonder if I was all right? Would he regret that he'd dumped me?

I'd be lying if I said that I didn't miss him. And yet, it was Jason I couldn't wait to hear from, not Carl.

For a moment with Jason, I'd felt myself let down a wall that had always been there with Carl: the emotional wall I'd erected around my heart to keep me from getting hurt. I knew first-hand that love could be taken from you in the blink of an eye.

The way it had been taken not just from my mother, but from an aunt whose husband had died in Iraq, and then again when the same aunt's only daughter had come down with meningitis and died two days later.

I'd been too young to remember the devastation my mother must have experienced at losing my father, but I could only imagine the pain was so intense it was why she had not only not remarried, but why she had never loved another man. She didn't have pictures of him in the living room, or in the bedroom. Apparently she wanted no reminders of the man she had loved and lost. My mother didn't even like to talk about my father. I knew that he'd liked to sing, that he had taught himself to play the piano, that his birthday had been in June. I also knew that his name was Leroy, but that was pretty much it. Every time I'd asked my mother questions about my father, her face had contorted with pain. Pain that hadn't healed with time. Eventually, I'd stopped asking, wanting to spare her any more grief. But I had many more questions about my father, questions that would never be answered.

The idea of loving someone so much that your heart would never heal scared me. My relationship with Carl had lasted for two years, and I liked him a lot, even loved him as a friend— but I wasn't *in* love with him.

I hadn't really examined why I'd dated someone I wasn't passionate about, but now the answer was suddenly obvious. I'd chosen Carl because if things ended between us, I wouldn't be utterly devastated.

Ashley was the exact opposite of me in that regard, but we had bonded because of what we had in common. I had grown up without a father. Ashley had also grown up without a father for most of her life. The circumstances of our fathers being gone were different, which, as far as I was concerned, explained why our approaches to relationships was so different.

My father was missing from my life, not by choice, but because he'd died. Ashley's father had abandoned her, no looking back.

She'd shared with me how devastating it had been, at the age of ten, to come home from school and find her mother sitting at the kitchen table, holding a letter and crying her eyes out. According to her, she had known before asking that something horrible had happened, something that would change her world forever.

Then her mother had told her that her father had left and was never coming back.

The abandonment had killed Ashley's self-esteem. In all her relationships, I saw her as seeking approval from men, perhaps as a way to show she was worthy.

Worthy of having a father who should have loved her forever, not abandoned her.

And yet, in every one of her relationships, Ashley set herself up to be hurt. She always chose the guy who wasn't going to respect her, who was going to hurt her, and ultimately leave her.

It was a cycle she couldn't seem to escape.

Was that what had happened on Sunday night? Had Ashley been drawn to a man, likely attractive and charming, who had seduced her with easy words and romantic gestures?

Had she been easy prey for a man with an agenda?

And would that agenda cost her her freedom—or her life?

Chapter
Twenty-three

ERICA LEFT a few hours later, and even though I didn't want to be alone, I realized it was for the best. Her emotions were in tatters, and she needed to be back home with her family.

We ate a late lunch at the beachside grill, then went back to the room and collected Erica's bags. I walked her to the front of the resort and waited with her while she got a cab.

As the driver put her bags in the trunk, Erica hugged me. "You be careful, okay? I don't like it that you're still staying here."

"I'll be fine," I told her, faking a bravado I didn't truly feel.

"Call me when you get back. Let me know you made it home all right."

"I will."

She smiled sadly as she got into the cab, and waved from the backseat until the taxi rounded the corner, and I couldn't see her anymore.

I turned, hugging my torso, feeling completely alone.

I went back to my room and lay on the bed for twenty minutes. Every so often, I could hear people laughing and talking as they walked past my room. People whose worlds hadn't been changed by a random act.

My eyes ventured to the cot, with Ashley's open suitcase still resting on top of it. Her mother hadn't taken it. I wondered why.

Because to take it would have meant that Ashley wasn't coming back?

I couldn't allow myself to believe that she would never return. How could someone so full of life simply be gone forever?

Ashley had a vibrant laugh, and one of the best smiles I'd ever seen. I'd give anything to hear her laughter in the hallway. To know that she was about to open the door.

One that would make her famous.

Megan's words sounded in my brain, and frowning, I rolled over. I still couldn't wrap my mind around the comment— around the insinuation that Ashley might do something like this on purpose for attention.

The Ashley I knew just wasn't that kind of person. She was sweet and trusting and naïve. Not cunning and manipulative.

Suddenly I sat up. A thought hit me with the force of a locomotive. Something I hadn't considered before, nor even remembered with all the madness going on.

Kevaughn and BJ.

I hadn't seen them since Sunday night in the club.

Since they'd drugged Erica.

A feeling of dread settled in the pit of my stomach, heavy and uncomfortable.

Whatever they'd given to Erica had rendered her damn near incapacitated. They had drugs. I knew that. What if Ashley had run into them at the club? What if they'd bought her a drink, spiked it with something, and waited for it to take effect?

"My God," I uttered. A tingling sensation shot down both arms.

I'd been so focused on Ryan and Blake, I had missed the obvious. The obvious being two guys out for no good with unsuspecting college girls.

I swung my feet over the side of the bed. I had to do something. Had to find them somehow.

But I didn't know their surnames. How could I find them when I didn't know who they were?

They played college ball, that much I knew. Something gnawed at my brain, the wisp of a memory. I closed my eyes, tried to force it into focus. There was something about them maybe playing for the NFL. No, not BJ. He'd said he wasn't good enough. But Kevaughn . . .

Which team? Cleveland? Green Bay? The memory was there, almost within reach.

And then BJ's words sounded in my brain like a gift from God: *The Arizona Cardinals are taking a serious look at him.*

Yes! That was it. I pumped a fist in the air, triumphant, knowing that I'd just remembered something that might lead the police to BJ and Kevaughn after all.

I slipped into my sandals and grabbed my purse. Then I hurried out of my room and to the front of the hotel.

Jason believed Ashley had been abducted into white slavery. And that was one theory. A theory he wanted to believe, based on what had happened to his own sister.

But what if the truth was something far more simple? That Ashley had met a couple of guys who'd seemed charming and fun. They'd given her a drug to reduce her inhibitions so they could take her somewhere and have their way with her without a problem.

But what if something had happened—something they hadn't expected? Maybe the toxic mix of alcohol and whatever they'd given her had rendered her unconscious, and they'd freaked out.

Jason had mentioned that on the north side of the island, the waves were strong and deadly.

That it was the perfect place to dispose of a body.

When I saw the taxi pull up to the curb, I ran toward it and opened the back door, only noting once I got into it that someone was protesting. I looked to the right to see an older couple staring at me with an outraged expression. Clearly, I'd gotten into their cab.

But that was the least of my concerns.

"Take me to Zack's Shack," I said to the driver. "As fast as you can."

I'd called Jason while en route to Zack's Shack, not expecting to get him, but wanting to leave a message nonetheless.

"I thought of something," I said. "Something that could explain all of this. Call me as soon as you get in and I'll tell you everything."

That was all I would say with the taxi driver able to over-hear me.

About twenty minutes later, I was at Zack's Shack, which had a small crowd on the patio. More smiling, happy people, their worlds sheltered from the horror of my own.

It was early in the evening, so I didn't expect the inside of the place to be busy. And it wasn't.

Just like the last time.

Different from the last time was the fact that I was alone.

I felt like a spotlight was on me as I walked toward the bar, with the few people inside turning to look at me, as if they thought it odd that a woman would enter an establishment like this on her own.

Of course, I could have just been paranoid.

Also like the last time, Sebastian was behind the bar. He had his back turned and was making a drink.

He turned around and handed a brunette a frothy red con-coction, likely a strawberry daiquiri or strawberry margarita. And then his eyes landed on me.

His smile instantly disappeared. He wasn't happy to see me.

No paranoia there.

I made my approach, settling on a bar stool. Sebastian bus-ied himself behind the bar, rinsing the blender and moving aside glasses. He was taking his sweet time—I was sure of that—so he didn't have to deal with me.

But after about a minute, he knew he couldn't avoid me any longer. He faced me, his expression serious.

"Hello, Sebastian."

"You shouldn't be here," he told me.

He no longer wanted to talk to me? Or did his words mean something else?

"I thought about something," I said in a low tone. "Something about that night."

He said nothing, as though he wasn't the least bit interested in what I had to say.

"I think I know what could have—"

"More allegations of pretty girls being kidnapped for sexual purposes? I don't need your problems in my bar."

"No, that's not what I was going to say. In fact, I think what happened to Ashley might have nothing to do with that. There were these two guys, from the States, African-American. One of them might have mentioned he had a shot of playing in the NFL? Anyway, they tried to give me drugs, and they did give some to my—"

"Stop," Sebastian said, holding up a hand. "I don't want to hear anything."

"But maybe you saw them. Maybe you can help identify who they are."

"I saw nothing."

"These guys would have stood out. They were tall, and very well built. Like football players."

"I saw nothing," Sebastian repeated. Slowly. Clearly.

I got the point. Even if he had seen something, he wasn't going to talk to me about it.

"I don't understand," I said.

"You don't understand?" He looked at me disbelievingly. Then he leaned forward and said in an angry whisper, "Take a look around, young lady. This place isn't nearly as busy as it was before yesterday. You're bringing heat on my establishment, costing me money—all because of your allegations. I'm sorry about your friend, but she made her own bed."

"Made her own bed?" I asked, aghast.

"Leave. I don't want you on my property."

I stared at Sebastian in disbelief. I didn't understand what was going on.

"Now." The word was firm. Harsh. Leaving no room for any doubt.

I stood up and took a step backward, keeping my confused eyes on his. I didn't understand.

A male customer approached the bar, and Sebastian broke our eye contact. I turned then, running toward the exit.

Emotion hit me as I stepped onto the street, and I doubled over, tears of frustration filling my eyes.

I didn't understand. Why had Sebastian turned so cold? Unless . . .

I righted myself as reality hit me.

No, the Sebastian I'd spoken with before wasn't such a cold, unfeeling guy. This wasn't his doing.

He was afraid. Afraid to be seen talking to me.

And could I blame him? A man had had his tongue cut out after speaking to me behind this very place.

Which only had me wondering if Sebastian knew more than he'd admitted.

Knew more, but had gotten the point that speaking out would get him killed.

Chapter
Twenty-four

I OPENED the door to my room, saw her packing her suitcase, and froze.

And then my heart leaped into my throat, my excitement and relief instantaneous.

"Ashley!" I exclaimed.

She spun around, her long blond hair whipping over her shoulder.

And then confusion. Disorientation. All in a nanosecond. But as my brain registered understanding, my heart split, and I felt anew the jarring pain of my friend's sudden absence.

It was Megan. Packing her sister's things.

She looked so much like Ashley . . .

I felt winded as I stepped into the room, my heart not wanting to accept what my brain knew was true.

"We came back," Megan explained. "You weren't here, so the manager let us in."

That's when I saw that the screen to the balcony was open. Anabelle stood at the balcony's railing, hugging her torso, staring off into the distance.

"Is your father here?" I asked. I didn't see him.

"*Bill* stayed at the guesthouse." And it was clear, with the way Megan had said her stepfather's name, that there was no closeness between them. He might have stepped in as a father figure, but she didn't see him as that. "He's making some calls," she added, and shrugged.

"Oh," I said. I wanted to ask her what she meant by her parting comment earlier, but I didn't. Instead, I asked, "Any news?"

"You should talk to my mother." Megan looked toward the balcony. "Mom!"

Anabelle turned. When she saw me, she stepped away from the balcony railing and immediately walked back into the room.

"I'm sorry," she said. "We came back, but you weren't here. The manager let us in so we could collect Ashley's belongings."

"No, it's okay." I was still winded, the shock of thinking I had seen Ashley almost too much to accept. "How did everything go?"

When Anabelle got closer, I could see that her eyes were red-rimmed. She'd been crying. "Who knows? I gave the police photos of her, told them anything I thought would be helpful. And we'll see. But I'm not sure . . ."

"Not sure what?" I asked.

She shook her head. "I just don't know if it will help."

4000

I got the impression that was not what she'd been about to say, but I didn't press the matter.

"I didn't know what she was wearing," Anabelle said. "That night. You can help by giving the police a description of what Ashley was wearing."

"Of course."

She reached into the front pocket on her denim skirt and produced a business card. "The officer gave us his card. His name is Sergeant Bingham."

As I heard the name, my stomach lurched. It was the same man I'd spoken with when I'd first tried to report Ashley missing.

He'd been so skeptical and unhelpful . . . I couldn't help feeling that he was the last person who should be heading up this investigation.

"At least they're now going to declare Ashley a missing person," Anabelle said, and shrugged.

Once again, I got the feeling that there was something else she wanted to say.

"What is it, Mrs. Hamilton?" I asked. "Did the police give you a hard time?"

She frowned slightly. "Not exactly. They seemed willing to help. But I got an odd feeling from the lot of them. I'm starting to wonder if your friend Jason is right . . . if there's a conspiracy going on. God help us if there is."

I said nothing, just nodded. I knew exactly what she meant.

"But the more attention I bring to this situation, the better," Anabelle went on, her tone saying she wouldn't give up. "My husband put in a call to a friend of his in the FBI. Hopefully they'll get involved in helping us find Ashley."

"That's great," I said, feeling the burden weighing me down

ease a smidgen. "If the FBI gets involved, that'll be incredible. They're so great at what they do."

It would be one more reason to be hopeful. To believe that for Ashley it wasn't too late.

The way it was for Jason's sister.

"I think through Bill's connection with the FBI, we can get a team of investigators here to hit the streets and search the island from one end to the other. This isn't a big place. I'm confident we can find her."

"Oh my God, that's excellent," I said, and drew in a shuddery breath. "I feel so hopeful. We're gonna find Ashley, and everything will be like it was. No, it'll be better than it was. Because we'll all appreciate each other that much more."

Anabelle looked at Megan, her expression a mixture of puzzlement and pain. It was a look that was heavy with meaning, yet I couldn't understand it. I glanced at Megan, who was shaking her head ever so slightly at her mother. Then she turned back to the suitcase she'd been packing, not meeting my gaze.

Anabelle faced me once more, not speaking, but seeming to study me. Had I said something wrong? Crossing her arms over her chest, she took a step toward me and said in a lowered voice, "Chantelle, I know you must have heard some . . . some *things* about our family. But I want to assure you that regardless of what Ashley may have told you, we both love her dearly and want nothing but the best for her. I'm sorry she hasn't always seen that."

Huh?

"I . . . I know you love your daughter," I said, confused. "I've never doubted that for a second. And Ashley sure didn't . . . doesn't."

"That's good to hear," Anabelle said, and her emotional

armor cracked, her face filling with angst. She sniffled. "Thank you, Chantelle. That means a lot."

I know you must have heard some . . . some things about our family.

I had no clue what Anabelle meant by that comment. And to whom was she referring when she said *we*? Her and Megan? Her and Bill?

I wanted to ask her to elaborate, but I knew this wasn't the time. All I knew for sure was that there were some problems in the family.

Whatever had been going on, I was surprised Ashley hadn't shared it with me. We talked about everything—or so I thought.

But maybe she just hadn't been ready to share whatever problems her family was going through. My guess—from seeing Anabelle and Bill together—was that there were serious marital problems. Ashley had already lost her biological father. To lose her stepfather as well . . . it might have been too devastating for her to talk about, even with her best friends.

"Bill has also passed along the names of the boys you mentioned. Even if they're not directly involved in what happened to Ashley, they may have information that can shed light on her disappearance."

"Good," I said. "If they're withholding any information, the FBI should be able to draw it out of them."

"Where's Erica?" Anabelle suddenly asked.

"She left. Her parents were scared. They wanted her to go home."

"What about your parents?"

"My mother isn't thrilled that I'm here, but I told her I'm staying." I shrugged. "I may be able to help. Like this info about what Ashley was wearing." Although I suddenly remembered that the photos of Ashley that night were on Erica's phone. I would have to get her to send them to me.

"And I remembered something else," I continued. "It could be a lead."

Anabelle's eyes lit up. And I thought of Jason, what he'd said about hope. How it was a blessing and a curse.

"What?" Anabelle asked. "What is it?"

"I don't know why I didn't think about it before. There were these two guys who were staying here. Americans. They were at Zack's Shack on Sunday night and gave Erica a pill that almost knocked her out."

I went on to explain our initial run-in with them at the resort, how they'd offered us drugs. How once again we'd seen them at the bar, and Erica had foolishly taken the pill they'd offered.

"Erica was disoriented and throwing up, so I went with her to the bathroom. It's possible they spoke to Ashley after that, bought her a drink. Maybe they gave her the same kind of pill they gave Erica." I paused, staring at Anabelle and Megan in turn. "What if that's what happened, and they left with her, and . . ." I didn't finish my statement. Because the ending of this scenario would be far worse than any scenario that involved white slavery.

Anabelle knew it, too. I saw the heavy rise and fall of her chest before tears glistened in her eyes.

"I mean, I don't know," I said. "But I haven't seen either of those guys since that night . . . God, I'm sorry."

Anabelle wiped her tears away. "No. Don't apologize. Anything you remember is important. No theory can be discounted. Not until . . . until we find Ashley."

Dead or alive.

Anabelle didn't say it. But I knew that's what she meant.

The depression set in after Anabelle and Megan left the room, Ashley's belongings in tow.

Here one minute. Gone the next. It was the worst way to lose someone, without any warning. But this situation was even harder to accept than a sudden death because of the not knowing.

Alone, and with no desire to hang out at the bar, I went to bed and tried to coax myself into slumber. But I was far too anxious to sleep.

Before Anabelle had left, she'd told me that a crew from CNN would arrive on the island in the morning, and that they would surely want to talk to me.

I'd turned on the television after they left, found CNN, and sure enough, the news had just broken about a college girl who'd gone missing in Artula. That was all they'd said, for now not identifying Ashley by name.

At some point I must have drifted off, because when my cell phone rang, it jarred me awake. I bolted upright, disoriented, my arms flailing.

In an instant, I remembered where I was, and registered that it was my cell phone ringing. I glanced at the bedside clock as I reached for my phone.

The digital numbers read 12:33.

Then I glanced at the caller ID. *Private name. Private number.*

My heart began to pound. Hope. Hope that this was the call that would make everything all right.

I opened my phone and groggily said, "Hello?"

A beat. "Chantelle."

My heart pounded harder, fueled in part by disappointment and surprise. It wasn't Ashley.

"Carl?"

"I just heard the news."

"You did?"

"Yeah." Pause. "Are you all right?"

"I'm okay. But things are crazy."

"Mad crazy. Why didn't you call me?"

"Well . . . I didn't think you'd want me to."

"Come on, babe. Yeah, things were tense when you left, but you know I'd want to hear from you with this shit going on."

"I guess," I said softly. Had Carl called as a friend—or as a boyfriend? "How'd you hear? CNN?"

"Naw. The word got back to me on campus. This shit's big news."

Ryan and Blake. They had to be back by now. "Have you heard anything about Ryan Sinclair and Blake Crawford on the news?"

"Like what?"

"Like anything."

"Naw."

"Hmm." I was thinking. Wondering. I still didn't like the timing of their leaving.

"Chantelle?"

"Yes?"

"I just wanted to say, I didn't mean what I said before you left. You know you'll always be my girl."

So he was calling as my boyfriend. As if we were just supposed to pick up where we'd left off and keep going.

"Carl, this isn't really the time. I'm in the middle of a crisis.

My best friend is missing. That's really all that matters right now."

"All right. I hear you. I just wanted you to know. Cuz something like this, it puts things in perspective. I love you, and I'm here for you."

I said nothing.

"So what happened, babe?" Carl asked after a moment. "How'd this shit go down?"

I wasn't up for this. I didn't know why. I just knew that I didn't feel like talking to Carl about any of this. At least not yet.

"Carl?"

"Yeah?"

"I'm really kind of tired. Tomorrow's gonna be a long day, talking to the police and probably the media."

"Oh. Okay. That's cool. We can talk later."

"Thanks for understanding. Good night."

"Hey," Carl interjected before I could hang up.

"Hmm?"

"You want me to meet you in Artula? You know—be there for you?"

It was the last thing I wanted. Before I'd left, I was upset that Carl had dumped me. But now I knew there was no going back. It had finally clicked that I wasn't in love with him, something I'd known in my brain, if not my heart. I didn't know how I'd let myself stay in a relationship with him for two years.

"No, Carl."

"You're sure?"

"Yes, I'm sure. I'll be fine. Spring break's almost over, anyway. Good night."

I hung up before he could say anything else, all too aware

that if Jason had been on the other end of the line, I wouldn't have been eager to end the call.

The room phone woke me up bright and early. I bolted upright, reaching for the receiver.

"Hello?"

"Miss Higgins." The male voice sounded authoritative.

"Yes, this is she."

"This is Sergeant Bingham. We spoke a few days ago."

I was suddenly nervous. I didn't like this man. "Yes. That's right."

"Mrs. Hamilton tells me that you have information that may be helpful to this investigation."

"I hope so."

"Can I send a car to pick you up and bring you to the station?"

The thought alone made my pulse race. I didn't trust the Artulan police, I realized.

But if they were finally taking Ashley's disappearance seriously, I would have to deal with them.

"What time?" I asked.

"How's twenty minutes?"

It was as good a time as any. "I'll be ready."

Chapter Twenty-five

I'D BEEN NERVOUS ever since leaving my room, but when, through the glass lobby doors, I saw the police cruiser pull up to the curb, my stomach fluttered with a sick energy.

I tried to act as casual as possible as I exited the hotel and approached the officer, who was now standing outside of the car, and identified myself. He nodded, then opened the door to the backseat of the cruiser for me.

Everyone within the vicinity openly stared, curious. I hadn't been placed in handcuffs, but I'm sure that didn't stop people from speculating that I was in some sort of trouble.

The only good thing was that no one from Lancaster was at

the front of the resort. Those who were awake at this ungodly hour would either be eating breakfast or lounging at the beach. But I would bet my last dollar that everyone from Lancaster was still in bed, asleep after another night of heavy drinking and partying.

I leaned back, resting my head on the back of the seat and closing my eyes. The officer drove to the station without speaking, which was the way I wanted it. I was in no mood for small talk.

I opened my eyes periodically, long enough to know that we were taking the road that led into town. The island was small, and I wouldn't have been surprised to learn there was only one police station that serviced the island's small population of seventy-five thousand.

As we neared the street that would lead us to Zack's Shack, my heart began to pound wildly, and my nape tingled with fear. I remembered that night in the alley, and suddenly wondered if I was really being taken to the police station. What if this officer was going to take me back to the alley, where I would be beaten and threatened, the way Jason had?

But instead of getting into the right lane that would lead us to Zack's Shack, he got into the left lane and turned that way. About a minute later, past the upscale shops, the cop turned right. A short while later, he turned left into the parking lot of a two-story building that had three other police cars parked out front.

The Artulan flag—red, black, and green—billowed in the breeze on a flagpole that stood in the center of a floral island. The sky was gray today, promising rain.

The officer parked the car, then exited the vehicle. He opened the back door so I could get out.

As I stood, I swallowed my nervousness. I felt ambiguous about this meeting, I realized, wanting to believe it would help, but wary that these cops didn't give a damn.

I climbed the steps behind the officer. He opened the door for me and gestured for me to enter. Goose bumps popped out on my skin as I stepped into the cool, air-conditioned interior.

A tall, dark-skinned man dressed in a white shirt and black pants turned when he heard the door. He was large and imposing, but had a nice smile. But it was the kind of smile that didn't hold any warmth.

"Miss Higgins," he said, moving toward me with an outstretched hand. "I'm pleased to meet you."

"Sergeant Bingham?" I recognized the voice.

"Yes," he said, his voice deep. "Thank you for coming in."

"No problem."

"This shouldn't take long." He opened a latch on a gate in the entryway, one that led beyond the public area of the station to the areas designated for law enforcement personnel. "Follow me, please."

I did, my pulse growing quicker with each step. Were the officers who'd harassed us and beaten Jason in here?

I examined the faces. There were about ten men in the open area, a mix of uniformed officers and plainclothes detectives behind desks. Some were typing at keyboards, some scribbling on notepads, and others on the phone.

But the cops from the alley weren't in here.

Sergeant Bingham walked all the way to the back of the room, veering toward an open door on the right. I followed him into the small, neat office.

"Take a seat," he said, gesturing to a chair opposite his side of the desk.

I sat, gingerly, my eyes sweeping over the office.

"I thank you for coming in today, Miss Higgins," the sergeant said as he rounded the desk and took a seat opposite me.

"I'm glad you believe that my friend is really missing." I was surprised that I'd spoken the words, but I was still peeved. Not only because the sergeant had not taken me seriously initially, but with how those officers had treated me, Erica, and Jason in the alley.

And the last thing I wanted was to be sitting here if this cop was only going to pay lip service to a very serious issue.

Sergeant Bingham grinned, but it was guarded, and I couldn't read what was in his eyes. "I understand you are frustrated by our first conversation, but I assure you that I do believe your friend is missing. I will do everything in my power to make sure that she is found."

I nodded. There was no response required for that statement.

"You can help by telling me exactly what happened on Sunday night when you were at Zack's Shack."

"I went to the bar with my friend Erica, and also with Ashley. It was supposed to be a fun night out. And we were having fun."

I went on to explain all that had happened that night, how Ashley had met Jason Shear and the two had spent some time together. How I'd also noticed her arguing with Ryan and Blake, presumably about a raunchy cell-phone video they had taken of her. I finished the story by talking about BJ and Kevaughn, and the fact that the pill they'd given Erica was clearly something designed to knock her out.

"Erica was really sick and out of it, and I knew I had to get her back to the hotel. That's when I searched the bar to find

Ashley so we could leave. I looked everywhere, but she was nowhere to be found. I also didn't see Jason anymore. I figured they'd both hit it off and maybe . . ."

"Maybe what?"

I shrugged. "I figured maybe she'd left with him. Not that I expected her to do something like that, but she'd been drinking, and he was an editor, and I could see her leaving with him to go somewhere else if it meant, hopefully, getting a connection to being published."

"Did you have a card for Jason Shear?"

"No."

"Then how did you come to speak with him? After your friend was missing."

"I remembered his first name, and the name of the publishing house Ashley said he worked for. When she didn't return to the room, I called the publisher and asked them to contact Jason on my behalf. He got back to me—and that's when I learned that Ashley wasn't with him."

The sergeant folded his hands together. "I'm curious as to why you believed him."

I frowned, confused by the statement. "I—I don't understand."

"You didn't know him. He could have been lying, and yet you chose to believe him."

"I'm a good judge of character, Sergeant Bingham. At least I think I am. I saw no reason for Jason to lie about something like that. And he was immediately willing to help me find my friend."

"Because of his belief that tourists on this island have been abducted into white slavery."

"I suppose. Yes."

The sergeant studied me, and though I didn't want to, I fidgeted in my seat under his intense gaze.

Breaking eye contact with me, he drummed his fingers on the desk. "All right. Back to the night you went out. What was Ashley wearing?"

"She was wearing a glittery red halter top and a white denim miniskirt. She'd styled her hair in big, loose curls. She looked gorgeous." I paused. "My friend Erica can e-mail you a picture of Ashley that night. She has one on her phone."

"Why didn't your friend come in with you?" Sergeant Bingham asked.

"She left yesterday. Her parents wanted her to go home."

"Yet, you're still here."

"Because I want to do whatever I can to help find my friend."

The sergeant nodded, once again studying me with that discomfiting gaze.

I changed the subject. "I find it suspicious that Ryan and Blake left the island days before they were due to go home. But there's also BJ and Kevaughn. Those two could just as easily be responsible for what happened to Ashley. They were obviously out to victimize someone."

"Does this mean you no longer believe your friend was kidnapped for the purposes of being a sexual slave to some rich prince in another part of the world?"

The way he asked the question made it clear he didn't believe for a second that was even a likely reality, that he was humoring the idea at best.

"I can't say. All I know is that my friend is missing and anything's possible."

"Hmm." The sergeant leaned back in his chair, once again studying me in a way that made me feel uneasy. "Would you be surprised to learn that many tourists, both women and men, sometimes drink too much, walk the short distance from the party zone to the beach, and end up drowning? Sometimes their bodies are washed out to sea and they end up caught in a fisherman's net. Sometimes the sharks get to them."

I swallowed at the idea of Ashley's body being eaten by sea creatures.

"The point," the sergeant went on, "is that the family and friends of these people almost always suspect foul play in the beginning. But the truth is, there is usually a simple answer for what happened to the missing person. Tragic, yes, but simple."

"I'm sure it happens."

"By your own accounts, your friend was drinking heavily."

"It's spring break. That's what college kids do."

"Hmm."

What did that mean?

"Thank you, Miss Higgins. The information will be helpful, I'm sure."

I stared at the man in surprise. "Don't you want to know Blake and Ryan's full names? A description of BJ and Kevaughn? Maybe they're still on the island. And if they are, they need to be brought in and questioned."

"I know how to do my job, Miss Higgins."

I opened my mouth, wanted to say something. Because I got the distinct impression that this man was going to come to the conclusion that Ashley had died by misadventure, that she'd been so drunk she'd wandered to the beach, and drowned.

But I wasn't stupid. I knew better than to push it. I wasn't in America. The last thing I wanted was to get thrown in jail.

Or worse. Like had happened to Jason.

So I said, "Yes. Of course. I didn't mean to say that you didn't."

He pushed a notepad across the desk to me, then handed me a pen. "Write down the names of these boys you've mentioned."

I did as instructed, writing alongside Blake and Ryan's names the college they attended, and the city and state.

"The other guys, BJ and Kevaughn, I don't know where they live, or their surnames. But if they offered me and my friend drugs, maybe they offered them to other women. Someone on the island may be able to tell you who they are."

Sergeant Bingham reached for the notepad and gave it a quick perusal. "You forgot a name," he said.

I looked at him quizzically. "Excuse me."

He began to write, then said, "Jason Shear."

"Jason?"

"He was with your friend before she went missing. By your own account, you assumed she had left with him."

"Yes, but—"

"I wouldn't be doing my job to the best of my ability if I excluded Jason Shear as a suspect in your friend's disappearance."

"If you thought that Jason had anything to do with what happened to Ashley, then why did you tell him to leave the island and head back to the States?"

"I did no such thing."

"Maybe not you personally. But someone from this station." When the sergeant didn't speak, I continued. "You brought him in a couple nights ago, and released him yesterday morning with the instructions to get off the island."

Surprise flashed in the sergeant's eyes, a look that made my pulse thunder in my ears. Because the look seemed genuine.

"Is that what he told you?" Sergeant Bingham asked.

"Yes, that's what he told me," I replied a bit testily.

"Considering I believe Mr. Shear might be crucial to this investigation, why would I—or anyone from this department— instruct him to leave the island?"

"I saw your officers arrest him!" I protested. "I saw them beat him in the alley. And I saw him yesterday morning—saw the bruises."

"Which officers?"

"I—I don't know their names. But they were in uniforms, and driving a police car just like the ones parked outside."

"I'm the sergeant at this police station, Miss Higgins. If Jason Shear was detained the night before last, I would know about it."

I stared at Sergeant Bingham in confusion, shaking my head.

"Are you telling me he wasn't brought in?" I finally asked.

"That's exactly what I'm telling you."

My mouth fell open.

"If that's what Mr. Shear told you, he lied."

"But . . . but I saw . . ."

"You saw what he wanted you to see."

No. No, it couldn't be true.

Jason wasn't lying. I'd seen those officers attack him.

"I think it's clear you don't know this Mr. Shear at all," Sergeant Bingham said, almost smugly.

My hands began to shake. Surely the sergeant was mistaken. Surely.

But what if . . .

I'd told Jason about the meeting in the alley. He could have had time to set up something that would seem believable, including real or fake police officers to take him down.

Oh my God.

What if there *was* a conspiracy—one that Jason Shear was smack-dab in the middle of?

Chapter Twenty-six

I FELT physically ill as I left the police station, so much so that I had to draw in slow, easy breaths and to clutch my stomach as the officer drove, fearing I would vomit in the backseat of the car.

I was sure of nothing anymore.

Least of all Jason.

But why would he lie? I asked myself over and over. Why? What could he possibly have to gain?

His story? Publicity for the book he was writing about white slavery?

Needing some fresh air, I pressed the button to lower the window. But it wouldn't budge.

Of course not. I was in the backseat of a police car, where prisoners normally sat. The window's power button had obviously been disabled.

"Excuse me," I said, leaning forward. "Can you please open a window?"

The officer looked over his shoulder at me. "You want the window open?"

"Please."

He lowered his own window halfway, and then did the same with the front passenger window. Fresh air blasted into the backseat.

As I leaned my head back, questions continued to race through my mind.

Could Jason really have lied about everything? Could he have set up that scene in the alley? Was he truly capable of that kind of deception?

I'd seen movies where the bad guy had shot himself in an effort to appear innocent. Always because he had done something heinous and wanted to hide his guilt.

If Jason had set up the whole meeting in the alley, had let himself get beaten as part of a ruse, then that meant only one thing.

He was behind Ashley's disappearance.

But his sister, I said to myself. *The article about her disappearance.*

Hope filled my heart once again, the hope that Jason was exactly who he'd represented himself to be. But the hope ebbed away when I considered that he was in publishing. How hard would it have been for him to create such an article as part of his cover?

I closed my eyes as my stomach rolled. Had I gotten my hopes up with a psychotic liar?

By the time the cop car pulled up in front of the hotel, I was on the verge of breaking down. The intensity of my emotions shocked me.

Was it that I had come to care for Jason so much in the short time I'd known him, or the fact that the person responsible for what had happened to Ashley could be back in the States—or God-knew-where at this point—never to pay for his crime?

I was so lost in my depressing thoughts that I didn't notice the various vans lining the hotel's circular driveway. Only as I got out of the car and saw a videographer filming the hotel's exterior did I realize that the media must have arrived.

Two Lancaster students were standing near the hotel's front door, and a woman with a notepad was talking to them, scribbling and nodding.

Yes, the media was here.

As I started toward the front door, my fellow students glanced in my direction. Then the reporter was spinning around and looking at me. And the next second, she was scurrying toward me.

"Chantelle Higgins?" she asked.

I stopped, my heart thundering. Did I want to do this? Give a statement to the media? Especially now, when I wasn't sure what to believe?

"Yes," I answered after a moment. Whether or not Jason had lied to me, he was right about one thing. This story needed to get out. "Yes, I'm Chantelle."

"My name is Molly Sandford from *The New York Times*. I understand you're a friend of Ashley Hamilton, the woman who's gone missing."

I nodded.

"And you were with her the night she disappeared?"

"Y-yes."

"Can you tell me what happened that night?"

So I did. Telling her everything I knew. Only this time, I concluded by saying that Ryan, Blake, BJ, Kevaughn, *and* Jason might have vital information regarding Ashley's disappearance.

"Jason Shear," Molly said.

I swallowed. "Yes."

"I spoke with him this morning." She flipped back pages in her notepad. "He says he met you, Ashley, and your friend Erica by chance on Sunday night, while on the island researching cases of missing women for a book he's working on."

"Mmm-hmm." I tried not to show any emotion.

"Can you speak to his allegations of police misconduct in this investigation?"

"I . . . I'm not sure. But I do believe they should have taken Ashley's disappearance more seriously when I first contacted them about it."

"What do you think of his allegations of white slavery?"

"I . . ." The videographer and a man with a microphone were around me now, along with someone else with a handheld recorder.

"I remember the case of Hilary Shear's disappearance," the woman went on, more to herself. "That was my first year as a journalist." She shook her head sadly. "It was a big story in New York."

Her words made my stomach roll again—but this time for a

different reason. Relief. Her words were outside validation that Jason hadn't lied about that.

And if his sister had gone missing years earlier, it made perfect sense that he would have devoted his life to investigating what had happened to her.

And to examining a huge conspiracy theory, if he believed one existed.

"I'm from CNN," the male reporter said. "What do you think happened to your friend?" He pushed the microphone forward, under my chin.

I was angry now, angry with Sergeant Bingham. *He* was probably the one who had lied to me. Played me for a bloody fool to get to me.

And he'd succeeded.

The truth was, if there was a conspiracy going on, then Sergeant Bingham was the one with the reason to lie.

"Jason Shear's sister went missing here in the late eighties," I began. "So have many other women since. Young, attractive women from all over the world, here in Artula for a vacation in paradise. Mr. Shear believes there is an organized ring involved with abducting these girls into white slavery. And I think . . . I think he may be right."

"Tell us why you believe that," the man from CNN said.

"Let me just say that I don't have much faith in the police here," I said, scowling, thinking in particular of Sergeant Bingham. "I don't think they're exactly forthright."

"What about the men you mentioned?" the woman asked. She referred to her notes. "Ryan Sinclair and Blake Crawford, the ones from Lancaster. And BJ and Kevaughn."

"I think they need to be questioned," I said. "Ryan and Blake were definitely at odds with Ashley. They took . . . they took a compromising video of her that she was understandably angry about. That video is the reason she broke up with Ryan, so who knows?" I shrugged. "Do I believe white slavery is a possibility? Yes. But there are other possibilities, too. All I really know is that my friend is missing, and someone knows what happened to her. That's really all I have to say."

Two of the reporters began to speak at the same time, but I held up a hand. "Really, that's all I have to say." And then my voice cracked. "Please—please get the word out. Please keep this story in the headlines. I want my friend to come home."

And then I hurried off, away from the cameras and the spectators, holding my tears in until I was away from the spotlight. I ran to the bathroom off the lobby, where I locked myself in a stall.

And that's when I burst into tears, letting myself finally feel all that I had tried to avoid feeling in the last few days.

My interview made it onto CNN by the noon broadcast, after which my cell phone rang.

Private name. Private number.

I flipped my phone open and held it to my ear. "Hello?"

"Hey."

At the sound of his voice, I began to cry.

"Hey. Chantelle . . . are you all right?"

"No, Jason. I'm not. This is a nightmare. I want to wake up and find that none of this has really happened, but I won't. And I'm trying to stay hopeful, but the truth is I don't know if any of this will help. I don't know if I'll ever see my friend again."

"Aw, sweetie. I wish I could be there with you."

A niggle of doubt came into my mind at his words. Maybe

it was irrational, but after what Sergeant Bingham said, I was still confused. I didn't know if anything was as it seemed.

"Are you sure about that?" I asked.

"What?"

"I spoke with Sergeant Bingham this morning. He said you were never brought into the station."

A couple of beats passed—too long, as far as I was concerned—and a sickening fear washed over my body like a giant wave. The fear that Sergeant Bingham hadn't been lying.

"Jason?"

"He's right," Jason said. "I never spent the night at the police station."

"Oh God," I cried.

"Chantelle, hear me out."

"You lied to me?" I asked, hysteria and rage bubbling forth in my tone. "If you lied to me about that, Jason, then—"

"I didn't lie, Chantelle. I just didn't tell you everything."

"A lie by omission—"

"*I didn't lie,*" Jason insisted, and damn it, I believed him. "You saw the bruises," he went on. "Those were real. I just didn't want to tell you everything." He paused. "Because I didn't want to scare you."

I wiped at my tears. "I'm listening."

"Those cops beat the shit out of me. After they put me in that cruiser, they drove me around the island. They took me to the north side I told you about, where the waves will swallow you in a matter of seconds. They dragged me out of the car. Dragged me to the rocks and held me over the edge. I thought it was over. I thought they were going to put a bullet in me and dump me into the crashing surf.

"But I think they realized they couldn't do that. That if they got rid of me, there would be too many questions. So they held me there, let me beg for my life for about twenty minutes, and then they made me swear I would get off the island and never return. That if I did return, this was exactly what would happen to me."

"Oh my God," I said softly. That would explain why Sergeant Bingham knew nothing about what had happened to Jason. Why the surprise in his eyes had been real. Maybe Bingham was innocent in all this, but someone in the department knew what was going on.

"Why didn't you tell me?" I asked.

"Because . . . because I wanted to protect you from this."

My pulse raced at the simple statement. And I got the meaning behind the words. That he cared about me. As much as I apparently cared about him.

"I saw you on CNN," Jason said after a moment.

"And? What did you think?"

"I kind of got the feeling you were throwing me into the pool of suspects at first."

I sighed. That's exactly what I had done. "I wasn't sure what to think after Sergeant Bingham told me you'd never been detained at the police station. I figured if you were lying about that . . . I—I'm sorry."

"It's okay. I'm not worried. My sister's story came out, so I don't believe anyone thinks I'm a suspect. But . . ."

"But what?"

"But I think some people are going to be angry. The authorities, for one. You basically said you didn't trust the Artulan police. And Ryan and Blake will be pissed for sure."

"Well, they can be pissed, I don't care. They took off in a hurry. That still doesn't sit well with me. If they have nothing to hide, they'll go to the authorities and try to help with the investigation."

Another beat passed. "I think you should come home. After what those cops did to me, and what you said on CNN—I can see them being livid. Wanting to silence you. I don't trust them."

Fear shot down my arms and my back. "You don't think they'd hurt me? After speaking out like I did, the last thing they would want is for anything to happen to me. That would only lend credence to your conspiracy theories."

"Maybe . . . but I don't trust them."

I didn't trust them, either. But I found myself saying, "I'll be okay. I've only got a a day and a half left here, and I . . . I want to be here when Ashley's found."

I spoke the words as though they were a statement of fact, not an unlikely and desperate wish.

"All right," Jason said after a moment. He sighed softly. "I understand. I've been where you are. I guess . . . I guess I'm being partly selfish in wanting you to come home. I really don't want anything to happen to you."

A soft smile touched my mouth as my heart began to pound. That thrill of desire, even at a time like this. "I know you don't."

"Watch Fox News later. They're going to interview me about my connection to this story—and what happened to my sister."

"Okay," I told him. Then, as much as I didn't want to end the call, I said, "This phone call is going to cost me a fortune."

"I know. I'll call you later, on the room phone."

I smiled again. "Okay."

. . . .

There were more calls, from my mother, and Erica, and other friends back home. I was brief with everyone, telling them to call the room phone if they really wanted to talk. Because I knew my cell-phone bill would be exorbitant. And it wasn't like I could afford it.

My mother did call me back on the room phone, pleading with me to leave Artula. Like Jason, she agreed that I had likely angered the Artulan authorities.

"I'm being careful," I assured her. "I've been in the room the entire day. And I'm going to call for room service." That was a little white lie, as the hotel's all-inclusive plan didn't include room service. But there was no need to worry my mother even more. I didn't believe I'd get hurt just by leaving my room for food.

When I went for the dinner buffet, I saw only a handful of students from Lancaster. I learned from one of the guys that in light of what had happened to Ashley, most had opted to leave early.

I went back to my room, wondering if Jason was right. If I should get out of here sooner rather than later.

I turned on the television and after thirty minutes of watching, I caught Jason's interview on Fox News. A team from Fox News was also on the island, because they'd interviewed Anabelle and Bill Hamilton. Even though they'd stood before cameras, hopefully to present a united front to the world, they had stood a good two feet apart, the gap between them clearly beyond a physical one.

Yeah, there was trouble in that marriage.

I was watching the replay of the Fox News segment at nine

when the room phone rang. Smiling, I answered, expecting to hear Jason's voice.

Instead, a pleasant female voice said, "Chantelle Higgins?"

"Yes."

"This is Claudette from the front desk. There's a package for you."

"A package?"

"Yes. Would you like to come retrieve it, or would you rather have someone bring it to your room?"

I needed to save any extra cash I had for my cell-phone bill, not tips. Every dollar would help. "I'll come get it."

The moment I hung up, I slipped into my flip-flops and left my room.

There was only one woman at the front desk, most likely the woman who had called me. I went up to her. "Hi. I'm Chantelle Higgins in room 1604. Someone called and said there was a package for me."

"Yes." The woman smiled warmly, then reached below the counter. She produced a small, flat, brown box. It looked like the size of a box that might hold one or two paperback novels.

"Here you go."

"Thanks," I said, accepting the box from her.

There was a white label, upon which my name and hotel address were typed. Missing was my room number.

Whatever was in the box, it was light. I wondered who it was from.

There was no other way to find that out than to open it, something I would do back in my room.

The box was taped shut, so in the room, I got my keys from my purse and used one as a knife to cut the tape along the seams.

I could see a slip of paper as I lifted the box's flaps. A note. I withdrew it and read.

GO HOME NOW.

My heart began to pound, a sixth sense telling me that whatever was in the box was going to be something awful. And though I knew that, I couldn't stop myself from lifting the dark plastic bag inside and opening it.

The bag was fairly big—bigger at least than whatever was inside of it. Holding the bag open, I tipped it upside down so that whatever it held would fall into my open palm.

A dark mass came out, about three inches long by two inches wide. I couldn't immediately tell what it was.

But as I examined it in my palm, felt its almost rubbery consistency, realization slammed into me with the force of a bullet to the head.

I dropped it. Dropped it and screamed.

Chapter
Twenty-seven

MY SCREAM DIED as bile rose in my throat. I ran to the bathroom, barely making it to the toilet before the vomit forced its way out of my mouth. My stomach convulsed as I threw up twice.

I stood hunched over the toilet, my hands braced on my knees. I began to quiver, a full body tremble.

Pressing my eyes tightly together, I tried to block out the image of what I'd just held. Tried, but failed.

A severed tongue, blackened as it had begun to decay. I was sure of it.

Gasping out a sob, I dropped down onto the bathroom

floor. I sat on the cold tile and cried, stricken with terror and not knowing what to do.

The tongue belonged to the man from the alley. To Paul Dunlop. It had to be his. And if not his, then someone else who'd been about to speak out regarding what had happened to Ashley.

Sebastian? Had he been killed just for talking to me?

Would I be killed?

My chest hurt from the effort to breathe. My arms and legs felt numb.

Go home now. That's what the note had said. The severed tongue was meant as a warning. A warning to shut the hell up. To keep my opinion about the police to myself. To keep my opinion about conspiracy theories to myself.

Or whoever had delivered that tongue would cut my tongue out, too.

I got the message loud and clear.

Go home now.

Still shaking and crying, I looked to my right, through the open bathroom door, to the spot where I'd dropped the tongue. The disgusting mass lay on the floor.

I'd touched it. A dead human tongue had been in my hand.

That thought was enough to make me rise, head to the sink, and turn on the water. I grabbed the small bar of soap and lathered my hands. Lathered them under the warm water. Washed them over and over and over. Washed my forearms, too.

It wasn't enough. Nothing would be enough to erase the horrifying image from my mind. Enough to wash away the feel of the tongue against my skin.

If I were back home, I would call the police and report this incident. Leave the tongue where it was and let them conduct an investigation.

But this was Artula, and I didn't trust anyone on this island, least of all the police.

Jason was right—I should have left. Now I would have to wait until the morning to get the hell out of here.

One more night I would have to spend on this island, in this room alone, a possible target for a ruthless killer.

The last thing I wanted to do was touch the tongue again. But I knew I couldn't call the police about this threat. It would be a waste of time. Calling the media into my room might bring light to the fact that someone on this island was trying to cover up a dirty secret. But that might very well cost me my life.

There was only one thing I could do. Get rid of the tongue myself.

Because I damn well wasn't going to sleep in the room with it.

I pulled off reams and reams of toilet paper, wadded it into a giant ball, and forced myself to walk back toward the severed tongue.

My hands shook as I stared down at it. I whimpered, not wanting to touch it. I was afraid, as though the tongue would come to life the moment I reached for it.

"Do it," I said. "Do it and get it out of here."

I had to. Otherwise I wouldn't be able to sleep in this room.

Not that I was going to sleep well anyway, if at all.

Not after this.

Grimacing, I lowered myself and scooped the tongue into

the wad of tissue. Then I ran to the balcony door, unlocked and opened it with my left hand, and rushed outside.

I didn't hesitate before throwing the tongue and toilet-paper ball as far as I could. I watched it sail through the air and come to land about ten feet from the base of a palm tree.

And that's when I got the feeling that someone was watching me.

My gaze flew to the left. To the right. Scanned the open area between my building and the one on the other side of the courtyard.

All I noticed was the rustling of the palm trees and bushes in the breeze.

I saw no one.

Goose bumps popped out on my skin as a weird tingling sensation spread down my arms. There was another option. One far more terrifying.

Someone could be in my room.

I turned slowly, fearing the worst, ready to vault over the first-floor balcony if necessary. My eyes quickly scanned the lighted room.

Again, no one.

But that's when I heard the knocking on my door.

I stood, paralyzed, wondering if I should climb over the balcony railing and run off.

"Hello?" I heard as the knocking continued. "This is hotel security. Are you okay in there?"

Security. Thank God.

I rushed into the room, and to the door. Only as I was about to open it did I get a second thought.

Was the person on the other side really security? Or the person who had sent me the tongue?

The knocking persisted. "If you don't open the door, I will have to come in."

I turned the knob, opening the door slowly.

A man in a security guard uniform looked me over with concern. "Ma'am, are you all right? Someone reported a scream coming from this room."

"I . . . I . . ." What could I say? "I was . . . having a bad dream. I—I must have screamed in my sleep."

The man peered over my shoulder into the room, as if he didn't believe me. "Are you alone in this room?"

"Yes." I opened the door wider, so he could get a better look. "I had a nightmare. I'm really sorry. I didn't mean to alarm anyone."

The security guard continued to peruse the room. Then his eyes settled for a moment to the area left of my shoulder, and I followed his line of sight to the box on my bed.

Did he know? Was he the one who'd delivered it?

I quickly looked back at him, but any sign of tension or concern on his face was now gone.

"Don't worry about having alarmed anyone," the man said. "We take our guests' safety very seriously. I'm just glad you're all right."

"I am." I forced a smile.

The man nodded. Then his eyes narrowed, and my heart accelerated again. "Ah . . . you're the young girl who was on the news earlier. Your friend is missing."

Hugging my torso, I nodded.

"I was sorry to hear the news. I hope your friend is found, and that she's unharmed."

The words sounded heartfelt. "Thank you," I said. "That means a lot."

"Have a good evening."

"You, too."

He started to walk away, and I closed the door behind him and bolted it. I went to the balcony door, closed and locked that, too, then drew the drapes together.

The next thing I did was get my cell phone. I punched in the digits to Jason's cell.

He answered on the second ring. "Hello?"

"Jason . . ." I had to hold in my tears. "It's me. Chantelle."

"Hey," he said, concern in his tone. "Are you okay?"

"No. No, I'm not. Something happened, Jason. And I'm scared."

"What?"

I took a deep breath and told him what had transpired.

"You have to come home. As soon as possible."

"I know. I'm going to call the airline as soon as I hang up with you, see if I can head out in the morning instead of on my evening flight."

"God, this pisses me off," Jason said. "These motherfuckers are behind what happened to my sister, your friend, the other women. They're willing to kill to keep their dirty secret."

"You're right," I said sadly. "I was hoping I'd get answers, but this conspiracy is too big."

"Yeah." Jason groaned his frustration. "Damn that fucking place."

"Jason, I'm sorry."

"For what?"

"Because I was hoping . . . that maybe through all of this, you'd get some answers. Finally learn what happened to your sister."

"It's been a long time. Too long for me to really believe that

I'll ever learn what happened to her. I've made peace with that."

"But still—"

"Look, we can't change what's happened, but we can affect the future," Jason said. "The future is getting you back here safely. The media's picked up this story in a big way, so maybe there'll be answers yet. But that doesn't matter now. What matters is you getting back here. As soon as you can."

He was right. One hundred percent. "I'll call the airline now."

"And will you call me back to let me know your flight schedule?"

"I will."

I called the airline next. I grimaced when I learned it was going to cost me an extra four hundred dollars to change my flight to the next morning. It was money I didn't have, but I certainly didn't want to take my chances with the stand-by option, so I gave the ticket agent my credit card number. I wanted to leave Artula as soon as possible, no matter the cost.

The cell-phone charges were an extra expense. Cutting the trip short was an extra expense.

What had started out as a cheaply priced vacation was costing me a lot more.

But the biggest cost of all was not the monetary price tag. It was the life of my best friend.

A friend I was starting to believe I would never see alive again.

Chapter
Twenty-eight

MY NEW FLIGHT was scheduled for eleven-thirty, so I left the hotel at eight. I wanted to call Ashley's parents, but I didn't have a number for them, and since they were renting a guesthouse, it seemed impossible to locate them.

I hadn't heard from them since Anabelle and Megan had come to take Ashley's things, but that was to be expected. They were no doubt going through their own private hell. I knew what I was feeling, and Ashley was my best friend. It had to be much, much worse for her family.

I stared out the taxi's window at the hotel, watching as it

got smaller and smaller in the distance. I was happy to say good riddance to the place. To the whole island.

Even if Ashley was found alive—and I prayed that she would be—what had happened here had changed me. I would never be able to think "spring break" and be happy. I would probably never be able to vacation on another island.

How could I, and not remember?

I called Jason from the airport. "Just wanted you to know that I got to the airport safely," I said. "I land in Miami around two-forty, and then it's back to Philly."

"Good. That's really great." He paused. "You should know— Ryan and Blake have been picked up by the authorities."

My heart leaped to my throat. "They have?"

"Yep. The news is reporting that the FBI is working with the Artulan authorities to solve Ashley's disappearance."

Even yesterday morning, this news would have made me happy. Now, I felt ambiguous. But worse than ambiguity, I felt guilt. Guilt I never expected I'd feel.

Because I suddenly had a pretty good idea of how this would play out. And it was all my fault. I had handed the Artulan police the perfect scapegoats.

"Oh God," I uttered.

"What?" Jason asked.

"This is my fault. Oh, shit. Jason, I fucked up."

"What, Chantelle?" Jason said, more urgently.

"The police will go after Ryan and Blake, probably conclude that they killed Ashley, either on purpose or by accident, and that'll be it. Everyone will be satisfied, and the conspiracy theory will die down—exactly what the Artulan authorities will want. Courtesy of yours truly."

"It's not your fault."

"And then another girl will go missing, and this nightmare will begin again for another family."

"Chantelle." Jason said my name firmly.

"Jason, I feel awful."

"Because you're giving yourself too much power. The Artulans involved are masters at deception. They have perfected their denial that anything untoward happens on their island. Even if there was no Blake, no Ryan, they'd come up with a way to deflect the truth. They always do."

Jason was right. I knew he was. But still, I felt bad.

"And we don't know that this will happen to another girl," Jason went on. "Maybe all this heat on the island is what is needed to stop it from happening again."

"But what about Ashley?" I asked. "If the authorities settle on Ryan and Blake as the prime suspects, they'll probably assume she's dead and not look for her. And if they don't look for her, how will we ever find her?"

"I know what you're feeling, what you're going through, but we can't give up on your friend, Chantelle. Not yet."

"I'm not giving up. I'm just . . . I guess I'm realizing this is going to be harder than I ever thought."

"You don't believe Ryan and Blake are behind what happened to Ashley?" Jason asked cautiously.

"Do you?" I asked, turning the tables on him.

"No. But I've never believed it. And I don't think that BJ and that other guy are responsible, either. If something got out of hand between Ashley and either of these guys, where's her body? How has she just disappeared into thin air?"

"The north side of the island?" I suggested.

"Sure, it's possible. But most tourists don't even know about it. And they'd need a car to dispose of the body. It doesn't seem likely to me."

"Yeah," I said, my voice barely a whisper. "But that's good. Because if Blake and Ryan *did* take her to the north side, that would mean . . . that would mean the worst-case scenario. But white slavery . . . at least there's hope."

As I finished my statement, I swallowed painfully. *Hope.* Both a blessing and a curse. A ray of light and an albatross.

Pushing the thought aside, I said, "I'd better go. I'll call you when I get to Miami, when it won't cost an arm and a leg to use my cell phone."

"Talk to you then, sweetie."

I got off the phone with Jason, and called my mother briefly. She actually began to cry happy tears when I told her I was at the airport, on my way home.

"Praise Jesus," she said, and continued crying, overjoyed with relief.

I couldn't help thinking about Anabelle Hamilton's tears. Unlike my mother's, they were fueled by grief.

One mother was devastated. The other relieved.

Life wasn't fair.

I didn't dare tell my mother about the incident with the tongue. She would probably insist that I move back home and never leave.

On the plane, once airborne, I stared down at the view of the island. *Are you down there, Ashley?* I thought. *Are you trapped somewhere on the island, where no one can help you?*

My gaze went from the lush greenery to the stretch of white sand beach and the gorgeous blend of turquoise and deep blue water.

What a difference seven days could make. When we'd been arriving, I'd looked down at this same view with such hope and happiness. But that's not what I saw now.

Now I saw hell.

I hadn't given any thought as to how I would get back to campus once I arrived at the Philadelphia airport. My only goal, after receiving that awful package with the tongue, was to get out of Artula.

When we'd been leaving for our trip, Ashley had arranged for a car to pick us up on campus and take us to the airport. A car was to do the same upon our return.

But obviously there would be no hired car now.

A taxi was going to cost a pretty penny. It might be better to do a one-way car rental.

I collected my suitcase and started toward the ground transportation area, where I planned to approach a few car rental companies and find out how much one would cost. But about ten steps into my walk, I stopped dead in my tracks, my mouth falling open.

Carl was standing a few feet away from me.

I stood there in shock, momentarily not believing my eyes. How could it be?

A relieved smile broke out on his face, and then he rushed toward me.

He wasn't a figment of my imagination. He was really here.

"Baby," he said, drawing me into his arms. "Thank God you're home."

I said nothing. I was too startled to speak.

He was still smiling as he pulled back and stared down at

me, clearly not picking up on my discomfort. He framed my face, gazing at me with an expression of pure joy.

And when he kissed me, I didn't pull away. This wasn't the time.

When he broke the kiss, I finally found my voice. "Carl, what are you doing here?"

"Your mother called me. Told me when your flight was arriving, said you'd need a ride back to Lancaster."

"Oh." Of course.

Ray held up one of his Lan-U jackets. "I brought you a jacket, in case you were cold. You know, coming from a warm place back to Philly."

"Right. Thanks, but I'm okay." I had taken the change of weather into account, and was already wearing a thick sweater-coat.

He took my large suitcase from my hands. "Here, let me get that."

"Thanks," I said softly.

I didn't ever remember seeing Carl look so happy. He had a bounce to his step, and his ear-to-ear smile seemed to be permanent. Like a man who'd reunited with a love he hadn't seen in ages.

I glanced down, feeling awful. Because my heart had already moved on from Carl.

To Jason.

And I felt guilty about that. Yes, Carl had broken up with me for going on this trip, but the truth was, my heart had never truly been his. I could see that now.

But none of this was something I was about to bring up at this point. Heck, I needed the ride back to Lancaster.

It wasn't like Carl to hold my hand, but that's exactly what he did as he walked with me out the airport doors and to the short-term parking. And once we got in the car, he took my hand in his once again. Even as he drove, he periodically lifted my hand to his lips and kissed it.

He was being far more affectionate than I'd known him to be—at least for a long time. Maybe it was this whole crazy situation with Ashley that had him realizing he could have lost me forever. Or perhaps he felt bad for pushing me away and was trying to show me how sorry he was.

I let him hold my hand. I didn't have the heart to pull it away.

For the first thirty minutes of the drive I didn't speak, and Carl didn't ask me any questions. I was grateful for the silence. I laid my head against the door frame, thinking. Thinking about everything.

Would the day ever come when I could close my eyes and not be haunted by what had happened? I didn't think so.

"Hey," Carl said softly.

I opened my eyes and looked at him. "Hmm?"

"How're you holding up?"

"Honestly? Not good. But I'm hanging in there."

"There's something you need to know," Carl said. His tone and expression were grim. "You haven't said anything, so I figure you haven't heard."

I lifted my head, my breath catching in my throat.

God, no. Oh God, no.

Carl's eyes widened slightly, in surprise, I think. And then I saw realization dawn on his face. He understood my emotion.

"No," he quickly said. "It's not that kind of news. But it's something that will shock you. And yes, it's about Ashley."

"What?" I asked, anxious.

"People on campus are talking, Chantelle. Some shit about Ashley being in porn videos. Something like that."

I stared at Carl blankly for several seconds, hearing his words but not making sense of them. There was no sense to be made of what he'd said.

And then—

"Oh my God. That son of a bitch!"

"What?" Carl asked.

"He must have e-mailed the video before I destroyed the phone. Shit!"

"What video?" Carl asked.

I clenched my right hand into a fist. I wanted to punch Blake's face in until his good looks were forever changed.

"Where's this coming from?" I asked, not answering Carl's question. "The news?"

"I think so, yeah."

I gritted my teeth. If this vile allegation had made the news . . . God, the pain this was going to cause Ashley's family. It was horrifically unfair.

I honestly didn't know what I would do when I saw Ryan and Blake. I didn't trust myself to maintain any semblance of control. As far as I was concerned, they were the lowest forms of life existing on earth and deserved to be treated as such.

"Will you tell me what's going on?" Carl asked. He looked at me a little too long, and the car drifted onto the shoulder.

"Carl!" I exclaimed.

He jerked the steering wheel to the left, returning the car to the proper lane. "I'm sorry. It's just, you've got me on pins and needles here, waiting for you to tell me what's going on."

I exhaled sharply, angrily. "In Artula, Blake took a video of Ashley . . . of her giving Ryan a blow job. This is where all the problems started. Ashley didn't know until after the fact, and she was devastated, and I found Blake and destroyed his phone, but he must have already e-mailed or texted someone the video. Now they're spreading the word about the video to the news media?" I shook my head, disgusted. "I can't believe they would stoop so low as to leak that story to the media now that Ashley's missing. Nor that stupid," I added, realizing it truly was a stupid move. "That video was the whole bone of contention between Ryan, Blake, and Ashley. So, duh, they've just shared their possible motive for hurting her with the world."

"Maybe it wasn't Ryan or Blake who leaked it to the media."

"Oh, please," I countered. "I get that they wanted to be assholes and share their raunchy video. But that was before Ashley went missing. Obviously they sent it to friends—and I can't see any of their friends going to the media with this unless they had their blessing."

"Maybe," Carl said. "But you know how these things are. You put them out into cyberspace and they take on a life of their own. Maybe it was some other person who got the video, realized it was the same girl missing in Artula, and he—or she—decided to make it public." When I looked at Carl doubtfully, he continued. "It's possible. I'm just saying, ya never know."

I continued to seethe for a few minutes, until what Carl had said finally registered. What if he was right? What if Blake had e-mailed the video before I'd destroyed his phone, and people had then forwarded the video to everyone they knew? There was no way to truly pinpoint what prick had thought it a good idea to send the video to CNN—or wherever they'd sent it.

My cell phone rang. I was about to reach for it. Until I realized who it might be, and knew that I couldn't.

"Aren't you going to get it?" Carl asked me.

I didn't make a move to even take my phone from my purse. What if it was Jason?

If so, I couldn't answer the call while in the car with Carl.

"I've been on my phone so much already, I won't be able to pay the bill," I said. That was true. "It's probably my mother. I'll call her when I get to my room."

Only when the phone stopped ringing did I reach into my purse and pull it out. Opening it, I pressed the button to display the number of the missed call.

I only needed to see the 212 area code to know it *had* been Jason. Now that I was back in the U.S., my Caller ID was once again working.

I glanced at Carl, who looked back at me. "Your mom?" he asked.

"Yeah, my mother," I said, wondering if he could tell that I was lying.

I surreptitiously turned the phone off.

Chapter
Twenty-nine

FIFTY MINUTES into our trip, we were almost on campus. I was feeling anxious about my return, knowing that the moment people saw me, they would want to grill me for details about what had happened. But I wasn't ready nor in the mood to talk about it. For many people at Lan-U, this would simply be gossip. For me, it was real. And it was hell.

"I heard the police were planning to bring Ryan and Blake in for questioning," I said. "Do you know if they've been arrested?"

"As far as I know, they were questioned and released."

"Released?" I asked, surprised.

"I don't know if they're in the clear or anything, but for the time being, they were allowed to leave. Something like that. I saw Blake when I was heading to the airport to get you."

"How nice. He and Ryan get to walk free, while Ashley is missing."

"Why do you say that?"

I didn't answer right away. The truth was, I didn't believe that they were behind what had happened to Ashley. Not anymore. But I no longer felt guilty that they might deal with being suspects for a long time. "I suppose I'd like to see them go to jail for being assholes, but that's not a crime."

"You think they hurt Ashley?" Carl asked now, doubtfully. "You said earlier that you thought it was white slavery. That the government over there was involved in the cover-up."

"I know." For me, the severed tongue had solidified that belief. No one delivered something like that to you with a warning to get lost when they weren't trying to cover up a dirty secret. "I'm just . . . I'm just pissed at how those two treated Ashley. And if they've sent this video all over the place . . ." I doubted there was a criminal statute on the books for what they'd done, but there should be.

We were approaching campus now, and Carl would head to The Hill, the area where my dorm building was. But I suddenly didn't want to go there.

"I want to see them," I said, the words surprising me as much as they'd clearly surprised Carl.

"What did you say?" he asked, his tone saying he was certain I *couldn't* have said what he'd heard.

"I want to see them," I repeated. "You know which dorm house they're in, right? It's on Lem Morrison Drive. The one where all the jocks live."

"Jesus, Chantelle. Why?"

"Because I need to give them a piece of my mind."

Carl made a face. "For what purpose?"

I felt a flash of irritation. And then I thought, *Jason would understand. He wouldn't ask me why. He'd just take me there.*

But I said, "Someone needs to. They hurt Ashley, disrespected her. Violated her. For Ashley's sake, I need to let them know what I think of them."

"Babe, why get into a war with them? Just put what happened behind you and move on."

"Put it behind me?" I asked, anger tingeing my voice. "You think I can just *put this all behind me*? My friend may be dead!"

I was taking my anger out on Carl, but he didn't truly deserve it. None of this was his fault. I was angry at the world for what had happened to my friend, and afraid that she was dead. And if not dead, gone forever.

Like Jason's sister was.

"Okay," Carl said, his tone placating. "I hear you. I know you're not gonna just get over this. That's not what I meant. But what do you really expect to get from confronting Ryan and Blake? If you think they hurt Ashley, then go to the cops. Get at them that way. If you don't . . . then what's the point in all of this?"

His question reminded me of what Erica had said, but now things were different. Now, that fucking video was out in the world for everyone to see. That I could never forgive.

"What's the matter, Carl? Scared of some football jocks?"

I knew the question would get to Carl, especially since he played basketball, and there was a definite rivalry between the Lan-U football and basketball players. That had been the point. Challenge his manhood, and he'd be forced to do what I wanted.

"This ain't about me being scared of no one. Shit, you just came back. After everything, I thought you'd want to chill."

"I have to see them," I said, stubborn. "And you can come with me, or you can drop me off there."

Carl grew silent, his lips pulling in a tight line. I knew him, knew him well. He would take me—but he wouldn't like it.

Instead of driving through the streets that would lead to The Hill, he headed to Lem Morrison Drive and took it around to the area that housed a cluster of newer male dormitories. He parked out front, frowning as he did, but other than that, he didn't voice another protest.

It was a chilly day, but there were a handful of guys outside, some hanging out near the base of the steps, and some standing near the maple tree, with girls. Two guys were heading to the front door, each with a case of beer.

It was still spring break, and people were still in party mode—as if a fellow student wasn't missing in Artula.

Together, Carl and I made our way to the front door. There, Carl stopped and turned to me. "Let me go in and see if they're there."

I considered the suggestion. "Fine. Yes, that's a good idea."

As Carl disappeared inside, I stood against the railing outside the door, gripping the cold iron as if my life depended on it.

What *was* I doing?

Defending my friend. Because her good name didn't deserve to be dragged through the mud because of Ryan and Blake.

A few minutes later, the front door opened. I held my breath as Carl stepped out, wondering if he'd found them.

The question was answered in the next moment. Ryan's head appeared behind Carl's, then Blake's.

Their eyes widened in surprise when they saw me. Carl obviously hadn't told them I was here.

One minute, I'd been second-guessing my decision to come
here. But at the sight of Ryan and Blake, both holding bottles
of beer, anger engulfed me.

Fucking pricks.

"Yo," Blake said. "You didn't tell me *she* was out here."

"Because you wouldn't have come," Carl explained, and I
was glad that he was defending me. "She's got something she
wants to ask you." Carl gave me a pointed look before facing
them again. "Just hear her out."

Ask? I wanted to kick these two in the groin and render
them impotent. I hated them for what they'd done to Ashley.

But I knew that instant anger would get me nowhere, so I
summoned all the strength I could to help me be calm.

"How could you?" I asked, looking at each of them in turn.
"And especially you, Ryan. A pastor's son and all. I thought
you'd have some sort of decency."

Ryan frowned at me. "I don't know what you're talking
about."

That was all it took for my anger to come to the surface.
"Oh, really?" I asked, all sarcastic. "No idea, huh? Okay, let me
make it clear: How could you send that disgusting video you
made of Ashley all over the place and defile her good name?
Especially now."

"What video?" Ryan asked.

Oh, so it was like that. I dug my nails into my palm. It was
the only way to avoid punching him.

I leveled an angry stare on Ryan first, then one on Blake.
"The one your friend here took of Ashley . . . and you. Together.
You know what I'm talking about. The reason I threw Blake's

phone in the hot tub, remember?" When they both looked at me dumbly, I rolled my eyes. "Maybe *you* didn't leak it to the media, but someone you sent that video to decided to send it on to the news. And now they're saying Ashley was in a *porn* movie. As if her family isn't going through enough." I took a breath and added, "You two are despicable."

Anger flared in Blake's eyes, and I got the sense that he wanted to hit me. But with Carl standing there, all six-foot-four of him, he wouldn't dare.

"Are you telling me you ruined my new iPhone because Ashley told you I'd made a video of her and Ryan making out?" Blake asked.

"You know damn well that's why."

And now Blake laughed. A pissed-off, I-don't-believe-this laugh.

"You need to explain the circumstances to the media," I said, the idea coming to me instantly. "Tell them that she was with her boyfriend, not performing for pay. That way, you can vindicate Ashley's name. She doesn't deserve this—and you know it."

"Ashley lied to you," Blake snapped. "Big surprise there, bro," he said, looking at Ryan.

"Yeah, big surprise." Ryan took a pull of his beer.

"Lied?" Were they actually going to deny what they'd done? "She came back to our room in tears after what you did. She was *devastated*."

"Maybe she was devastated because she knew her little se-cret was about to come out," Ryan retorted.

I stared at them, trying to make sense of their riddles. "What secret?"

"Turn on the news to CNN," Ryan said smugly. "The porn

they're talking about isn't some amateur cell-phone video. It's the real deal."

I heard the words, and I wanted to snort in derision, but the looks on Ryan's and Blake's faces were far too smug.

Far too confident.

"Looks like your sweet and innocent friend had a secret that no one knew about," Blake said, exaggerating the words "sweet" and "innocent."

"And that's what our fight was about in Artula," Ryan added. "That's what we were going to tell you when we talked to you. But we didn't get to."

"Because you left!" I said angrily, letting the words hang between us like an accusation. "And why? What was so urgent that you had to leave the island days before the trip was over?"

Ryan and Blake exchanged glances.

"Why?" I yelled.

Carl reached for me. "Chantelle—"

I slapped his hand away. "No." My eyes went back to Ryan and Blake. "You two take off from Artula days early, right after Ashley goes missing, and you don't think that's suspicious?"

"We got into some shit with some people," Blake said. "That's why we left."

"What kind of shit?"

"Nothing that concerns you," Blake said. "All you need to know is that your friend is a liar. I didn't take any sex video of her. She did that shit for cash, because she was a whore."

I slapped him. Slapped him good.

"You'll discover the truth soon enough," was all Blake said. "You can kick me, punch me, slap me—make as big a fool of yourself as you want. That's not going to change the facts."

I couldn't take any more. I stepped backward quickly, as though that could shield me from the awful picture they were painting. I hit the first step and stumbled, crashing down onto the concrete with my knee.

"Babe!" Carl immediately reached for me, but before he could touch me I got to my feet.

Got to my feet and ran back to the car.

But I couldn't outrun their words.

Chapter
Thirty

FIVE MINUTES LATER, Carl was pulling up to my dorm building, the M residence hall. Before the car had even come to a full stop, I was opening the door.

"Chantelle, chill for a second. You're gonna get yourself hurt."

I jumped out of the car nonetheless, not caring if I got hurt. A sprained ankle, a broken wrist—that pain would be far preferable to the pain I was feeling in my heart.

Carl parked the car and got out, shaking his head. While he went to the trunk, I retrieved my purse and carry-on bag from the front seat.

We made our way inside in silence. I walked several steps ahead of Carl while he carried my suitcase up two flights of stairs.

I opened the door to my room and stepped inside, glad to see it was empty. I didn't want to see anyone.

"Chantelle . . ."

At the sound of Carl's voice, I faced him. "I'm tired, and I'm stressed," I began without preamble. "I just want to go to bed."

"Let me be here for you, babe. That's all I want."

"I—I can't. I can't be with anyone right now. I need to be alone right now." When a pleading look streaked across his face, I added, "Please."

"All right, babe. All right."

I moved toward him and gave him a brief hug and a chaste kiss on the cheek. The disappointment in his eyes said that he was hoping for more than that.

"I'll talk to you later, 'kay?"

"Okay." Grudgingly, he backed out the door, and I closed it immediately, turning the lock.

I shared this half of my quad room with Erica, while two other girls shared the other half. The two sides were separated by a wall, but we all shared a bathroom.

I hadn't expected to find Erica. The whole ordeal had been so hard on her, I knew she would have gone home for the remainder of spring break. Maybe even longer.

I could hear no sound on the other half of the quad, which I hoped meant Sheila and Kate were still away.

After a few minutes of silence, I was satisfied that I was alone in the room. I found the television remote and quickly turned it on, going straight to CNN for the latest news. I knew it would only be a matter of time before the story about Ashley would be featured.

I didn't have to wait long. When Ashley's face appeared on the screen by way of photograph, the caption below it read, COLLEGE GIRL'S SECRET LIFE?

The reporter went on to speak about the newest "developments" in the Ashley Hamilton disappearance, explaining that a porn video of her had surfaced.

I still expected there to be a description of the cell-phone video Ashley said Blake had taken of her. Perhaps *wanted* was a better word. It was hard enough dealing with Ashley being gone. I didn't want to accept that maybe I hadn't known her at all.

The fresh-faced, innocent shot of Ashley faded from the screen, and the one that replaced it was so shocking, I gasped.

The new photo was of a blonde with wild, teased hair, wearing harsh makeup. Dark eyes, tons of mascara, maybe even fake eyelashes. Her pinky finger was crooked between her parted, glossy red lips in a come-hither look.

It was an all-out glam sex-kitten photo—one like the many I'd seen on guys' walls before. So that in itself wasn't shocking.

But I'd gasped because it *was* Ashley. Oh, she looked different. Very different. But underneath all the makeup, I knew it was her.

Ashley Hamilton, who apparently went by the stage name of Mint Trix.

The reporter went on to talk about the *various* films Ashley had made over the last year, how she was quickly making a name for herself in the porn world.

I turned off the television. And then I stood, numb, for several seconds.

I was too stunned to be devastated.

Ashley had lied to me. About everything.

Even her story about Blake making a video of her and Ryan together had been a lie.

Lord have mercy.

I plopped myself down on my bed and lay there, my breathing shallow, my body numb.

Who *was* Ashley? And how had I not known the truth about her at all?

She'd told her sister that she would have a story that would make her famous by the time our trip was over. Had she been talking about her double life as a porn star?

Was, as her sister had wondered, the whole missing-in-Artula story just a big publicity stunt?

"What the fuck did you do?" I whispered. "Ashley, what the fuck did you do?"

My question bounced off the four walls of my room.

But they gave me no answers.

The thought came to me later that night, that the one person who might know *something* of Ashley's double life was her roommate.

I desperately needed answers.

One way or another, I would get them.

Ashley and her roommate, Lina, weren't very close, but neither were they enemies. They shared one side of a quad in Graves residence hall, meaning Lina had plenty of opportunity to see Ashley's comings and goings, and even to overhear her end of various conversations. Lina might know something that would help me understand this latest news better, even indirectly. Something that would help shed light on who Ashley really was, and the double life she was leading.

And because Lina wasn't Ashley's close friend, she wouldn't be blinded by friendship when I asked her questions.

And failing getting answers from Lina, I knew that Ashley kept diaries. She also kept journals where she scribbled story ideas. Maybe there were clues in there.

I wasn't sure what kind of clues I expected to find, but I knew what I was hoping. That something would point to this whole porn angle as being a complete misunderstanding. A practical joke when she was a freshman, perhaps—where she'd taken crazy pictures for fun. Now, out of context, people were misconstruing those very photos.

It was a long shot, but possible.

I left my room once darkness had settled. I didn't want anyone to see me. I was in no mood for anyone to ask me about Artula, and what had happened there. Especially not in light of the latest news.

I walked past Terrell dining hall, cutting across the grass and through the patches of trees, taking the shortest route from my residence building to Ashley's. Mostly, it was quiet. Until I got close to Graves residence hall.

I should have expected what I saw. The white vans in front of the building. The spotlights. The news cameras and reporters. I slowed my pace, standing across the street near a thicket of trees, wondering how I was going to get past the crowd to get into Ashley's building.

The trees and darkness gave me cover, allowing me to take my time as I checked everything out. I could see now that a few students were standing in front of the reporters, probably answering questions that had to do with Ashley's secret life.

With the news of her involvement in porn, the story had most likely gone from the *missing* angle to the *sensational*. I could only imagine the scandalous headlines that would sell papers for days, and had to wonder if anyone cared if Ashley was found at all.

Worse, with her character under attack, would people start believing she *deserved* whatever had happened to her?

The thought made me only more determined to get inside Ashley's building, but I had to do so without being noticed. Thankfully, there was another way to enter the residence hall, at the back. The reporters and everyone else were at the front.

I doubled back a little, to position myself in line with the farthest corner of the building. And then I cut across the street, walking nonchalantly so as not to draw attention to myself. Every few seconds, I looked in the direction of the cameras.

No one was looking my way. I was just a college kid walking about.

Nice and easy, I rounded the far side of the building, walking quietly across the grass to the building's back door. Normally it was locked, a measure to keep strangers from entering, but the students had a habit of taping off the lock's insert so it wouldn't catch. More than one had been out late, drinking, and forgotten the building's key.

I tried the door. It opened.

Quietly, I climbed the backstairs to the second level. There I paused, listening for sound. Hearing nothing, I opened the door and stepped onto Ashley's floor.

No one was in the hallway. I had a feeling that those who were back from spring break were downstairs, taking in the media show.

Ashley's room was two doors down on the left. I moved slowly, soundlessly, feeling like a thief in the night. Reaching Ashley's door, I again paused to listen for sound. It was quiet on the other side of the door, but that didn't mean Lina wasn't inside.

I knocked softly.

A few seconds passed, and no answer.

I knocked again, louder this time.

Still no answer.

Obviously, Lina wasn't in.

I suddenly realized the kink in my well-laid plan. How to get into the room.

I didn't have a key.

Frowning, I stood there, contemplating what the heck to do. I needed to get into the room.

Digging into my jacket pocket, I withdrew my own room key, wondering if it would work. Or at least allow me to fiddle with the lock enough to pry it open.

What the heck? I had to try something. I pushed my key into the slot—and to my surprise, the door eased open.

I frowned at the door, not understanding. How had it opened with no effort?

And then I understood. Like the building's back door, the lock hadn't properly been latched.

I shrugged, figuring Lina likely *was* around and had been careless in closing the door when leaving the room.

Her negligence worked for me. Because now I could head inside and search for Ashley's diaries without any questions.

Pushing the door open wider, I stepped into the room.

And felt a jolt of panic.

The room was in total disarray. The mattresses were turned over. Desk drawers dumped onto the floor and the contents spilled. The closet doors were open, clothes strewn about.

What the hell? was my first thought.

And then, *Why?*

Why would anyone do this? Why would someone tear apart Ashley's room?

My stomach churning, I walked on tiptoe across the room to the desk. It was a mess, with papers strewn about, but I could see some notebooks among the mess.

I lifted one and flipped through it. Spanish notes. I lifted another notebook from the debris. Sociology.

And then I saw what I'd come for. The glittery pink notebook that Ashley used to write her stories. She took it with her every time we met to talk about our writing.

Flipping the notebook open, I began to peruse its contents. Then ice spread through my veins. Had I heard a sound?

Nervous, I glanced over my shoulder in the direction of the door.

No one had entered the room.

Nonetheless, I was suddenly very uneasy. Someone had come into this room looking for something. Something valuable enough that they'd torn the place apart to find it.

I closed the notebook and held it to my chest. I had to get out of here.

I took a step toward the door, then hesitated.

Ashley's diaries. I needed to find those as well.

She liked to use a diary she could lock, ensuring privacy. I'd seen at least a couple of them in this room when I'd visited Ashley in the past.

I searched the desktop once again. No diaries.

Using the tip of my shoe, I carefully kicked around the papers on the floor. Again, no diaries.

Doing a one-eighty, I slowly scanned the room, looking for anything that stood out.

That's when I noticed her laptop was missing.

Her diaries. Her laptop. Someone had taken them.

My spine tingled with fear, and I hurried toward the door. Once there, I held my head against the wood, listening for sound outside.

Hearing nothing, I carefully opened the door and stepped into the hallway. Then I jogged to the door that led to the back staircase.

I ran now, my heart pounding. Something was going on here. Something bigger than I understood.

On the main level, I gazed out the back door. In the darkness, I saw no one.

Opening the door, I slipped out. I wanted to run, but I couldn't risk drawing attention to myself. I didn't want anyone recognizing me and pointing me out to the media.

I walked quickly and steadily, a college kid out for a stroll.

With each step that took me farther from Ashley's dorm building and away from the media camped outside, my breathing became calmer. And when I rounded a corner that would block me entirely from their view, I exhaled in relief.

It was about a minute later that I sensed someone behind me. Sensed so surely, a chill danced across the nape of my neck.

I spun around.

There was a figure behind me, no doubt about it. Probably one hundred feet away. A man, by the shape of the person.

My heart thundered in my chest. Was the person following me? Or was I being paranoid?

I picked up my pace, hustling for about ten seconds before I dared to look over my shoulder again.

The man was jogging to keep up with me.

I broke into a sprint, adrenaline fueling my run. I ran, panting, terrified. One more glance over my shoulder, and I saw the man still in the distance, the gap between us wider now.

But beneath a street light, I could see that he had dark skin. Someone from Artula?

My whole body consumed with fear, I ran as fast as my legs would carry me. Someone was exiting my building as I came to the front doors, and I whizzed past her.

"Chantelle?" the girl said, concerned.

I didn't stop. Holding the notebook to my chest, I charged up the stairs and didn't stop until I'd reached my room.

Chapter
Thirty-one

THE POLICE. I had to call them. Not just because of the man who'd been following me, but because Ashley's room had been trashed.

But I was too scared to do anything other than sit in the darkness of my room, hoping that if anyone came into the building, they would think no one was in here.

For ten minutes I stayed still, holding my knees to my chest as I sat against the wall farthest from the door. The only sound in the room was that of my heavy breathing.

As the minutes ticked by, my breathing became calmer. No

one had come to my room. I was beginning to think that paranoia was getting to me.

In the darkness, I made my way across the room to the
closet. It was fairly large, and we kept a flashlight in there for
emergencies.

Feeling around on the floor, I found the flashlight. I clicked
it on, positioned myself fully inside the closet, then closed the
door.

I may have been paranoid, but I didn't want to take any
chances.

For about a minute I sat in the closet with the flashlight on,
almost afraid to open Ashley's notebook and search for the
clues I was desperate to find.

What I wanted to do was call Anabelle Hamilton and ask her
what she'd meant by her comment that every family has its
problems. Or better yet, I would talk to Megan. Siblings often
shared secrets with each other they would never dare share with
their parents.

But I couldn't talk to Anabelle or Megan. They were still in
Artula, and CNN had reported that they couldn't be reached
for comment in the wake of the reports that had surfaced
about Ashley.

I inhaled a deep breath and opened the notebook, praying
I would find answers to make sense of everything.

The first several stories were ones Ashley had brain-
stormed with me about. A daughter dealing with the breakup
of her parents when the father leaves for another woman.
This had been loosely based on Ashley's experiences when
her own father had left the family and never returned. Another story was about a teen drug addict whose baby is taken

away by the courts. Another was about a girl and her sister's suicide pact.

They were all depressing, something we'd talked about. I'd asked her how a person as bubbly and outgoing as she was could write such dark stories. She told me that she put all of her fears and hurts and disappointments into her fictional stories as a release. Writing for her was like therapy.

I understood that. It was for me, as well.

The fourth story was one Ashley hadn't talked to me about before. A girl trapped in the cycle of abuse with a boyfriend she was afraid to leave.

But the fifth story—also one she hadn't told me about before—made my body tremble.

A title was scrawled at the top of the first page: AT LAST. Unlike the other stories in the notebook, this one was only four pages long. I figured it wasn't completed.

What made me tremble was the fact that as I read this story, I got the feeling that I wasn't reading fiction.

It is late, some time in the middle of the night. I am not sleeping. I don't sleep well anymore. Not after the first time he came into my room.

I always know when he'll come. When my mother is at the hospital with a patient in labor. It gives him all the time in the world to do what he wants to do to me. Things a father shouldn't do to his daughter.

My head swam, and I had to close my eyes in order to keep my equilibrium.

I thought of Anabelle's cryptic comment about things Ashley

might have told me. I thought about Megan always standing close to her mother, on the side away from Bill. And about the way she had almost violently shrugged away from Bill's touch and run to her mother.

I thought of the fact that Bill Hamilton had given me a bad vibe, period.

Bill Hamilton. Ashley and Megan's stepfather.

Dear God, no.

Slowly, I reopened my eyes, then read the rest of what Ashley had written in a state of morbid fascination, feeling as though I was glimpsing into Ashley's tortured soul.

She wrote about her stepfather coming into her room at night, and how she had learned not to protest when he wanted her to have sex with him. How she let him do what he needed to do to her so that he wouldn't touch her younger sister.

As I finished reading what Ashley had written, I was softly crying. This was a piece of the puzzle. I knew it.

Bill Hamilton had raped my friend and left her scarred.

So much made sense now. The way Ashley jumped into re-lationships so quickly, as though desperate to have someone love her. As though seeking approval.

She gave her heart and body too freely, set herself up to be hurt over and over again because that's what she knew.

And the porn . . . I drew in a sharp breath, stifling a cry. I'd once heard some ridiculous figure like 80 percent of the women who'd gotten into the porn business had been sexually abused.

As I cried for my friend, I thought about the injustice in the world. Ashley was missing—maybe dead—while people like Bill Hamilton still got to live.

It wasn't fair.

. . .

My butt began to hurt on the hard floor. I eased up slowly, stretching as I did.

Keeping the flashlight on, I exited the closet. I'd been in my room for a while without anyone coming to my door. It was safe to say that whoever had chased me didn't know where I was.

If someone had been chasing me at all.

But just in case, I went to the door and stood there for a moment, listening. Better paranoid than sorry.

Only the sound of my slow and steady breathing filled the room.

I flicked the light switch on, anger and hatred brewing inside of me. For what he had done to his daughter, Bill Hamilton deserved to go to jail. Had the pig touched Megan, too?

I wanted to call the police and have them arrest him. But a fictional story in Ashley's notebook could hardly be considered evidence.

So much had come to light in the last twenty-four hours. Was this the story Ashley had been talking about that would make her famous? The story of a stepfather's abuse, and how it had ruined her life, made her a prime candidate for the sex trade?

I wanted to call Jason. Share all of this with him.

After talking to Ryan and Blake, then watching the news, I'd been so sick with shock that I'd forgotten to turn my cell phone back on. I made my way over to the armchair where I'd placed my purse and rummaged around for my cell inside.

I punched in the code to retrieve my messages. There was

one from Erica, asking me to call her about Ashley. She'd called the hotel and learned that I'd checked out. And there were three calls from Jason.

"Chantelle, this is Jason. I assume you're back. Call me and let me know how you are. And call me because . . . because there's something I've got to tell you," he added in a lower, sadder tone. "About Ashley."

I knew what he wanted to tell me. The news that had broken about her secret life.

The second message was similar to the first, but in the third one, left an hour earlier, he expressed more concern. "Hey, Chantelle. It's Jason again. You're still not answering your phone. I'm guessing you heard the news, and that you're upset. Call me. I'm here for you."

As soon as I was finished listening to the messages, I dialed his number.

"Chantelle?" he said, answering after the first ring. "Where are you? How are you?"

"I'm back at Lan-U, and I'm fine." I paused. "No, that's not true. I'm not fine." I closed my eyes. Squeezed my forehead with a thumb and forefinger. "This nightmare keeps getting worse. How can this be possible? How can anything be worse than my friend being missing?"

It was a rhetorical question, and Jason didn't offer me an answer.

"I'm sorry," was all he said.

"You didn't know, did you? That's not the 'big secret story' she was hoping to sell to you?"

"She never told me what her story idea was. Only that it was a doozy, and that it'd make a great memoir."

College girl's secret life as a porn star. Yeah, that was a doozy of a story.

"Jason, there's more going on," I said after a moment. "More serious than Ashley's secret life."

"What?"

"I went to her room tonight. The door was locked. And the place was trashed. Someone was in there looking for something."

"You're kidding," Jason said.

"I wish I were. And there's more." I paused, inhaled a shaky breath. "Someone followed me tonight when I was heading back to my room. I couldn't see who it was, but it was a black man. My best guess is it's someone from Artula—" I stopped abruptly, another thought hitting me. "Oh my God."

"What?" Jason asked.

"I . . . I just realized. BJ and Kevaughn . . . What if . . . what if one or both of them are here at Lancaster? What if they're angry because of what I said on the news and they want to hurt me?" It made sense. Either BJ or Kevaughn could have been the man in the distance, watching me. Following me.

"I'm coming over," Jason said.

"What? You're going to get in a car or on the train, and head here from New York?"

"I'm already here."

He spoke softly, and I was sure I hadn't heard him correctly.

"What did you say?"

"I said I'm here. In Lancaster."

A delicious thrill shot through me. But I was calm as I asked, "Why?"

"Because I wanted to see you," he said. "And I didn't want to wait."

"Are you serious?" I asked, and inhaled a shuddery breath.

"As a heart attack." A beat passed. "Can I come over? I'll understand if you say no."

I didn't speak right away, though I immediately knew what my answer would be.

Yes.

But Jason clearly read my hesitation as reluctance. "I promise I'll be a perfect gentleman. I just . . . wanted to see you. You know, after—"

"Yes," I said.

"Pardon?" Jason asked.

"Come over," I told him, my voice soft. "I don't want to be alone. Especially not now."

"How do I get to you?"

I told him. "And when you get to my building, call me. I'll come down and open the door for you."

"See you soon."

Chapter Thirty-two

WHEN, ten minutes later, my cell phone rang, my heart began to pound. I was nervous and excited. More nervous and excited about seeing a guy than I ever remembered being.

"Hey," I said, my voice husky as I answered the phone.

"Hey, yourself."

Why was my heart pounding so hard? "You're downstairs?"

"Yeah."

"I'll be right down."

I smiled as I ended the call. Then I looked in the mirror, checking out my appearance. My face was bare, and my eyes were undoubtedly tired, but I still looked cute.

I fluffed my hair, giving it some life, then hurried down to the front door.

I lived in the one female-only residence in The Hill, but boyfriends came into the building all the time.

Besides, it was still spring break, and the place was mostly empty. Jason and I could have privacy.

I opened the door and there he was, standing with his legs askance on the stoop, a black leather jacket on his wide shoulders, his hands stuffed into the front pockets of his jeans. His wavy blond hair was unkempt. And sexy.

God, he really was sexy.

He smiled when he saw me. I smiled back.

Then he rushed toward me and scooped me into his arms. And Lord, it felt so good to be in his embrace.

I didn't understand this carnal reaction to him. I only knew I loved how it made me feel.

We pulled apart, and I stepped backward. Then I averted my gaze, slightly sheepish. I was happy to see him, but nervous at the same time.

Nervous because of the feelings inside of me.

A hot flush swept over my body from head to toe. And then I felt guilty. Ashley was missing, maybe dead, and here I was getting turned on by seeing Jason. It didn't make sense.

And yet, I couldn't control it.

"So," Jason began, "are you gonna invite me in?"

He may as well have been asking if he could sleep with me, because my pulse quickened with expectation at the question. *What the hell is wrong with me?*

"Of course," I replied, trying for nonchalant. "My room's on the second floor."

I led the way up the staircase, with Jason following closely behind me. All the way to my room, butterflies danced in my stomach.

My reaction to simply being near to Jason was unlike anything I'd ever experienced before. From the butterflies in my stomach to my shallow breathing to my quickened pace. And the excitement. Oh God, the excitement.

I honestly didn't remember ever feeling like that before. I'd definitely never experienced that with Carl.

Reaching my room, I paused only briefly before opening the door. I stepped inside while still holding the door wide enough for Jason to follow.

Once he was in the room, I closed the door. Inhaling deeply, I turned the lock.

Slowly, I swiveled on my heels and faced Jason, meeting his gaze again. It was amazing how much his presence seemed to fill the room.

"So," I began, "why are you here in Lancaster?"

Jason took one step toward me. One step, but it seemed to bring him several feet closer. Again, I sucked in a deep breath.

"I wanted to see you."

A simple answer, but it may as well have been a whispered promise of a naughty sexual act. Another rush of heat shot through me.

He took another step, and this time I took one toward him as well. And the next thing I knew, he was wrapping his arms around me, and pressing his mouth against mine, and oh it felt so good.

My body came alive with sensation, tingling and throbbing everywhere. I clung to Jason's shoulders, digging my fingers into his jacket and kissing him with all the fascination of a woman kissing a man for the first time.

Jason slipped his hands beneath my shirt. Not in an aggressive, college-boy way. But gently, with a groan that said he was feeling the same rush of exquisite pleasure that I was. For a moment, I thought about pulling back, telling him we couldn't go any further.

But the wonder of what I was experiencing was too intense for me to pull back. Too intense for me to want to stop.

So as he kissed a path along the underside of my jaw, I didn't say no when he began to pull my shirt up. Instead, I raised my arms.

He continued to kiss me as he reached his hands around my back and unsnapped my bra. My large breasts spilled free. My lips parted wider, his tongue delved deeper.

And when he backed me toward my roommate's bed, I knew what was going to happen next.

And I wanted it. Very much.

Jason and I made love three times during the night. And that's exactly what it felt like—making love, not just screwing. Every one of his touches was a caress ripe with meaning.

I never imagined that a sexual connection with someone could be as intense, as explosive, or as deep as it had been for me and Jason.

We were still snuggled in my single bed, his arms wrapped around me from behind, when a knock on the door roused me from sleep. I glanced at the digital clock, saw that it was forty minutes after nine.

That's when my body grew tense.

Even before the second, more urgent knock, I pretty much knew who had to be at my door at this hour.

And it meant trouble.

Another knock. "Chantelle. I know you've got to be in there. Open the door."

Jason eased up on an elbow. The knocking had woken him up, too.

"Shit," I muttered.

"Who is it?" Jason asked.

Before I could answer, there was another knock. "I know you're avoiding me, Chantelle. Open the door. If you want me to leave you alone, tell me that to my face."

"Is that your boyfriend?" Jason asked, and in his tone was a hint of shock. Shock that I could have been intimate with him if I was involved with someone else.

"He's someone I need to deal with," I said, not facing him, and getting off of the bed.

I didn't look back at Jason as I headed to the door. I couldn't bear seeing a disappointed expression on his face.

Just as Carl's knuckles connected with the door again, I opened it. But just a crack.

"Why are you here so early?" I asked, testy.

"You didn't call me all last night," he countered. His face held a mixture of confusion and relief. "You didn't return my texts. No e-mail."

Carl wanted answers, and he deserved them, but this wasn't the right time to tell him it was over.

"Can we talk later?"

Carl laughed, a sound dripping with sarcasm. "Right. Like you called me last night." A beat. "There something you want to tell me, Chantelle?"

"Not right now," I told him.

"So you *are* still pissed with me." He pressed his lips tightly together and shook his head. "I was stupid," he said. "I already apologized for being a jerk about your trip."

I shrugged, not wanting to say anything with Jason in my bed.

Carl's eyes widened slightly, and I saw the moment he knew. Knew that there was no going back for us.

"So it's like that, is it? Even though I said I was sorry."

"Carl . . . it's not about the trip and what you said." I glanced quickly over my shoulder—a stupid move—because when I turned back to Carl, I saw another expression on his face.

Incredulity.

"You got a *dude* in there?" he asked me.

I swallowed. Hard. And then I stepped into the hallway and closed the door behind me.

"Fuck, Chantelle." Carl's eyes were hard as he stared at me. "You *do*. So in the seven days you were gone, you already found yourself someone else?"

What could I say? I couldn't very well lie about it now.

"It's not what you think," I said.

"No?" His eyebrows raised in challenge.

"No. We met because of Ashley. They were hanging out the night she went missing, and then—"

"So, he was fucking your friend, and now you're fucking him?"

"He wasn't fucking Ashley," I snapped, angrier than necessary. And I knew why.

Because Jason *had* kissed her, something that didn't sit well with me, even though I believed his story about it being one-sided. I hated that they'd shared any moment of intimacy whatsoever.

I continued defensively, "They were talking because he works for a publishing company—"

"Ohhh." The exaggerated word was accompanied by an exaggerated eye roll. "Now I see what's going on here."

"No, you don't. It's not about me getting a publishing deal. It's about the connection we made, Carl. He understands me."

"And I don't?"

I didn't want to be having this conversation. "Please don't do this. I'm not trying to hurt you."

"Could have fooled me."

I said nothing, just stood there and let Carl scowl at me.

"Look—"

"How does he understand you more than I do?"

"Carl—"

"Tell me!"

I sighed. "He understands what I'm going through. And no, it's not just because he was in Artula when Ashley disappeared. There's another reason, but I'm not gonna get into it."

Carl's eyes traveled over my body, full of scorn. "I bet you understand each other real well."

Carl couldn't have said he believed me less if he'd come right out and said that I had slept with Jason in hopes of getting published.

"I didn't ask him to come here." It was important that Carl knew that. "He showed up because he . . ." I didn't bother to finish my statement. There was no need to rub in that we both felt a connection that was bigger than each of us.

"So let me get this straight. He talks to your friend. Then she goes missing. Now he shows up at Lancaster and you open the door—and your legs—to him, no questions asked."

The words stung. But there was no point in trying to convince him that being with Jason hadn't been about an easy lay, or an easy path to publication.

"I heard that Ashley's room was ransacked," Carl went on. "Someone wanted something. And this guy *conveniently* came here because he couldn't stay away from you. What's wrong with this picture?"

My heart began to beat fast, his words getting to me. Was the timing a coincidence—or was Carl right?

But I shrugged, trying to play cool. "I'm sorry, Carl. I really am."

"Hmm." He didn't believe me. And I couldn't blame him. "I hope you can live with yourself," he added, then stormed off down the hallway.

I slipped back into the room and turned the lock. But distancing myself physically from Carl didn't distance me from what he'd said.

And this guy conveniently came here because he couldn't stay away from you. What's wrong with this picture?

"Hey," Jason said, gently. "Are you all right?"

Slowly, I turned to face him.

Wondering if I'd just given my heart to a devil.

Chapter
Thirty-three

"ARE YOU all right?" Jason repeated.

I stared at him before answering, saw genuine concern in his eyes. And slowly, my doubts began to ebb away.

What we'd shared last night was real. A connection I couldn't explain. And I knew from the way he'd touched me, looked at me, that he felt the same way, too.

Besides, Jason hadn't been in Artula when the severed tongue had been delivered. So what if he'd come to Lancaster to surprise me?

He'd wanted to see me, as I'd wanted to see him. Because something had ignited between us in Artula. Something real.

Why was I letting Carl, who was clearly jealous, get to me?

Because he has a point, whether or not you want to accept it.

Jason sat up. "Chantelle?"

I tried to smile, but I'm not sure I pulled it off. "I'm okay."

"You're sure?"

"Yeah, I'm fine."

Jason got off the bed and started toward me. "So . . . that was your boyfriend?"

"We broke up before I went to Artula," I explained.

"Before you went to Artula," Jason said, nodding. "So, you had some sort of argument that time and distance has put into perspective."

"Exactly." His eyes widened in surprise, and I knew he'd misconstrued my response. I moved toward him. "For me, that perspective has shown me that I should have broken up with Carl a long time ago. For him . . . he's wishing he didn't push me away." Reaching him, I snaked my arms around Jason's neck. "But it doesn't matter. We weren't meant to be together." I smiled up at him and added, "I'm right where I want to be."

"Are you sure about that?"

I had expected Jason to return my embrace, or at least smile down at me in return. Maybe even kiss me and take me back to the bed. When he didn't, I was jerked out of the amorous moment—doubts beginning to creep into my brain.

I lowered my arms from his neck. "Yes, I'm sure. But what about you? Did you come here for me . . . or the story?"

My eyes searched his for an answer. As much as I didn't want Carl's words to have affected me, they were.

I didn't believe for a second that Jason was anyone other than who he claimed to be. There was no way he was behind the ransacking of Ashley's room. He wouldn't even know where it was.

But did he want to be close to me only because of my connection to Ashley and the story he was writing?

"You think last night was about a story?" he asked, and the astonishment in his eyes assuaged my skepticism.

"I . . . I had to ask."

"And I could ask you the same thing. Do you like me for me, or are you only interested in getting published?"

His eyes searched mine, and I could see that he had his own doubts.

"Of course not," I told him.

"Look," he began frankly, "we could both be using each other, but I prefer to think we've found something here. Something worth exploring. I hope we can trust each other."

"I trust you," I said, the words spilling from my lips quickly, no hesitation at all. "Trust you enough for last night to have happened. I've never . . . fallen into bed with anyone so quickly."

"Neither have I," Jason said.

I made a face as I stared at him. "A guy like you? Women must throw themselves at you."

"If I said no, never—you'd think I was full of it. Sure they do. Sometimes." He slipped his arms around my waist, and my stomach fluttered. "Especially when they learn I'm an editor." He paused, smiled, letting me know he was teasing me. "But you're the only one I've ever felt an instant connection to."

My body grew warm, and my lips curled in a grin. I believed him. I believed him because I was feeling the exact same thing.

He began to kiss me, and my body went from warm to hot in about two seconds.

It took us another two seconds to get back to the bed and begin to make love all over again.

"I have to go," Jason told me hours later.

"What?" I asked. "You've only been here a day."

"I know." He stroked my face. "Like I told you, I came here just to see you. But I have to get back to New York. I've got a couple of interviews lined up about my sister. And Ashley." He shrugged.

I knew what the shrug meant. He was hoping that all of this attention would lead to answers. Even if they were the ones we didn't want to hear.

"And be prepared for the phone call from *Dateline* or *20/20*, or both. Yeah," he said, responding to the surprise in my eyes. "This is a big story. They're gonna want to interview you. For sure."

I didn't want to think about that. I couldn't stand the fact that Jason was leaving.

A stab of sadness pierced my heart. "When will I see you again?"

"We'll work something out."

I missed him already. Again, a reaction I'd never experienced before. I couldn't bear the thought of him being gone one day, much less more than that.

How had my mother survived losing my father, knowing that with each day that came and went, she would never see him again? No wonder she hadn't been able to give her heart to another man.

The direction of my thoughts startled the hell out of me. Was it possible I'd fallen in love with Jason?

"I'll call you," he said. "Often. And we'll text, and e-mail."

I nodded. Emotion had clogged my throat, preventing me from speaking.

"It's not like you need a guy hanging around all the time, distracting you from your studies," he added, smiling softly.

He was right, but still I didn't feel better.

"I can come back on the weekends, or you can visit me in New York."

"I don't have the cash to rent a car or take the train on a regular basis," I told him.

He placed a finger beneath my chin and tilted my face up. "Hey. Don't worry. I make a decent salary. And it could be worse—you could live in California."

"True."

"We'll make this work," Jason assured me.

I don't know what was more surprising—that he was talking about something long-term, or that I was thinking it.

Either way, we were on the same page.

"All right," I said, and gave him a soft kiss on the lips. "We'll find a way."

We started necking, deep and hot, the kind of kiss that would send us right back to the bed. I wouldn't have minded.

But Jason groaned and pulled away. "Chantelle, I really do have to get going."

"I know," I said, but I didn't release my hold on him. I wanted to savor the feel of him for just a little longer.

"Chantelle, Chantelle." Staring into my eyes, Jason swayed his body against mine. "I'm just gonna say this, and I hope it doesn't sound bad." He paused, trailed his fingers over my neck.

"Despite everything that's happened, and how shitty it's all been, the one good thing through it all is that I met you. I'm not saying I wouldn't change things so that Ashley was still here, but—"

My pulse quickening, I put a finger on his lips. "I understand." A bittersweet feeling of warmth and sadness flowed through me. "Even the darkest clouds have a silver lining. Me and you—we're that silver lining."

My eyes misted, but then Jason was kissing me again, effacing my sadness, leaving hope in its wake.

The hope of a future that I prayed included Ashley.

After Jason left, I kept a low profile. I might have been mistaken about a man trying to follow me, but I didn't want to take any chances.

Because the more I thought about it, the more I believed that BJ or Kevaughn *could* be following me. The news had let the world know I was a Lancaster student. How hard would it be for one or both of them to have headed here in search of me? I'd branded them suspicious to every media outlet interviewing me, and that could easily have pissed them off.

I didn't head out to Terrence Hall for food, instead snacking on a bag of Doritos and other junk food in my room. When early evening rolled around, I ordered a pizza.

Other than that, I chilled, spoke to my mother to assure her I was fine, and followed some of the news.

It all focused on the racier side of Ashley that had been unveiled, so much so that I couldn't stomach watching it for long. I didn't want to learn more about the missing college girl's "secret life."

Just after seven, my cell phone rang. I'd been expecting to hear from Carl all day, but I guess the fact that he knew I had another man in my room was enough for him to realize it was irrevocably over.

I grabbed my cell phone from my desk and glanced at the display screen. What I saw made my skin prickle with anticipation.

Private name. Private number.

My heart began to accelerate, the response I'd had every time this week I'd seen those words on my caller ID. I quickly placed the cell phone to my ear, cautiously hopeful and sick with anxiety at the same time.

Please, let this be the call.

"Hello?" I said, then held my breath as I waited for a response.

Scratchy static filled the line, evidence of a bad connection. I strained to hear the person on the other end of the phone.

And then, the faint sound of *something* on the other end of the line. A voice, a movement—I wasn't sure.

"Hello?" I repeated. "Is someone there?"

"Chantelle . . ."

My back went rigid. I was certain now. Someone had whispered my name.

"Help . . . please."

"Ashley?" Excitement washed over me in waves. The voice was faint, but it was female. It had to be her. "Ashley—is that you?"

"Help me . . ."

"Why are you whispering? Where are you? Who's there with you?"

"I was stupid," she went on, sobbing between her words. "This was . . . all a mistake. A stupid decision. And now . . ."

The rest of her words were drowned out by the static.

"Ashley? Ashley!"

When I heard more soft sobbing, I was relieved. For a moment, I thought the call had been disconnected.

"Ashley, we must have a bad connection. Can you speak up at all? Tell me where you are. I'll come get you. Or I'll send someone."

I strained to listen, hearing static and the faint sound of a voice. So faint I couldn't make out the words.

"Ashley, please speak up." Now I was crying. I was relieved, but terrified. I had to get to my friend. Save her. "Please tell me where you are."

"I . . ." More crying. "I . . ."

My voice rose an octave as hysteria set in. "Where are you?" No answer. "Ashley? Ashley!"

The dial tone sounded in my ear.

The line was dead. And Ashley was gone.

Just like a ghost.

Chapter
Thirty-four

FOR THE NEXT minute, I waited for the phone to ring again. Prayed that it would.

When it didn't, I quickly went to my phone's index of the people who had called me, knowing it would yield no results. The number for the person who had just called me was unknown.

"Fuck!" I uttered. I sat on the edge of my bed and buried my face in my hands, wondering what I should do.

Call the police? What would I tell them? What *could* I tell them?

Only that Ashley was apparently alive.

And if she was alive, it meant that her disappearance had been an elaborate scheme. And for what—to help her sell a damn book?

Anger gripped me. Anger that Ashley would put me, her friends, and her family through unnecessary heartache for selfish goals.

But my ire faded quickly. Whether or not this had all been a game for Ashley, the reality was that she was in trouble. She was alive, and that was what mattered most. I would deal with my fury over her unthinkable stunt later.

I paced the floor in my room, feeling helpless. And then I had a thought.

Ashley must have called me from her cell phone.

Her cell phone . . .

I quickly pressed the button on my phone that was preprogrammed with Ashley's number, then held my phone to my ear.

I waited, not breathing, for Ashley's cell to ring. At least five seconds of dead silence passed. Then an automated message began to play.

"The voice mail belonging to—"

I clicked off, having heard this message too many times already over the past week. Ashley's mailbox was full.

Was I fooling myself? So desperate to believe Ashley was alive that I was misconstruing the phone call?

I shook my head. No, I wasn't fooling myself. Who could have been on the other end of the line if not Ashley?

I felt it in my heart, believed it in my soul. Wherever she was, she'd found a way to call me. But God only knew if she was somewhere in Artula, or in the Middle East, or on a boat to some other place.

Plopping down onto my bed, I punched in Jason's number

on my phone. I needed to tell him what was going on and ask for his advice. But my call to him also went to voice mail.

Feeling helpless, I stood again, pacing nervously. Thinking. I supposed there was only one thing I could do, and that was to call the police. But not those incompetent jerks in Artula. I'd have to call the FBI, and hope to hell they could do something to track down my friend with the scanty information I could provide them.

Before I could make that call, my cell phone rang again. I immediately flipped it open and placed it to my ear.

"Hello?" I said anxiously

"Chantelle, don't hang up."

For a moment, I was silent, confused. It wasn't Ashley. "Who is this?"

"It's Ryan."

I said nothing. I was too shocked to speak.

"I'm sure you don't want to talk to me. Trust me, the feeling's mutual. But some shit's going down." He paused briefly. "I just got a weird call. And I think . . . I think it was from Ashley."

The words would have surprised me, if I hadn't gotten my own strange phone call. A phone call that I'd *wanted* to believe was from Ashley. Now, hearing Ryan say he'd gotten a weird call too, my heart soared with hope.

Because it meant I wasn't deluding myself with wishful thinking. Ashley was alive.

"I got a call not too long ago myself," I said.

"From Ashley?" Ryan asked. He sounded excited. And as hopeful as I felt.

"I . . . I think it had to be. And if you got a call from her, too . . ."

"So I'm not crazy," Ryan said. "I knew it. I knew it was her. She barely got a few words out before the line went dead. I waited for her to call back, but she hasn't yet. What'd she say to you?"

"That she was in some kind of trouble. That everything was a mistake that got out of hand. Obviously, she's alive somewhere. I didn't want to believe it, but I think . . ."

"What? You think what?"

"I . . ." My voice trailed off. I didn't want to accept that Ashley could have done something so horrible. Let us all believe she was dead for her own personal gain.

"What?" Ryan demanded.

"Maybe this whole disappearance thing was all a ploy," I said softly. "Something she set up so she'd have a story to sell."

"What?" Ryan asked, sounding stunned. "Are you telling me that this was all a game to her?"

"I don't know for sure. But someone suggested that."

"Someone suggested that, and still you roasted me in the media? Made it sound to anyone who would listen like I had something to do with what happened to her?" Ryan's voice rose in anger.

"You're the one who wouldn't talk to me!" I countered. "I tried to talk to you in Artula, remember? Get your side of the story!"

"I know," Ryan said, sounding immediately contrite. "You're right. But I think we need to talk now."

"Why?"

"Because if Ashley's in trouble, we have to figure out what to do."

"You'd want to help her?" I asked. "Now, after the truth is coming out?"

"I'm not a villain, Chantelle. Yeah, she clearly lied, and I'm pissed with her—really fucking pissed—but I don't want to see her die or anything. She lied to you. You don't want her dead, right?"

"No." I was angry with her, but she was still my friend. "Of course not."

"Neither do I. Finding her is gonna help clear my name. Don't you think we should work together to help bring her home?"

Ryan was right, and as much as I wasn't his biggest fan, not even close, maybe if we put our heads together, we could figure out the best way to handle the situation.

"I can go to you," Ryan said. "Or you can come to me." When I hesitated, he continued. "Okay, let's meet outside then. In public, if that'll make you feel better."

"How about in front of Terrence Hall?"

"No problem."

"We should do it now," I said. "Ashley doesn't have much time."

Stepping outside, I hunched into my hoodie. Not just to ward off the coldness in the air, but hopefully to obscure my identity.

Just in case of any media.

Or in case BJ or Kevaughn or someone else from Artula was hiding in the trees, waiting for me to show up.

I walked briskly along the path that would lead me to the dining hall, glancing over my shoulder only occasionally to make sure that no one was following me.

Ashley was alive. I was overjoyed, but still terrified. Terrified because of what her call had represented. That she was somewhere in trouble. Somewhere in need of help.

"Oh, Ashley," I whispered as I walked. "What the hell have you gotten yourself into?"

For a moment, fear got to me, making my limbs numb and my heart heavy. The fear that there was nothing we could do to find her.

But she called, I told myself. *If she could get a call out to you and to Ryan, she can do it again. You can't give up hope.*

And I wouldn't. Whatever it took, we would find her.

As I rounded the corner of the Knapp residence hall, a shadow stepped out from behind a tree and into my path. My heart slammed against my rib cage, and then my body froze.

But a moment later, I relaxed. It wasn't some stranger who had stepped into my path, but Ryan.

I should have been happy to see him—I was meeting him, after all—but after everything he'd done, I felt guarded. Wary.

But what *had* he done? I'd come to hate him based on what Ashley had told me about the cell-phone video, but that had been a lie.

"Hey," he said softly.

My feelings were still mixed about him, based mostly on Ashley's lies and my own misconceptions. I would have to work hard to erase the slate in my mind. Because as much as I'd thought him the world's biggest jerk, he was here right now, ready to help find Ashley. Given her lies, he certainly didn't have to be.

"I just want to say," I began without preamble, "I'm sorry for . . . jumping to negative conclusions about you."

"It's all right. Ashley lied to you. She lied to all of us."

I nodded, knowing he was right, but still I felt bad. Because

I knew I'd never truly like him, perhaps never really trust him, and it was all because of what Ashley had said and what had transpired over the past week.

Even in the face of contrary evidence, it was hard to change a person's opinion. Like the way I felt about Ashley. I was mad at her, yes, but this whole angle about her secret life as a porn star—I kept waiting for someone to report that it had been a vicious lie.

And I would believe that report, without question, even if the *National Enquirer* was the one to publish it. Because the Ashley who'd been my best friend simply didn't seem capable of that kind of life.

I pushed the thought from my mind, because I only wanted to concentrate on the task at hand, and that was figuring out what to do to get Ashley home safe and sound.

"So—"

"Do you think we should go to the police?" Ryan asked at the same time I'd started to speak. "Let's face it, I've been portrayed as a suspect in the media, and the cops will probably think I've got some motive to lie if I go to them with this story about Ashley calling me, but it might be the only way."

"I can vouch for you," I said. "I got a phone call from Ashley, too."

Ryan nodded. "So we call the cops, then. Tell them that we heard from Ashley, and run by them the idea that Ashley's disappearance was all a hoax for publicity." He paused. "Or . . ."

"Or what?"

"I don't know."

"No, what were you gonna say?"

He shrugged. "I think it'd be good to have more to give them. Some sort of direction they can follow."

"I don't understand."

"If Ashley planned this, I really doubt she got to Artula and just thought of putting this hoax into play. She had to have been working on it before."

Because before Ashley left on this trip, she said that before the week was over, she would have a story to sell. One that would make her famous.

Megan's odd comment sounded in my mind, no longer seeming so odd.

"What?" Ryan asked when he saw my puzzled face.

"Ashley's sister . . . she made a comment I considered weird at the time. But maybe it proves that Ashley was planning this from before."

"And if she was, there's got to be some proof of that," Ryan said, a hopeful glint in his eyes. "Something we might be able to find in her room."

"You want to search her room?"

"What else can we do?"

"I don't know how helpful that will be. Someone trashed her room. I'm sure you heard."

"Shit. You're right."

"Her computer's gone. I don't know what else we could find that would help. I took one of her notebooks with her stories, and I've been going through that."

"You have one of her notebooks?" Ryan asked.

"Yeah."

"Have you read all the stories?"

"No." I didn't bother saying that I'd read one about sexual abuse, and it had so jarred me that I'd had to stop, unable to read more about Ashley's secret pain.

"Then maybe there's something there. Some notes about her idea, maybe even a contact name and number."

"You think so?" My voice rose, hopeful. What if he was right?

"Who knows? It's worth checking out, right? I mean, if her room was trashed, it means someone was looking for something."

Feeling a chill, I whipped my head around. I knew now, with certainty, that I hadn't been paranoid the other night. Someone *had* been following me. Maybe not BJ or Kevaughn, but quite likely someone from Artula who might have been a part of Ashley's plan. The pieces of the puzzle were finally fitting together.

"Oh my God," I uttered.

"What?" Ryan asked.

"It's all making sense now," I said, more to myself than to Ryan.

"What?"

I inhaled deeply before speaking. "When I first got back here, I saw someone suspicious. He appeared to be following me from a distance. I got the eerie feeling that he was from Artula. Then I found out Ashley's room was searched. I couldn't imagine why, but if this whole disappearing act was a hoax, she probably had proof in her room. E-mails, Web searches. Whatever. Now that her scam has gone bad and someone has truly abducted her—maybe for cash, since her family's got money— the people behind the abduction want all of the evidence that could possibly point to them."

It was a wild theory, but it felt right.

"Why don't we check this notebook you mentioned," Ryan

suggested. "The minute we find anything, we can call the cops with that—and our theory."

Once again, I glanced around, my eyes sweeping the dense trees. I got the feeling someone was out there, watching us.

"Come on," I said to Ryan, anxious now about being out in the open. "Let's go to my room."

Chapter
Thirty-five

A SHORT WHILE later, we were in my room, and I was heading right for Ashley's notebook. I felt a slight twinge of guilt when I passed it to Ryan, knowing Ashley wouldn't want me sharing her deeply personal words with him.

But if there was a clue in there that could help find her, what choice did I have?

"I don't know if this will really help," I said. "I think it's likely that any info connecting Ashley to whomever she was working with will be on her laptop, which was taken." I shrugged. "But it's worth a shot."

Ryan took the book from me and began to flip through it,

not looking at the content of the stories but scanning for anything that stood out.

"Maybe we ought to go back to her room," I suggested. "She could have hidden something there that someone overlooked."

Ryan's eyes scanned my room. "Or . . . she could have hidden it here."

"Here?" I asked, surprised.

"She hung out in your room a lot, didn't she? She could have slipped something here for safekeeping, knowing you'd eventually find it."

"I doubt it," I said, "but I suppose it's possible."

I heard my doorknob turn, and whipped my head in that direction, fear gripping my body and rendering me paralyzed from the neck down. As it began to open, I had one terrifying thought. That whoever had been following me the other night from Artula had figured out which room I was in, and was about to enter and shoot me.

But instead, as the door came fully open, I saw Blake standing there.

Instead of being comforted by his appearance, a new wave of dread washed over me.

"Hi," Blake said casually, as if we were expecting him, and stepped into my room.

"I sent Blake a text and asked him to come over," Ryan explained, and only then did I whirl around to look at him. "I figured six eyes were better than four," he added with a sheepish smile.

I felt uneasy for some reason, but nodded nonetheless. "If you think it will help. But I really don't think anything's here."

Blake walked over to my dresser and opened the top drawer without even asking permission.

"There's nothing in my drawers," I insisted. "I would know."

Blake ignored me, rummaging through my drawer, tossing my bras and panties aside without any concern for my privacy.

I felt violated.

As Blake finished with the first drawer and moved on to the second, Ryan suddenly cursed. "Oh, fuck." He was looking at something in the notebook, his face contorted in anger. "Look at this." He angled the notebook toward Blake so that he could read whatever was written there, leaving me in the dark. "Look at what she fucking wrote."

Blake looked at the page, his growing wrath making his face turn bright red.

"What?" I asked. "Is it a name?"

"It's proof," Blake said. He went at my belongings almost violently now, throwing my clothes left and right without a hint of common decency. "Proof of her fucked-up plan."

Ryan flung the notebook onto the desk and headed to the closet.

"There's nothing in my drawers," I said to Blake, who continued to ignore me. But my attention was drawn to Ryan when I heard something land on the floor with a thud.

A box with last year's textbooks that had been on the top shelf was now on the floor, the books spilled out.

"What are you doing?" I asked.

"It's got to be here," Ryan said. But I didn't get the sense that he was talking to me.

In fact, I suddenly got the sense that this wasn't about me and Ryan looking for answers, but something else altogether.

Blake moved to the next drawer while Ryan flipped through the text pages. My eyes volleyed between the both of them. They seemed determined, intent on finding something.

Almost as if they knew what they were looking for.

"You finding anything, Blake?" Ryan asked.

"Nothing here. But it's gotta be somewhere." Blake glanced over his shoulder at me, his gaze almost accusing.

"What?" I asked. "What do you think is in here?"

Neither answered me. I watched as Ryan held up a large textbook and shook it, trying to free something that might have been hidden within the pages.

When nothing fell out, Ryan threw the book aside in disgust. It slammed into the desk lamp and sent it crashing to the floor.

Then he turned to me, his eyes darkening in anger.

"You know where it is." It was a statement, not a question, one that made an icy nip slither down my spine.

I said nothing. I wasn't even breathing.

Because I suddenly had the awful feeling that something was very, very wrong.

Ryan started toward me, and I should have tried to move, but fear had me rooted to the spot.

"Where is it?" he asked me.

"This isn't about helping Ashley, is it?" I asked, my voice low, my chest tight. "What are you really looking for?"

"Where is it?" Ryan repeated.

"I have no clue what you're talking about."

"I saw that look on your face outside."

"What look?" My heart began to beat faster.

"And the way you've been looking at me and Blake now."

"I'm looking at you like I'm confused," I said. "Because I am."

"You read the fucking stories," Ryan went on. "You know what's going on."

The stories? Did he know about Ashley's sexual abuse? Even if he did, that didn't explain his behavior now.

Confusion had me exasperated. "You're not making any sense!" I yelled. "I'm completely in the dark."

"The pictures!" Ryan shot back.

"Pictures?" More confusion. Nothing was making sense.

"An envelope. A flash drive. *Something.* Something that Ashley told you she wanted you to hold for her, even if she never explained what it was."

"I don't know what you're talking about!"

Ryan stared into my eyes with a probing gaze that left me frigid. I shot a nervous glance at Blake. He, too, was looking at me with a hard expression.

"Honest to God," I said, "I have no clue. I—I don't understand what's going on."

"She said it was with a friend," Blake said with a calm tone that didn't match the evil vibes he was sending out. "Someone she could trust. And you two are about as tight as two people can be."

"So tight that I didn't know what she was doing in her spare time?" I shot back, my tone rhetorical. "Look, I don't have any idea—"

In a flash, Ryan closed the distance between us, wrapped his fingers around my upper arm and squeezed. Hard. "Cut the bullshit. You know what I'm talking about." He shook me. "Tell me where it is!"

"Yo," Blake said. "Ryan—"

"She knows!" Ryan spat out. "She's playing me, biding her time. Time we don't have."

"I don't! I swear!"

Blake clamped a hand down on Ryan's shoulder and pulled

him off of me. "Calm down," he said, slowly, deliberately. And then, in a whisper, "If we lose control of this situation, we lose everything. Chantelle is our only hope."

Their only hope . . . ? I wanted to ask Blake what he meant by that, but I was too afraid to speak.

"It wasn't at her place, and maybe it's not here, but it's somewhere," Ryan said to me, the veins in his forehead popping as he spoke in a low, angry tone. "So put your thinking cap on and think of a place that Ashley would hide something."

"Pictures?" I asked. "That's what you're looking for?"

Ryan took a step toward me, and reflexively I stepped backward. But I bumped into Blake. I whipped my head around, surprised to find that he had encroached on my personal space from behind.

"You really don't know what I'm talking about?" Ryan asked me.

My eyes jerked from Blake back to Ryan. I was trapped between the two of them, the last place I wanted to be. "No."

"All right," Ryan said calmly. He actually sounded nice. "I'm willing to believe that. But you're gonna help us find the pictures."

I nodded jerkily. "Yes. Okay. I'll help you."

Ryan grinned. "Good. You help us, nothing happens to you."

The sickest of feelings washed over me. They were going to hurt me. Possibly worse. And I had no clue why.

"You're sure Ashley left nothing hidden in your room?" Ryan asked. He almost sounded friendly.

"I'm—I'm sure," I stammered. "But I think . . . I think I know where—"

Ryan's eyes lit up. "You do?"

"Yes. Maybe." I was lying. But I had to. It was critical for me to get out of this room.

In this room, I was vulnerable to whatever Ryan and Blake wanted to do to me in their quest to get ahold of whatever pictures they were after.

"Where?" Ryan asked me.

"Ashley has this friend. Someone she went to high school with. She—she lives in the Quad. What you want—I think it could be there."

"Why?"

"Because as we were leaving for Artula, Ashley had the driver stop at Keller Hall. She said she had to drop something off for . . . for Brittany." I chose a name randomly, a common one on campus. "It was a large manila envelope, and I remember wondering what could have been in it. But Ashley didn't say, so I didn't ask."

Ryan's lips curled in a cold, evil smile. He looked toward Blake. "Sounds like it."

"I'll take you there," I offered.

"Brittany Jenkins?" Ryan asked. "Or was it Brittany Sheffield?" Before I could answer, he nodded. "Yeah, I can see it being her. The bitch has never liked me."

I didn't know a Brittany Jenkins nor a Brittany Sheffield. I didn't know any Brittany in Keller Hall.

"I . . . I don't know her last name," I said. When Ryan's eyes narrowed with doubt, I quickly added, "But I'll know her when I see her. Let's go now. I'll point her out to you."

Most students were returning from their spring break vacations and trips home. So it was likely I'd find a "Brittany" at Keller Hall.

But more important, I'd be around other students. Ryan and Blake wouldn't dare hurt me with any witnesses.

Ryan gave me a shove toward the door. "Get moving."

I stumbled, but caught my footing, then made my way to the door. I breathed a sigh of relief when I stepped into the hallway. I was no longer trapped in my room with two men I was certain could kill me.

A cry bubbled in my throat. Had they killed Ashley? Killed her for whatever it was they were looking for?

I couldn't allow myself to cry. I needed to stay strong until I was safe.

They spoke in hushed tones behind me as I led the way downstairs. I couldn't make out everything they were saying, only snippets.

". . . bad move, man . . ."

"I'll worry about that."

". . . Artula?"

"I fucking said I'll . . ."

". . . deal with it here . . ."

". . . once we have the pictures . . . Don't worry."

I opened the front door and stepped into the cool night air. But it wasn't the chill in the air that made me feel cold.

It was the reading between the lines of their chatter, and coming to the conclusion that they were no doubt arriving at also.

Once we got to Keller Hall, they wouldn't be able to control the situation.

The situation being *me*.

Less than an hour ago, I'd received that strange phone call and had been so hopeful. The connection had been bad, but everything about the call had made me believe it was Ashley on the other end of the line. A girl in trouble, reaching out to her best friend.

Alive.

And if she was alive, she could be saved.

That's what I'd believed—until I began to put the pieces into place once things had taken a dark turn with Ryan and Blake.

Ryan had claimed he'd gotten a phone call from Ashley too, and I'd believed him. But now I realized that the phone call from Ashley must have been a setup on his part. He'd gotten someone to call me pretending to be Ashley, using some technique to fake static on the phone line. He had wanted me hopeful, unsuspecting, easily deceived when he called and told me that *he* had heard from Ashley. For his plan to work, he needed me to believe him and be willing to talk to him. Willing to let him into my room under the guise of helping Ashley, when all he really wanted was to search for whatever damn pictures he was so desperate to get ahold of.

And I hadn't even considered this until now—how would Ryan have had my cell-phone number?

Only if he had Ashley's phone.

And if *he* had Ashley's phone . . .

Lord help me.

Maybe he'd gotten my number another way, but a picture was still developing, one I didn't want to see. Because it was terrifying.

Ryan and Blake had gotten someone to call me, pretending to be Ashley, as a way to set me up so I'd help them find whatever they were after.

Photographs.

But photographs of what?

What was so important they were willing to kill for it?

Because that's what they had done. I was certain now. They hadn't come right out and said it, but based on the pieces of their conversation I'd heard and what they were doing now, it was clear to me that they were behind what had happened to Ashley in Artula.

If they'd set me up with a phone call to believe that she was still alive, then it meant only one thing.

That Ashley was dead.

Chapter Thirty-six

I SWALLOWED a gasp of sorrow. But that was the only sadness I could afford at this point. Because if these two assholes had killed Ashley . . . what were they going to do to me?

A hand came down on my shoulder, and I jumped.

"Wait a second," Ryan said.

I turned and looked up at him. "Why?"

"It's a far walk. We should drive."

I'd already started in the direction of the Duncan residence building, hoping that there would be people milling about so I could make my escape. But there was no one in the parking lot. No one hanging around the building's exterior. My next

best hope was the Hollifield residence, which wasn't too far. If
that too proved to be a ghost town, I would be steps from
Samford Avenue, where I at least could try to flag down a passing car.

"But your dorm is just as far as walking to the Quad," I said.

"Yeah, but I drove to your building," Ryan explained. "And
so did Blake. We can take either of our cars."

I didn't like this. Not at all.

Apparently, Blake didn't, either. He shook his head, his eyes
jittery. "Fuck, Ryan. This is a bad idea."

"Shut *up*, Blake!"

Another revelation. Ryan was calling the shots.

I met Blake's gaze. He looked away. But I saw in his eyes a
level of frustration—frustration that wasn't directed at me.

He didn't really want to be a part of whatever Ryan was
doing.

A plan was formulating in my mind. And I would have to
act quickly. Because if I got in a car with them, I was as good
as dead.

"Come on." Ryan indicated the opposite direction with a
jerk of his head.

"What's he going to do to me?" I asked Blake. "Hurt me?
Kill me? And you're going to let him?"

Blake didn't answer, and when I glanced at Ryan, he looked
a bit surprised.

"No one's gonna hurt you," Ryan said, and forced a hey-
why-are-you-freaking-out chuckle.

"Really?" I asked. "Because you pretended you were interested in helping Ashley. But all you want are some photos you
think she has."

Ryan held up his hands. "Okay. I lied about the photos. But they're . . . they're part of the clue. We heard from someone in Artula, okay? There are some pictures of . . . of Ashley and some government official . . . when he was visiting the States. They want them back in exchange for Ashley being returned alive."

I narrowed my eyes as I stared at him. The story was almost crazy enough to be true. Stranger things had happened. And with the news of Ashley's secret life, it certainly *could* be true.

I might have believed it—if Ryan had presented this angle before.

Now I saw it as another of his lies. One meant to regain my trust.

But it gave me an opportunity to play into his hands.

And in doing so, hopefully execute my plan.

"That's what this is about?" I asked, acting as horrified as I could. "Pictures of Ashley and some government official?"

Ryan nodded. "Yeah."

"Why didn't you just say so in the first place? This is the missing piece of the puzzle." I paused. Looked at Blake. He still wouldn't meet my eyes. But the expression on his face told me it was hard for him to stomach the bullshit Ryan was spewing.

"I figured there were enough surprises about Ashley," Ryan said. "I was trying to spare your feelings."

Right. But I said, "Oh. Well, I can see that."

"I say you and I go to Keller Hall," Blake said to Ryan. "Get the fucking pictures and . . . deal with the rest of this crazy shit."

"That's what I'm trying to do. Deal with this shit," Ryan said, and it was clear to me he was trying to convey a message to Blake.

He planned to kill me.

I wouldn't let that happen.

My pulse picked up speed. I had to act. And act now.

So while Ryan and Blake exchanged glances, I kicked Ryan in the groin as hard as I could.

In the nanosecond that followed, his eyes jerked to mine, widening in surprise. He was too surprised even to make a noise.

But the next instant, he doubled over and howled in pain.

It was the window of opportunity I needed. I took off.

"You're dead, bitch!" he cried out. "Fucking get her, Blake!"

A thicket of trees bordered the parking lot, and I ran toward them as fast as I could. I needed the cover of trees and darkness to hide from them.

If I could lose them, I'd make my way to the main road. Once there, I'd throw myself in front of a car if that's what I had to do to make one stop. Without my cell phone, I didn't have another choice.

As I moved into the trees, I threw a glance over my shoulder. Blake was quickly gaining on me. Ryan, half running, half limping, was a good ten yards behind his friend.

My eyes frantically searched the area in front of me. Where could I hide? Where? I darted to the left, but when I looked over my shoulder, Blake had followed my movements.

That's when my stomach sank.

I'd run into the thicket of trees hoping to escape them, but instead I'd given them the best spot to murder me. It was dark, and private.

The perfect place to kill someone.

I should have run to the doors of the Duncan residence and

banged on them. Created such a ruckus that Ryan and Blake would have fled, not wanting to get caught.

I began to whimper, fearing the worst. Even if I could outrun Ryan right now, I was no match for Blake's speed.

Don't give up! I told myself as I pumped my legs harder. *You can make—*

I screamed when I felt the brush of a body against mine, and the next second, I was tackled to the ground. Blake's hard body landed on top of mine, knocking the wind from my lungs.

My lip had split. I could taste the blood. And my chest hurt. But I kicked and squirmed with all the fight I had in me, managing to get onto my knees. Once again, Blake knocked me down. My face hit the hard earth, a twig scraping against my injured lip.

I continued to kick while trying to get up, but the next thing I knew, Blake was securing my hands behind my back. He jabbed a knee into my spine to keep me on the ground.

No! God, no! It couldn't end like this.

"You dare to kick me, bitch?"

Ryan's sneakers appeared before my face, and I closed my eyes, bracing myself for when he would kick my face in. When he didn't, I opened my eyes and slowly looked up at him.

And into the eyes of a devil.

"I lied," I said, not ready to accept that I would die here, at their hands. "The pictures aren't at Keller Hall." It was the only thing I could think of to say, and I prayed it bought me a bargaining chip.

"I don't care where the pictures are." Ryan's voice was cold. He was pissed. Pissed enough to get rid of me, right here, right now.

I tried to angle my head over my shoulder to look at Blake, but he pushed my face down. Tasting dirt, I fought to raise my head. "Don't let him do it, Blake. Don't let him kill me."

"No one's killing anyone," Blake said. "All we want are the pictures." He spoke softly, almost gently, like he was trying to make me trust him. "Ryan, calm down and remember the main goal."

Ryan said nothing. I braced myself for the pain that would come as he kicked me in the face. "As much as I'd like to re-arrange your face," he finally said, huffing with anger, "we need you. Because if we can't find the pictures, at least we've got you. A fair trade."

"What?" I tilted my chin up and looked at Ryan again, con-fused by his comment. I caught his look of surprise a moment before he said, "Shit!"

And then I heard a thud, and felt the weight of Blake's body on me again. He was going to smother me in the dirt. This was it.

I screamed. But he didn't press my face down. In fact, his hand was limp beside my face.

What was happening?

Before I had a moment to even think about what was going on, I saw a flash of movement. I glanced up. Saw a large stick strike Ryan across the face. He groaned and went down, land-ing on the ground with a soft thud.

Terrified and baffled, I maneuvered my body from beneath Blake's limp one and turned onto my back. Fear pulsed through my body when I saw the man standing over me.

Dark skin. It had to be the man I'd glimpsed my first night back at Lancaster.

I hadn't been paranoid. Someone *had* been following me.

Not BJ or Kevaughn, but someone from Artula.

"Please," I begged. "Please don't hurt me."

Something flashed in the man's eyes. An expression of sadness? And then he did something that surprised me.

He extended his hand to me.

Breathing hard, I stared at his proffered hand, then met his eyes again. What was he going to do? Take me someplace and grill me about photos? Or grill me about something else that Ashley had done?

"Please . . ." I said again, and the next thing I knew, I was softly crying.

The man lowered himself to his haunches, and I could see then that he was staring at me with kindness. Maybe even affection.

"Chantelle, I'm not going to hurt you," the man said quietly, and then reached out to touch my face.

I jerked my head backward, away from his hand.

"It's okay, baby," he cooed. "It's okay."

I regarded him warily. There was something about him. Something familiar . . .

"I would never hurt you, baby." He reached for me again, and this time I didn't flinch when he stroked my cheek. And then he smiled at me. Smiled even as tears filled his eyes. "Chantelle. Oh, my sweet baby. I'm your father."

Chapter Thirty-seven

THE WORDS stunned me. Left me breathless.

My father.

How could it be?

My father was dead.

And yet . . .

I heard a groan. His smile fading, the man looked beyond me, to Ryan and Blake, then quickly stood. "I better call nine-one-one."

My father? How could this be true?

I had a million questions, but the answers would have to wait. Because the man who'd claimed to be my father had his cell phone to his ear, and was instructing the operator where to find us.

I glanced around. Ryan was writhing on the ground. Blake, however, was still out cold.

"It's over, young man," the man said to Ryan. "The police are on their way."

My gaze went back to him—to this man who had claimed to be my father. I was both baffled and a little afraid. Not afraid of him—I believed that he had come to help me. But afraid that he was exactly who he claimed to be.

Because that would mean that my mother had lied to me. For my entire life.

I didn't want to believe that my mother would lie to me, not about something so vitally important. And yet, I *knew* this man. Knew him from the photo I'd kept in my wallet for so many years.

He was older and heavier than he'd been twenty-two years ago. But it was him. My father.

Alive. Real.

The campus police were the first to arrive. I explained to them everything that had happened, ending with the story of how I had been rescued. I didn't identify my rescuer as my father.

But with each minute that passed, the more I stole glances at him, the more I was certain.

His eyes were my eyes. His nose was my nose.

I could see myself in him. That was something I couldn't deny.

My father was alive. Resurrected from the grave my mother had buried him in.

But after a week that had given me so much to deal with, I didn't know how to begin to wrap my mind around this.

. . .

Hours later, after a trip to the police station to give a statement, I was informed that Ryan and Blake had been arrested for my assault. I wasn't sure what would happen next, but I was pretty certain this was the beginning of what promised to be a long, ugly road. I imagined the two of them turning on each other as the damning truth came out.

My father—it was still weird to think of him that way—had gone with me to the police station, and he was there now, as I prepared to exit.

As his eyes swept over me, I recognized something in his expression that I'd never expected to see.

A father's love.

I offered him a small smile as I walked toward him, probably the first smile I'd given him since he'd saved me from Ryan and Blake. I was finally coming to terms with all that had happened, at least as much as could be expected under the circumstances.

I'd had a little more than two hours to process the latest shocking bit of information in barely a week's time. But this—the news that my father was alive and well—was the easiest to accept.

And the most welcome.

"I know you have questions," he said, and I was glad that he spoke first, because I didn't know where to start. "Where have I been all this time, why haven't I been in your life."

I eased onto the seat next to him in the police station's waiting area. "All these years, I thought you were dead," I began softly. I wasn't angry. I only wanted to understand. "Where were you?"

"I . . ." He looked toward an officer who was walking by. "Maybe we can go somewhere and talk. Somewhere we can have some privacy."

I nodded. "I'd like that."

"Do you mind going in my car with me?"

I'd ridden to the police station in a squad car, and they would have given me a ride back to campus if I'd wanted.

But I didn't fear my father. And the cruel lessons of the past week had me realizing that life was too short to waste even a moment.

I wasn't about to waste time being angry. Not when I'd been given a second chance at a relationship with the man I'd always longed for.

"We passed a pancake house on the way here," I said. "Why don't we go there?"

A short while later, we were sitting at a table in a corner of the restaurant, two mugs of tea on the table in front of us. He was talking. I was listening.

He'd started by assuring me that he'd always loved me, that a day hadn't gone by when he hadn't thought about me. How the day I'd been born had been the happiest of his life. That he never knew if he'd ever find me again.

"I'd lost track of you and your mother," he said. "She wanted nothing to do with me, and I can understand that. And then I saw you on the news. Talking about your missing friend in Artula. And that's how I learned you attended Lancaster University. And I came here from California as soon as I could, walking the grounds every day and night on the off chance that I would see you. But when I did, you ran from me. I'd scared you."

"I thought you were someone else," I explained. "Someone from Artula. I didn't have a good experience there. If I'd known it was you, I wouldn't have . . ."

My father reached for my hand. "It's okay," he said. "I knew I'd scared you. I didn't see exactly where you'd run off to, but I had a general idea. So I waited. Waited for my chance to see you again. After nineteen years, I would wait as long as it took."

Thus far, he hadn't explained why he'd been gone. He'd made sure to assure me of his undying love, but I still had no idea what had happened to him.

"My mother said you were dead," I said.

"I'm not surprised," my father said. "But I don't want you to be mad at her for that. She did what she had to to protect you."

Perhaps because of all that had happened in the last week, I wasn't feeling angry. I'd gone through so many taxing emotions, I couldn't muster any anger at my mother. At least not right now.

Maybe later, when I talked to her. But for now, I only wanted to understand.

"Protect me, why?"

"Because . . . because I wasn't the best person when I knew her. I . . . I'm not proud of some of the things I did. I made a lot of mistakes when I was young and stupid. Mistakes that landed me in jail."

He paused after he said the words, and I could almost see him tense. Bracing himself. Waiting for my reaction. Perhaps expecting revulsion. Or at least shock.

But I didn't react. Not even a flinch. All I wanted was to hear him out.

"I didn't hurt anyone," he went on. "I want you to know that. No one except myself. I got addicted to drugs. Real bad. Crack.

Heroin. Anything that'd give me a damn high. It was all I lived for. I guess I'm lucky—because some of my friends, the shit killed them."

My father. A drug addict. I only nodded.

"I screwed my life up royally and got ten years in prison as a result. But I'm glad for that. The time in prison helped me get off the drugs. I even learned a trade while in there. Someone gave me a chance when I got out, gave me a job as a carpenter. I did everything I could to make a good life for myself, always hoping that one day you would be a part of it.

"I tried contacting your mother once I was sober, but all of my mail was returned unopened. She cut me out of your lives and moved on. Moved across country so I'd never be able to find you. I can't say I blame her. I put her through hell."

Again, I nodded. It was all I could do as I tried to comprehend what he'd told me. And I felt a bit numb, unsure how I was supposed to take it all.

I could be upset with my mother for her decision to tell me he was dead, but my father was right—she'd done what she'd done in an effort to protect me. I could be angry with my father for choosing a lifestyle that would ensure either death or imprisonment, both of which would have kept him out of my life.

And I could also be angry at the lies my best friend had told me, which had all contributed to the hell I'd gone through while trying to find her.

But what would anger over any of these situations accomplish? My mother loved me. I didn't doubt that. Even though her lie had kept me from my father, I knew she'd never meant to hurt me. And as far as my father was concerned, what mattered was that he was here now, that he loved me, and that he wanted to be a part of my life.

And Ashley. Oh, my dear friend, Ashley. Despite her secret life, she had truly been my best friend. We'd shared similar goals and dreams.

And I'd loved her. So had Erica. How would we go on without Ashley?

Suddenly, a tear fell down my cheek. I brushed it away.

"Oh, baby," my father said. "I'm sorry. I . . . I know this is a lot to digest."

"No," I told him, waving off his concern. "I'm glad you're here." Now I was the one to reach for his hand. "Life is too short to live it being angry over what you can't change. It's too precious to let resentment keep you from accepting second chances with people you love. Maybe because my mother told me you were dead, she never saw any reason to bash you. So all my life, I felt nothing but love for the father I'd tragically lost. And now we have a second chance." I swallowed so that I didn't cry. "That's why I'm sad. Because I'll never have another day with my best friend again. She's gone, Dad."

"You're sure?" he asked me.

"Yes, I'm sure." I sniffled. "I don't know if Ryan and Blake have admitted it, or if they ever will. But I know they killed her. I suppose one of these days we'll find out why."

I began to cry, unable to stop the flow of tears. In that moment, I realized that I would have forgiven Ashley. If she'd come home alive, I would have wrapped her in my arms and hugged her as hard as I could and forgiven her for her lies.

I would have hugged her hard enough to try to heal all the pain that had pushed her into her secret life.

But I would never get that chance.

Chapter
Thirty-eight

MY FATHER had just paid the food bill when my cell phone rang. Retrieving my phone from my purse, I looked at the caller ID.

Private name. Private number.

My entire body tensed as the phone rang a second time. Every time I'd seen those words on my phone's screen this week, I had been hopeful. Now, I felt ill. Because I no longer believed I would ever hear Ashley's voice again.

The phone rang a third time, and I pressed the talk button before it could go to voice mail. "Hello?"

"Miss Higgins?"

"Yes?"

"This is Officer Vogl. We met earlier this evening."

"Yes, of course." The tall, red-haired officer who'd driven me to the Lancaster police station. I wondered what he could possibly want at shortly after midnight.

"I'm sorry to call so late, but I have an urgent request from Ryan Sinclair. He said he'd like to speak with you. He can't use the phone, so if you agree, it'll have to be in person."

My eyes darted to my father's. He gazed back at me in concern.

"You don't have to," the officer explained. "But he's shackled, and he's in a holding cell. You'll be safe."

"Did he say what it's about?" I asked.

"Only that it's very important. Something about Ashley that you'll want to hear right away."

I swallowed. Hard. And then tears filled my eyes. Because I knew what Ryan was going to say. He was going to tell me where Ashley's body was buried. Or, if not buried, where he and Blake had thrown it out to sea.

My father reached across the table and took my free hand in both of his.

"We think he may want to clear his conscience with you, her best friend, before confessing to us what he did to her."

"Oh God."

"You can think about it," Officer Vogl said. "You certainly don't have to."

"But you think it will help," I offered. "Get a more speedy confession."

"It might."

I closed my eyes. Inhaled deeply. "All right."

"You can come in the morning if you like."

"No," I said. "I'm not far. I'll come now."

"Thank you, Miss Higgins."

"What is it?" my father asked as I hung up.

My head hurt. The moment of truth was arriving. The moment when the last bit of hope would be snuffed out. "That was the police. Ryan wants to . . . to talk to me. They think he wants to clear his conscience with me."

My father squeezed my hand tighter. "You don't have to go."

"Yes." I thought about Jason, of the closure his family had never gotten. "I do. For Ashley. And her family."

"All right." My father nodded. "Then let's go."

Ten minutes later, we were back at the police station. My legs were trembling as I followed Officer Vogl. My father held my hand as he walked with me, his warmth and love enveloping me.

I was surprised to see Ryan and Blake in a cell with one other person. But there were only two cells in this police station, and the second one was currently home to an angry-looking middle-aged woman.

Ryan immediately rose from the hard bed when he saw me. As he walked toward me, he looked defeated. That was the only word for it. Blake, sitting in a corner on the floor, didn't give me more than a passing glance. He wasn't happy—but who could blame him?

Ryan walked right up to the bars, wrapped his fingers around the metal. I stayed a good two feet back, fearing he might try to reach for me.

"Chantelle, I'm sorry," he said. His voice was low and rough.

I said nothing. Just gripped my father's hand tighter.

"I wanted to see you because I have a message for Ashley. I figure you're going to hear from her at some point. Tell her . . . tell her it's a go. She'll get what she wants."

I'd been holding my breath, and now I gulped in air. "What?" Ryan's words made no sense. *"What?"*

"Tell her she's won. But for God's sake, please tell her to destroy those pictures. They'll kill me. Kill my family. My father expects her total cooperation."

My head was spinning. I was trying to comprehend the incomprehensible. "Are you saying . . ." He wasn't confessing. "You didn't kill Ashley?"

"No, we didn't kill Ashley. And we weren't going to kill you." He looked and sounded earnest. "All we wanted were the pictures."

Ashley's alive. Hope came to life again, filling every part of my body, leaving me warm where I'd been cold. I was giddy with it. Elated. "You know where she is?"

Ryan shook his head. "But she'll surface at some point. If she wants to get her money."

"Her money?"

"Just tell her. If you hear from her. Better yet, send her an e-mail. I'll bet she's checking messages."

I stood, holding my father's hand tightly, watching as Ryan retreated. Watching as he sat on the hard bed and buried his face in his hands and started to cry. Weeping sobs I'd never expected to hear from a man.

But through his pain, I felt joy. He was telling the truth. He hadn't murdered Ashley.

She was still alive.

At least I prayed she was.

The first thing I did when I got back to my dorm room was search for Ashley's journal, the one Ryan had tossed aside in frustration. Something in there held a clue. A story, or random words scribbled somewhere. Whatever it was that he'd shown to Blake, but not to me.

After about five minutes of reading and scanning the pages, I found it, near the end of the notebook. It was a story, one called "Taboo." As I read it, my mouth gaping open in shock, I knew that it wasn't simply a fictional creation. It was a story based on a true experience. I was certain of that, the way I'd been certain that Ashley's story about a sexually abusive step-father was also based in truth.

His friend stroked my hair while Ray kissed me, a sign that he wanted to get in on the action. So I turned and kissed Brian, his friend, the same deep kiss I'd shared with Ray. But then Brian did something I didn't expect. He pulled away from me and began kissing Ray.

Two men. Two strong men. Best friends. Kissing each other with the same kind of passion they had just kissed me. It was fascinating to watch. It was taboo.

It turned me on.

They kissed me again, both of them at the same time, all of our tongues tasting each other's. Then they stripped me naked before turning to each other and doing the same thing. As they pulled at each other's clothes, they grunted with excitement—the excitement at trying something new. Alcohol had helped weaken all of our inhibitions, but it was pleasure, pure and simple, that drove their need to make out with each other.

The words burned my eyes. Burned as I read the sordid account of what two male friends had done to each other

one hot night in January. How they had taken part in taboo
pleasures.

Ray and Brian.

Ryan and Blake.

And Ashley.

Holy shit.

This was what they were after. Pictures that had documented
them together having gay sex. Ashley must have taken the opportunity to photograph them with her cell-phone camera.

I sat on the bed, the open notebook in my hands. Were
Ryan and Blake gay? Two men who bled testosterone?

No, I thought, shaking my head. They couldn't be. And not
just because they were football stars and two of the biggest
womanizers on the planet. But because in this day and age,
people didn't feel the need to hide their sexuality. They didn't
go to the lengths Ryan and Blake had gone to in order to try
and protect the truth about their sexuality from coming out.

No, they were likely two guys who'd gotten caught up in a
ménage-a-trois with a beautiful woman, everyone experiment-
ing with each other. For two popular jocks—one a minister's
son—the idea of that experimentation becoming public knowledge had to be beyond terrifying. Terrifying enough to have
them trashing rooms in a desperate attempt to find the evidence they hoped to destroy.

Terrifying enough that they would have killed to keep their
secret, if they'd had the chance?

Maybe.

But the chance hadn't presented itself, and Ashley was blackmailing them. For money. I found that surprising, and the one
bit of news that gave me pause. First of all, Ashley's family was

pretty well off. Second, the Ashley I knew was sweet and giving, and wouldn't be capable of exploiting people for money.

But the Ashley I knew was only one side of the real Ashley. She had a dark side, one caused by what she'd gone through in her life, one that she had never dared to share with me. And maybe that dark side was willing to exploit people for as much as she could take from them, simply for the thrill of it.

I closed the notebook and massaged my right temple. So many twists and turns. So much startling news.

After I tried to come to terms with all I had learned, I called Jason. I filled him in on the latest developments: my father's sudden appearance when Ryan and Blake had attacked me, Ryan's and Blake's arrests, how I'd believed Ashley was dead, and now, with Ryan's bombshell, that I believed she was still alive.

"Pictures?" Jason asked. "Money?"

"Yeah, I know. It's crazy. Ryan didn't come right out and say it, but it sounds like Ashley was blackmailing him. His family. His father is a very prominent televangelist, and the family has lots of money. Something like this would be scandalous if it came out."

"You think he's telling the truth? He could be lying, trying to mess with you and the police."

"I considered that. But it was the look on his face, one of pure desolation. I believed him."

"I don't know," Jason said. "I kind of figure someone would have heard from Ashley by now if this was all a blackmail ploy."

"True," I agreed, but only halfheartedly. I *wanted* to believe that Ashley was alive. Even if everything that had happened had been fueled by her selfish greed. Even if the truth about her was something I could never truly swallow.

"I honestly don't know what to think anymore," I said. "What to expect. I did send an e-mail to Ashley, as Ryan suggested I do. Just in case."

"This doesn't feel right to me," Jason said. "After everything that happened in Artula—me getting beaten, the tongue being sent to you—I still believe Ashley was abducted into white slavery."

Jason made a good point, as he had from the beginning. And I couldn't forget all that had happened in Artula. There had to have been a reason for it.

"I absolutely believe there's a conspiracy going on on the island involving the disappearance of young women," I said after a moment. "I'm just not sure Ashley was abducted. Maybe I'm stupid and I want to believe Ryan. But his words . . . they gave me hope. And I can't let go of that hope, not yet."

Jason was silent, not voicing the doubts I knew he had. Time would tell if hope would become my albatross or my salvation.

"You have a father now," Jason said softly, changing the subject. "How are you dealing with that?"

"Gosh, Jason. It's all so unexpected. But I'm happy. I thought I'd lost him forever, but knowing that he's really alive, and that he never stopped loving me . . . If this whole thing with Ashley hadn't happened, he never would have found me."

"Another silver lining."

"Yes," I agreed. Just like Jason had been.

"Have you talked to your mother yet?" he asked.

"No." I sighed. "Maybe tomorrow. I've had enough to deal with today."

A pause ensued. "I hate that I'm in New York right now," Jason said after a moment. "I should be with you. Holding you."

I said nothing. Why entertain the idea of being with him when I knew that wouldn't happen any time soon?

"Chantelle?"

"I'm here."

"I know there's a lot going on with you right now, and you're gonna want to spend time with your father. But can I come see you? Tomorrow? Or the next day?"

Warmth spread through my body at the idea, and I smiled softly. "But you just went back."

"I know . . . but don't you have a book you were going to pitch me? I could write the trip off as a business expense."

"Don't tease me . . ."

"I'm serious, baby."

God, I loved the way he said "baby." "Jason—"

"In fact," he went on, "we could discuss the idea of you writing a book about your recent experience. No joke."

My smile faltered as his words made me think of Ashley, of the story she'd told her sister would make her famous. The past week had been excruciatingly difficult for me, and the pain was still fresh and raw. If Ashley's disappearance had been a selfish ploy for profit on her part—if she had intentionally caused me and everyone who loved her unbearable pain—I wasn't sure I could ever write about the experience.

Jason must have read my thoughts, because he said, "Of course, you don't have to. But it's a doozy of a story. Horton House would love to buy it. And you can donate the proceeds to the efforts to find the missing. Or whatever cause you deem worthy."

Like abused girls who see no other future than a life in the sex trade, I thought.

"I'm not sure," I said.

"Just throwing the idea out there. Whatever choice you make, it will be the right one."

"I think you need to come down here so we can discuss the idea," I said, feigning a business tone.

There was a pause, and I pictured that sexy smile I loved spreading on Jason's face. "Is tomorrow too soon?"

I grinned from ear to ear. "Not a chance."

Epilogue

TWO DAYS AFTER Ryan and Blake were arrested for the attack on me, news broke on the island of Artula. A young woman, blond and beautiful, was reported to have gone missing. On a solo vacation after a nasty breakup, her family didn't worry when they hadn't heard from her for a week—the same week Ashley, Erica, and I had been in Artula.

It was only after the woman, Kimberly Cross, aged twenty-four, didn't return to Arlington, Texas, as scheduled that her family and friends became concerned. The family had dismissed the stories about white slavery after the unflattering truth about Ashley Hamilton had come to light, choosing to believe that Ashley had likely met with foul play during some sort of kinky escapade. But with their daughter-sister-friend now missing, they were turning to the media, fearing that Kimberly, the same type of blond beauty as Ashley, might actually have been abducted as a sex slave.

My heart broke for the family. Because if Ryan had been telling the truth, and Ashley was possibly missing for reasons that had to do with greed, this young woman's disappearance explained a lot. Paul Dunlop's talk about a ship leaving, his subsequent murder, the police beating Jason. The tongue I'd been sent as a warning.

The corruption on the island was evident. They had a dirty secret to hide.

News media from all over the world had converged on the island of Artula, reporting on the disappearance of not one, but two young women who could have passed for sisters.

I held out hope. The hope that Ashley was alive and in hiding. Not a captive for a depraved wealthy man.

As each day passed, I checked my e-mail. My voice mail. Waiting for word from Ashley. I received nothing, and couldn't help, ten days later, fearing the worst. No matter what had happened, Ashley was my friend. My best friend. Why would she want me to suffer with not knowing if she was alive and able to reach out?

I threw myself back into my studies, and tried to resume my normal life of hanging out with Erica and my other friends. I talked to Jason every day. Our relationship was going strong, something I was happy about. But despite that happiness, my heart was broken over Ashley. I tried not to think the worst, but the flicker of hope was fading fast.

After a full two weeks passed, I entered my room after a

biology class and saw an envelope on the bed. My roommate was out, but she must have put it there. Easing my backpack off, I approached the bed. Noticed that the envelope had a post-mark on it.

I reached for it, my heart accelerating as I did. The stamp on it told me the letter had been mailed from Artula.

I jabbed a nail beneath the corner of the flap, tearing the envelope open. I pulled out the two folded sheets of paper, unfolding them as quickly as I could.

Chantelle, please forgive me.

I can only imagine how worried you've been. Please know that I never meant to hurt you. I never wanted you to worry. But it was the only way.

By now, you've heard some of the stories that have come out about me, and I wish I could say they weren't true. But know this. Everything I've done has been for a reason—a good reason. To save my sister.

I could never bring myself to tell you that my stepfather is a sick bastard. Yes, in that way. It hurt too much to tell anyone—especially after my mother chose to believe him over me. But now that I'm free, and now that Megan is free, I can talk about it. That has been my whole goal, to get free of him. And to save my sister from him. I did a lot of things I didn't want to do, including the porn movies they talk about on the news, so I could earn enough cash to escape.

And then I got lucky. Maybe I'll call you one day and explain all the details, but the basic story is that I got incriminating photos of Ryan and Blake together—photos I knew Ryan's father would pay to keep secret. They're not the sort of pictures a prominent min-ister would want floating around.

I'm not proud of what I did, but I had no choice. Protecting Megan was my first priority. I'm sorry I had to hurt anyone else in the process. Ryan and Blake are jerks, but maybe they didn't deserve what I did. But mostly, I'm sorry for hurting you and Erica.

Ryan's father sent me one million dollars, the amount I blackmailed them for. As I write this, Megan is on a plane to meet me. I won't say where we're headed. It's not that I don't trust you, I just have to take all precautions. Sebastian, the guy from Zack's Shack, told me you were really worried about me. He's been a godsend. He helped me orchestrate this plan flawlessly.

Megan and I will be safe now, and I wanted you to know that. Please don't hate me. Try to understand that I did what I did because I had to protect my sister from a monster. My mother wouldn't do it; she failed to protect me. I'm sending her a letter, too, the moment Megan arrives safely, letting her know that we're okay. Then she'll never hear from us again.

I'm excited about where we're headed! It's beautiful, and we're going to have a great life. Maybe one day you'll come visit.

I love you, Chi-Chi. I promise, I'll be in touch when I can. Please don't hate me. I love you, and I love Erica. Please tell her that.

Until next time,

xoxo Ashley

I was crying. My tears spilled onto the paper I held. But I was crying happy tears.

I understood now. Understood everything. My heart broke for Ashley and what she'd gone through, but I also felt joy that she was in a happy place. Away from a monster. Her sister away from a monster.

A monster who was a child psychologist and should have helped children. Not taken advantage of them in the worst possible way.

Ashley hadn't been a greedy, immoral bitch. She'd been a selfless, loving sister, willing to do whatever it took to protect Megan from a total creep.

I held the letter to my chest, my tears continuing to fall. "I love you, Ashley," I whispered. "I love you, too."

The Depths of Friendship
The Price of Loyalty
The Bonds of Sisterhood